It was in this frame of mind that I keyed in my software, but instead of my usual menu coming up on the screen a message appeared.

If you are sensible, you will now accept that the events in Moscow are no concern of yours. You have been given examples of what happens to those who meddle, so take heed. Your friend no longer exists.

I stared at the screen and a new attack of panic made the glass of claret shake in my hand. Even with my limited technical knowledge I knew that all computers are open to attack by alien viruses, but this was too personal to be a random invasion.

Born in 1926, Bryan Forbes served in British Intelligence during the war. From 1969 to 1971 he was head of Production for EMI Film Productions at Elstree Studios and has directed numerous films. He is married to Nanette Newman and they have two daughters.

BRYAN FORBES

The Twisted Playground

Mandarin

A Mandarin Paperback
THE TWISTED PLAYGROUND

First published in Great Britain 1993
by William Heinemann Ltd
This edition published 1994
by Mandarin Paperbacks
an imprint of Reed Consumer Books Ltd
Michelin House, 81 Fulham Road, London SW3 6RB
and Auckland, Melbourne, Singapore and Toronto

Reprinted 1994

A CIP catalogue record for this title
is available from the British Library
ISBN 0 7493 1088 X

Printed and bound in Great Britain
by Cox & Wyman Ltd, Reading, Berks

This book is for
Gillian, Bernard and Patric
with much affection

A man must swallow a toad every morning
if he wishes to be sure of finding nothing
more disgusting before the day is over.

Chamfort

1

THE PRESENT
1991

It was a shock to sight my old friend Henry at Venice airport when, officially, he had been dead just over a year, found hanged in the closet of a Moscow hotel shortly after the Cold War ended with a whimper.

Having flown in earlier I was killing time in the Arrivals hall waiting to meet my American editor, Bill Borland, who was joining me from New York. We were both attending a conference on fellow writers jailed as political dissidents, one of those well-intentioned, but usually inconclusive gatherings that mollify individual consciences while sadly achieving very little.

Henry (for I was certain it was he) was with a girl, not his wife Sophie but, from a distance, sufficiently alike to be Sophie's clone; Henry's sexual taste had usually run to the familiar. I stood transfixed for a moment and saw them kiss. As Henry broke from the embrace he looked straight at me and the recognition appeared to be mutual. I started to raise my arm to hail him but before I could complete the gesture he had disappeared into Passport Control. It was all over in a matter of seconds.

I ran to the barrier, getting there too late to catch another glimpse of him and came face to face with the girl. At close range I was surprised to see how young she was; I put her age at no more than seventeen. She had Slavic features, with full lips and high cheek-bones. Her hair was cropped in an urchin cut, and she was wearing the standard, unisex mixture of clothes that the youth of all nationalities sport. I would describe her as attractive rather than beautiful and missing Sophie's remembered delicacy.

'Could I ask you something?' I blurted, and she reacted by backing away, understandably because the initial shock had given my voice an aggressive edge.

'Sorry, excuse me, I didn't mean to startle you. I just wanted to ask if that was Henry Blagden you were saying goodbye to?'

Her eyes flicked away from me and I tried another language, repeating the question in my halting Italian.

She still made no answer and at that moment an elderly man came between us, taking the girl's arm in a proprietary manner. He was dandyish, not of this age, like somebody who had strayed from a Henry James story: a cream linen suit impeccably pressed, purple tie, white patent shoes, the whole topped off with a Panama hat which he now raised to me revealing sparse white hair.

'May I help you?' His thin lips twitched in what could have been a smile and his tone was courteous but with ice in it. He spoke in English, but I detected the remains of a foreign accent.

'Thank you, I was asking this young lady about an old friend of mine. Henry Blagden. I thought I saw him with her a few moments ago.'

The thin smile stayed in place. 'No. You are mistaken. We know no such person. I regret not being able to help you.' He steered the girl away towards the water-taxis outside.

The abrupt way in which he had dismissed my enquiry strengthened rather than lessened my conviction that it had been Henry I had glimpsed. With my heart still surging from the encounter, I rushed to the Information desk. There were three imminent departures – Vienna, Leningrad and London – and I made determined efforts to discover which flight Henry might be on, but met with the usual stonewalling officialdom, (why is it that airports seem to be specifically organised as disinformation centres?). Politeness having failed, I lost my rag. 'It isn't a bloody State secret, is it? Just a simple enquiry. Isn't that what you're here for, to help passengers?' The man stared past me, unmoved, then turned away to answer the telephone.

The entire episode produced a mixture of feelings – bafflement, fear, the anguish of uncertainty. Could it have been a pure mistake on my part – a trick of light, perhaps, momentarily transforming certain features into a familiar likeness? Had I been misled by the double coincidence of seeing him with a girl who reminded me of Sophie? I don't believe in ghosts, but I had been devastated by Henry's death – in so many ways inexplicable, not the act of somebody I had once counted as my best friend and whom I believed I knew as well as anybody.

I was still rattled when Bill finally arrived, but I decided not to bore him with the story; like other people's dreams, anecdotes without a pay-off are seldom worth relating.

Bill and I had a love-hate relationship. He was a fine editor and had been an engaging drinking companion over the years, though perhaps too inclined to the belief that he had inherited Maxwell Perkins' mantle. This had led to creative differences between us in the past, for we authors are fragile creatures where our work is concerned. He arrived wearing a strange collection of clothes as though everything had been acquired, haphazardly, from a mail order catalogue.

He greeted me with, 'You look much too relaxed and healthy. I'm stressed out, I've been sitting for eight hours next to a child who puked his way across the Atlantic.'

We were both booked into the Gritti Palace, a hotel I had returned many times to in the past, usually out of season when Venice is cold and deserted, leaving before carnival time since manufactured gaiety is not my scene; I detest the corrosion of tourism, nor have I ever enjoyed mingling with the fashionable set at the Lido with its now unavoidable associations with the Visconti movie. It was routine for me to hole up in the Gritti to work on the final draft of a novel in solitude, always in the same room. I admit to being a confirmed creature of habit.

We exchanged reunion pleasantries as our water-taxi sped across the deep-water channels of the lagoon. As always, perched on every marker post was a solitary, ruffled seagull, indifferent to our passage. When the Turneresque outline came into view, I thought of the visit Sophie and I had made at the start of our affair many years before. It seemed the obligatory romantic gesture for lovers at the time. I remembered her reaction when she noticed fishermen with thigh-high waders standing in the waters beyond the designated taxi channels, for the shallowness of the lagoon always surprises the first-time visitor.

'Do you think something like that explains the miracle of Jesus walking on the water?' Sophie had asked me.

She had often jolted me with remarks like that. 'Maybe. You might well be right. Why didn't I think of that?'

The only miracle I had been thinking of was the way she looked, bright with that happiness of the very young. I could not wait to get to our room and make love to her. Memories of that trip came crowding back, now tumbled together with the puzzle of Henry's apparent resurrection. Nostalgia struck me like a sudden pain.

I urged Bill to stand in the cabin doorway. 'You mustn't miss your first sight of Venice, because it stays with you all your life,' I said pompously – the seasoned traveller who cannot resist offering advice.

He did as I suggested, bracing himself against the door jamb while he fumbled, inexpertly, with a camera.

'Don't bother with that, you'll be able to buy much better postcards at the hotel,' I said. 'Just look.'

He reacted with predictable amazement as we slid between the shiny damp walls broken here and there with the coloured patina of exposed brickwork and weathered shutters. As we entered the eastern end of the Grand Canal the low sun caught the tops of waves in an endless dazzle, but it was not in Bill's nature to be over-enthusiastic about anything for long, and as our boat bounced between the wakes of larger craft his conversation turned to the reason for our visit.

'D'you think this conference will achieve anything?'

'I doubt it,' I said. 'We'll pass some worthy resolutions and issue a finely worded statement at the final session, but I don't suppose our deliberations will have any lasting effect.' The Salman Rushdie affair was still high on the agenda, that sad, long-running nightmare that none of us were likely to solve with speeches.

'Ah, well, never mind, it's a welcome relief to get away from New York,' Bill said. 'Too many palace revolutions recently for my taste. We've been bought and sold twice this year. Publishing houses are becoming like football teams.'

'Does it seem odd to you that publishing was once known as an occupation for gentlemen?'

'For "gentlemen" now read "corporate raiders." We need gum shields and flak jackets these days. In the beginning was the word, in the end was the hype. Talking of which, how's your latest coming along?'

'It isn't. I'm going to bin it.'

'Why, for God's sake? The last time we spoke you said you were pleased with the way it was going.'

'Well, I changed my mind. It's been overtaken by events. The old spy formula's dead. We're all going to have to think again.'

'Gee, that's bad news. Can't you come up with some new villains? We were counting on a new novel from you this year.'

'You don't have to remind me,' I said, 'but at the moment the old brain cells haven't come up with anything.' To divert him from pursuing the topic any further I pointed to the outline of Santa Maria della Salute. This time he was visibly impressed.

'Now, that's the kinda church that could make me take up religion,' Bill said.

When we docked I discovered that whatever else had

5

changed in the world it certainly wasn't the cost of staying in Venice: our taxi-driver relieved us of 40,000 lire each for the short journey. There was another irritation when I found my old concierge no longer on the staff and my customary room already occupied. After some terse exchanges at the desk I finally managed to secure a third floor alternative overlooking the lagoon, but it meant waiting until the occupants left later that evening. I dumped my bags in Bill's room and we went down to the terrace bar to meet some of the other delegates and have a drink.

Venice has a calming effect no matter what your mood; maybe it is the absence of the motor car, the quality of the light, the fact that wherever you look you are staring at the undisturbed past. Yet despite this, three Bellinis and the pleasant, cocktail-party small-talk amongst fellow writers, I could not prevent my thoughts from returning to the episode at the airport.

Forcing myself to be attentive I listened to a tale of woe from a pushy German woman who had spent three years writing a biography of Bernard Shaw only to discover at the end of her labours that Michael Holroyd had pipped her to the post. 'There is room for two, don't you agree?' she kept repeating and I had an uneasy feeling, later to be confirmed, that her manuscript would come my way. 'Especially since I am bringing out in detail what others have missed. I am talking, of course, of Shaw's sexual deficiencies.'

'Really? How interesting.'

'I have my own theories why this is so. The title of my book will be *The Professional Virgin*.'

'Should sell with that,' I said. 'It sounds as though you have done some very original scholarship.'

Having visited the depressing shrine at Ayot St Lawrence I could readily believe that it had not been a Passion Flower Hotel during Shaw's lifetime, but I had no desire to delve further.

'Before we leave I hope we can discuss this again,' she said with ominous finality.

Luckily I was rescued from further revelations by a member of the hotel staff who informed me that my room was now available. I excused myself, whispering to Bill that we should escape the mob and have a quiet dinner alone.

Rather than rejoin the others after unpacking, I sat at my open balcony window to savour the passing scene below. It was while watching the gondola flotillas crammed with ecstatic Japanese float past on the Grand Canal that I saw the old dandy and the girl again. They went by directly beneath me in a private speedboat driven by a muscular young man in a T-shirt, heading out of the Grand Canal and into the lagoon. Their reappearance quickened my heartbeat again. The old man was wearing the same outfit, but the girl had changed since the airport. They sat side by side, holding hands, for all the world like father and daughter, except they didn't seem to fit together. I guessed they were going to dine on one of the smaller islands. I watched them until they were out of sight.

My thoughts were far away throughout dinner which made me a somewhat remote companion, something that Bill remarked upon. I excused myself by saying that the flight had given me a headache and we made an early night of it. I slept fitfully, racked by a recurring dream in which Henry and I were endlessly searching for Sophie and failing to find her.

I awoke with a genuine headache and while waiting for my expensive continental breakfast to arrive I went to the journal I always carry with me to look for the entry I had made on the night I learned of Henry's death. Curiously there was just the terse statement: *Henry found dead by his own hand in Moscow*, nothing else. Further down on the same page in a reference to the dramatic turn of events in Russia, I had made the fairly mundane comment that all previous enemies having been pushed off stage, doubtless a new cast was waiting in the wings, fully rehearsed and anxious for the show to go on, there being no business like the war business, et cetera.

The night the news reached me I had been alone in my risingly fashionable Islington flat, sitting in front of my word processor attempting to recover a lost passage of the novel I was writing. The software had been described by the salesman as 'user friendly' – employing computer terminology in an effort to quieten my fears of anything mechanical. It had been less than friendly that particular night; half a chapter had disappeared, something I likened to the destruction of a whole city, for I had been writing against the clock, on a roll for once, and presto! a wrong key struck in haste, in tiredness, and the muse had vaporised. In my case a particularly hideous event since I never make notes or lay out the plot on wall charts, and now my mind, like the screen, was a blank. I consulted the instruction manual, but for all it conveyed it could have been written in Sanskrit. I was consumed with thoughts of taking a cold chisel and performing a lobotomy on the bloody machine's brain, anything to make those lost words I had slaved over reappear. I do have a tame expert that I ring when the chips, literally, are down – one of those manic enthusiasts who can't write novels but is able to make any rogue computer give up its secrets – but I hesitated to expose my stupidity yet again. I poured myself a whisky and read the section headed *Trouble-shooting* in the manual for the fifth time. *Re-boot*, it said, *check for lost data using your DOS Undelete Command* – messages from an alien planet. I hit the keys as per instructions like a child picking out 'Chopsticks' on the piano, but salvation was still denied me. It was then, when I had decided to risk waking my mechanical brain surgeon and plead with him to perform an emergency operation, that the phone rang with that insistence peculiar to the hours of darkness. There is something unreasonably menacing about a phone ringing at night in an otherwise silent house.

The moment I lifted the receiver, spilling my whisky in the process, a confident male voice I could not immediately place addressed me by my first name.

'Martin?'

Some instinct made me cautious. 'Who do you wish to speak to?'

'Martin Weaver, please.' The first ploy having failed, the voice took on a politer tone. 'Is that Mr Weaver speaking, by any chance?'

'Who wants him?'

'My name's Anderson. I just wanted a quick word with Mr Weaver.'

'What about?'

'Is that Mr Weaver speaking?'

'Hold on, I'll get him.' I put my hand over the mouthpiece, giving myself time to try and identify anybody by that name who might have reason to call me at such an hour. The only possibility I could think of was some new arrival in my New York agent's office – Americans often assume immediate intimacy with complete strangers. When next I spoke I attempted to change my accent, but the effect was pitiful.

'This is Martin Weaver.'

'Ah! Sorry to bother you this late, Martin,' – he reverted to first-name basis, then wondered, in a voice devoid of wonder, whether I would care to comment on the news just in.

'What news is that?'

'You didn't watch television tonight?'

'No, I've been working, and I've had my fill of television for one week. What's happened now, has there been a second coup? Who are you, by the way?'

'Sorry, didn't I say? I work on the Sun.'

I have found that whenever members of the media ring out of the blue invariably there is good and immediate cause to regret ever answering their call.

'I'm sorry to be the bearer of bad tidings, but an old friend of yours, Henry Blagden, was found dead today in a Moscow hotel. It's believed he committed suicide . . . Hello? You still there?'

'Yes. How awful . Suicide, you say?'

'That's the story we have. He hanged himself. Sorry if I took you unawares, I assumed you would have seen the television item. Am I right in saying that at one time your name was connected with his wife?'

'Connected' is a danger word in tabloidese, saturated with carnal implications.

'A long time ago, perhaps . . . both Henry and Mrs Blagden were friends of mine.'

'Intimate friends, as I understand.'

'Yes, though we somewhat lost touch in recent years.'

'It was a happy marriage, though?'

'I've no reason to believe it wasn't.'

'There were rumours that it was going through a sticky patch.'

'Were there? They didn't reach me.'

Conversations with journalists quickly assume the character of a forced collaboration: two total strangers with nothing in common fencing with the truth.

'So you wouldn't have any idea why he would suddenly take his own life?'

'No.'

'None at all?'

'No.'

'When did you last see him?'

'When? . . . Er, we had lunch together at my club about a year ago, possibly a bit longer, I can't remember exactly.'

'How was he then?'

'Fine.'

'He acted normally?'

'Yes. Look, what is the point of these questions? A man, a friend, has committed suicide you tell me, though presumably that's still hearsay, and I don't intend to speculate as to what brought him to that point in his life.'

For some reason it was Sophie, Henry's wife, who was uppermost in my mind as I fielded his loaded questions. Perhaps the thought-waves transmitted themselves to him, for next he asked: 'Will you be talking to Mrs Blagden?'

'I've no idea where I'd contact her.'

'Oh, I'm sure we could trace her for you.'

'Well, no doubt I shall be writing to her in due course, but I hardly think she'd wish to be bothered at this particular time.'

'Does that mean you're no longer very close?'

'What sort of question is that?'

He caught the growing note of irritation in my voice and again apologised for disturbing me. 'Just that we're running the story tomorrow and we're trying to gather as much detail as we can.'

'Detail about what? His death or my friendship?'

'Well, you're the obvious person to approach. Somebody like you, your comments carry weight. After all, he was a public figure and in view of everything happening in the Kremlin, the story has added news value. I don't suppose you know why he was in Moscow at this particular time?'

'No, I don't. I've already told you, we haven't spoken in months.'

'There is a theory that he had connections with the intelligence services.'

'Is there?'

'Yes. He seems to have put his fingerprint on a number of pies, and naturally anything to do with intelligence is hot right now. So, you can't comment on that?'

'No.'

'Even with your own contacts?'

'My contacts are very peripheral I'm afraid.'

'But you write about spies, you're taken to be something of an expert.'

'I make up stories,' I said. 'One doesn't have to be a murderer to write detective fiction.'

'Except you're often praised for being so accurate.'

'Just like your newspaper I'm at some pains to get the facts right.' I had no idea whether he detected the irony, but he changed tack.

'OK, well, can you think of anybody else who might be able to give us a quote?'

'Quote?'

'What sort of man he was.'

'He always struck me as a very diligent MP.'

'Diligent? That's a good word. Did you ever think he should have gone further?'

'What d'you mean by "further"?'

'The fact that, despite his abilities, he was continually passed over for a ministerial post.'

'I've no idea. I'm not a very political person.'

'But he was ambitious, wasn't he?'

'I imagine you have to be to even think of making politics a career.'

'Did he ever discuss that side of his life with you?'

'Yes, people usually like to talk about what interests them most and most politicians of my acquaintance are one-track.'

'Can you remember anything about his relationship with the Prime Minister, for instance? He wasn't one of her inner circle, was he?'

'I don't have a tape recorder running when I meet with friends, Mr Anderson. I'm sure he had the normal outlook of anybody in politics . . .'

'Meaning?'

He was cute and on the ball, digging for dirt, but I did not fall for it. 'He's dead,' I said, 'so, the rest is conjecture. I know you've got a job to do and I'm sure you do it to the best of your ability, disagreeable though that must be at times. I've really got nothing more to add.'

'Well, before you ring off, sir,' – I had been elevated from Christian name to condescension – 'just one final point, how do you like to be described?' He exited my life as he had entered it with a false sincerity.

'Kindly,' I said.

'Ha, ha, don't we all?' His phoney laugh gurgled in my ear like disappearing bath water. 'Shall we say "author"?'

'Why not? It covers a multitude of sins.'

The moment the line went dead I forgot all about my vanished work-in-progress. It's difficult to grasp that somebody you have known for the best part of thirty years would never be around again. So many moments experienced together – trivial, desperate, happy, poignant and sorrowful moments – flashed through my mind, I remember, as the realisation sank in. The years we had shared appeared on the screen of memory in quick succession as though activated by one of those automatic projectors – some in sharp focus, some blurred, for memory plays tricks. I could see Sophie more clearly than Henry. Maybe that was a case of the subconscious deliberately protecting me; I didn't want to think of his hanged face – the only point of reference being newsreel shots of World War II partisans strung up by the roadside, like bloated rag-dolls twisting, lifeless. If I had ever thought of suicide victims before, they had always conjured calmer images – bodies sprawled on beds, the empty bottle of pills within reach of the outstretched hand. Hanging was something else, too much to take in. Another slug of whisky dulled my perceptions, but not enough. I had a vision of a Moscow hotel room devoid of comfort, the furnishings trapped in a time-warp, drained of colour like an old black and white film. What had Henry used for the act – braces, a piece of flex, his White's tie? Did he kick away a feeble bedside chair in those last seconds, had he judged the noose correctly, did his neck break or did he slowly throttle, bubbling last regrets?

I paced my living room thinking about the irony of the time and the place he had chosen: just when hope was beginning to spread like flood waters over the bleak landscape of the Soviet Union, this had been the moment Henry had chosen to extinguish the future. Why? Had he been one of my fictional inventions I would never have portrayed him as a potential suicide. From the first days of our friendship at the university I remembered him as a master of bravado, flying in the face of convention and convinced that better times were always around the corner. Possessed of no such general optimism myself these were qualities I admired and envied in him, and I confess to an element of hero worship.

Early on in our relationship I discovered that we both

shared a lasting affection for those compelling, if repetitive, tales of Greyfriars School which once flowed from the pen of Frank Richards, and had been the staple diet of our adolescence. If anybody had sought to explain our friendship (and I daresay there were many who did) the answer was to be found in the pages of *The Magnet*: he was Vernon Smith, the 'bounder' of the Remove to my Harry Wharton, ever daring to break the rules, always the instigator of any escapade we shared. A couple of years older than me, he displayed a sophistication in most things that made me a willing captive to his more forceful personality. He could make me believe anything in those days. I remember being immensely impressed when he told me his great-grandfather on his mother's side had been a member of the Souls, the nickname of that close-knit collection of late Victorian aristocrats. He often referred to this and liked to give the impression that he had inherited many of the attributes of that all-but-forgotten, brilliantly clever and vivacious group. Knowing nothing of the Souls, his boast sent me scurrying to the library to find out more, since I hadn't wanted to expose my ignorance. Armed with a little instant knowledge, I felt bold enough to point out that the true Souls had, almost to a man, shared a blighted romanticism. Far from taking this amiss Henry found the comment gratifying.

'Yes,' he said, 'but they acted on the assumption that whatever they did they would come out near the top.' He could always turn criticism to his own advantage, scoring many a quick point in the Debating Society, a quality which, early on, must have fed his future political ambitions.

Despite these efforts to upgrade his social standing he was, like me, forever trapped in his middle-class origins, and it bothered him. I know it bothered him because he was always at great pains to divert attention from his background. His father had been a country solicitor and his mother, who died while Henry was still in short trousers, a parson's daughter, though even this fact had to be elevated in Henry's telling of it. 'Her father, the Bishop,' he would say, forgetting he had once shown me the family snapshot album which contained no trace of the purple.

His method of dealing with any such self-sensitive issue was to sidle away from it, like a crab, although in other situations he displayed tenacity, a desire to lunge where others feared to tiptoe. I still believe that during his formative years he remained essentially an idealist, always harbouring, it seemed to me, a longing for a woman who matched some childhood dream of chastity and beauty.

Looking back, I see now that his was an invented life from which, ultimately, he could not extricate himself. The stories he trotted out whenever he had a new audience were constantly embellished like a Lego monument to vanity, for he was desperate to impose on strangers an improved account of himself. In the full flush of our friendship I was willing to forgive these conceits since they amused rather than repelled me. I was content to bask in his shadow, and if I admitted to myself that certain things did not add up, I kept such thoughts hidden. I know that others found the closeness of our relationship odd; many were turned off by his flamboyance and couldn't understand the attraction he held for me. But who can ever explain the attraction of opposites, the happily married couple, Laurel and Hardy physically, who yet complement each other? With the benefit of hindsight I realise now that what I took from Henry was a sort of spurious, second-hand glory. Whilst not sharing his philosophy of life I was still able to admire certain aspects. I might have suspected that much of his life was a pose but, then, whose isn't? We all choose to invent portions of ourselves for if we were to admit all our faults life would be intolerable. If I was unable to pin Henry down as to chapter and verse regarding his antecedents, my emerging sense of the dramatic still allowed them to appear glamorous. There is a note in my journal of that period which reveals as much about me as it does about Henry.

H at his most bombastic this evening. I wish he didn't feel the need to impress me all the time. I like him enough to tolerate his prejudices without having them rammed home. I know that most people find him garrulous and irritating, but they don't see the other side of him. I think basically he is frightened of revealing his real emotions. There are times when our friendship could splinter, and then he suddenly becomes contrite and generous, pathetically so. C annoyed me by hinting that Henry is a fairy in wolf's clothing. We almost came to blows about it. The trouble with C and his set is that they are always trying to recruit for their own way of life, they can't bear to think that a friendship such as H and I share can be innocent. I of all people would know if H was that way inclined.

If Henry was attracted to anything, it was wealth. He made it his business to learn the secrets of those who had it; I firmly believe that is what made him choose merchant banking as his first career. In his eyes the very rich had a mystique about them that allowed him to overlook what was often their appalling lack of any taste. It was his anxious socialising in those waters that eventually contributed to the diminution of our friendship. He took up shooting and even rode to hounds on a couple of occasions, two pursuits which are anathema to me and which, in fairness, even he admitted he only used as a means to an end. I unearthed an old copy of the *Tatler* the other day in which there was a photo of Henry resplendent in his hunting pink posed amongst a gaggle of vacuous faces – a Brideshead scene which happily he never revisited. When he first entered Parliament he was widely tipped as somebody likely to gain high office, but for some reason his star never ascended. Perhaps he was basically too bright, since the Tory Party has always been reluctant to promote cleverness and is quick to smother those who threaten the status quo. I think it must have been the first time Henry realised his charms could not unlock all doors. Others cast in the same mould must have seen through his pretensions with less tolerance than me. Lands he could not conquer he quickly vacated, for he couldn't handle rejection.

He was complex and baffling, and yet there were occasions when he overwhelmed me and I came as close as I could to that love which has no sexuality in it but still consumes us. He was one of those best friends we all need in order, from time to time, to betray and, in turn, be betrayed by.

2

THE PRESENT

I had a second espresso on the terrace with a slightly
hungover Bill before our party travelled in a river-bus to
disembark near the Ca' Sanudo, chosen for our first session
because it was the home of the sixteenth-century diarist; the
organisers of the conference were nothing if not literal. There
we debated the fate of writers in the South American
dictatorships, an official of Amnesty International being the
principal guest speaker. He showed some grisly slides to
support his case during the hour-long discourse, and this
was followed by a question and answer session. I felt there
was a certain unstated irony in the situation. There we all
were, cocooned in our easy freedoms, listening to tales of the
deprivation, torture and deaths of distant colleagues. Doubtless everybody felt that they had made a moral commitment
when the resolution for the press release was passed unani-
mously, but I was left with a sense of self-disgust.

My mood lingered throughout the subsequent lunch we
were treated to on the island of Torcello. Afterwards most of
us wandered around visiting the ancient church in an
attempt to walk off the effects of over-eating. There were
some small stalls selling linens and tourist kitsch and it was
while Bill was deciding on a gift for his wife that I was
astonished to see the old dandy from the airport once more.
This time he was with a new companion, a mature man
wearing one of those black, Italian suits made familiar by the

Godfather films and somehow always sinister. Together they made a study in contrasts, for the old boy was again wearing his cream suit. They passed quite close to me and although our eyes met, he betrayed no sign of recognition. My heart jolted as I watched them out of sight and something must have shown in my face for Bill asked: 'You feeling OK?'

'Yes, fine.'

'You look as though somebody just walked over your grave.'

'Too much grappa,' I said.

I was to see the old dandy one last time as we made our way back to the boat. This time he was standing outside the ornate gates of a large villa and seemed to be arguing with the same companion. I was sure he was aware of me because as I drew closer he turned his back.

A certain holiday atmosphere persisted on the return trip to Venice. Most of the delegates produced cameras, some had even brought camcorders. Bill fiddled endlessly with his Nikon complete with telephoto lens. I had noticed him studying the instruction booklet during the meal. He was attempting to shoot the solitary seagulls atop the marker posts, but our boat was moving too fast. 'Damn,' he kept saying, 'the bloody thing keeps going in and out of focus.'

'Try panning with it,' I said, airing a superior knowledge I had acquired on film sets. 'And brace yourself, otherwise everything will be blurred.'

It was then that I noticed something sufficiently odd to make me look twice. Ahead and to one side of us a score of gulls were whirling and swooping low around a deserted post. There were no fishermen in the vicinity, yet the predatory birds were obviously disturbed by something in the water.

'Lend me the camera for a minute, will you?'

I took it from him and lightly pressured the auto-focus button until the distant post became sharp. I could make out an indeterminate shape in the water lapping up against the post as the swell from our boat reached it, but the low sun flared the lens, making identification difficult. I used the zoom to take a closer look and what I now saw alarmed me.

'Somebody tell him to slow down,' I shouted. 'I think there's a body in the water.'

One of our party spoke fluent, colloquial Italian and the driver cut his engine allowing us to drift closer to the post. I was right. It was a body. Our driver skilfully manoeuvred alongside, then produced a grappling hook and with the help of several of the men managed to flop the corpse on to the deck where anxious hands turned it face upwards. My German friend of the night before suddenly screamed and covered her eyes. As the crowd parted I saw to my horror it was the girl Henry had kissed at the airport. Her head lolled at an unnatural angle on the wet deck for her throat had been cut, the bloodless flesh gaping like a gutted fish.

I felt compelled to give a statement to the Italian police, not that there was much I could tell them other than that I had seen the girl on two separate occasions in the company of the old man in the cream linen suit. At the time it seemed too complicated, and indeed pointless, to include my supposed sighting of Henry, though I did describe the young man in the T-shirt driving the motorboat and he, rather than the old dandy, elicited more interest than anything else. Nothing had been found on the body to identify the girl, nor had anybody of her description been reported missing. I daresay that had it not been for the fact that she was a murder victim they would have filed her as an unknown tourist who met with a tragic accident.

The incident left me in turmoil, perhaps because I could not avoid the association with my first mistake. At the airport I had fleetingly mistaken the dead girl for Sophie; now past and present images fused together and I was prey to premonitions I found impossible to dismiss. My conjured sense of the dramatic had always served me well in the pursuit of my craft, but in fiction murder is casual compared to reality, turn the page and the crime starts to be solved. I could solve nothing, for nothing made sense and I was not in control.

The incident sobered everybody at dinner that night; the confrontation with an actual death had more significance than the Amnesty official's recitation of events in distant lands and my tenuous involvement gave me a spurious glamour in their eyes that I could have well done without.

'I was amazed when you said you recognised her,' Bill said. (I have to add that he and several others had clicked their cameras at the corpse.) 'What made you remember her?'

Since we were not alone, I prevaricated. 'Force of habit, I suppose. I'm always on the lookout for character detail. It wasn't the girl that stuck in my memory so much as the old man I first saw her with.'

'Why, what was distinctive about him?'

'He seemed to be in a time-warp. The way he dressed, he wasn't quite real. That and the difference in their ages.'

'Well, I take my hat off to you. I don't remember faces at all, lands me into all sorts of trouble.' Then professional considerations took over. 'Hell of a jumping-off point for a new book. Just what you're looking for.'

'Maybe.'

The police contacted me again the next day and showed me a number of mug shots hoping I could pick out the young man in the T-shirt, but I drew a blank. The detective who questioned me this time was the size of Pavarotti and gave off a pungent smell of garlic. He spoke excellent English and probed me for more details.

'I'm curious, Mr Weaver, as to why the victim, whom you say was a total stranger to you, should have made such a big impression.'

'As I've already explained, it was the poor girl's companion, the strange old man, that stuck in my memory.'

He nodded, then seemed to change his mind before asking his next question. 'And the first time you saw them was at the airport?'

21

'Yes.'

'The second occasion was in the boat in the evening?'

'Yes.'

'They had just arrived at the airport, like yourself?'

'I've no idea. I believe they were saying goodbye to a friend.' It was the first time I had mentioned the presence of Henry and he immediately pounced on it.

'Oh, so there was a third person there?'

'Yes.'

'Man or woman?'

'A man. I saw them saying goodbye to each other before he caught his plane.'

'Describe him for me, please.'

'I didn't see him all that distinctly.'

'Well, as best you can.'

'Middle-aged, about six feet tall, respectably dressed. I'm sorry, but I can't recall anything odd about him, he was too far away.'

'And what time was this?'

'Approximately three in the afternoon. I had come in on an earlier plane from London and stayed at the airport to greet a colleague who was travelling from New York. He came in on the flight from Frankfurt about an hour later.'

He nodded. 'Nothing else?'

'I don't think so.'

'I have to ask you this, you had no prior knowledge or relationship with the victim?'

'No. I'd never seen either of them before. As I've told you, I'm just here for the conference. Tell me something, please, have you identified the old man?'

'Not so far. The population of Venice changes by the hour at this time of year. Did you hear him speak to the victim?'

'No, but I did see him again on Torcello, the day the murder was discovered, this time with a man.'

'The same man as at the airport?'

'No. From the way he was dressed I took him to be a local.'

He stared at me, then made a pencilled note. 'It's quite a

coincidence, isn't it? Here you are, a visitor newly arrived, and yet on three separate occasions within the space of twenty-four hours, you see this same man.'

'The odds are long, I agree.'

'Especially with the number of people in Venice at this time.'

'I can only say it happened.'

'There is, of course, the further fact that it was you who happened to be on the boat when the body was discovered.'

'Yes, I admit that shook me.'

'Do you play the lottery, Mr Weaver?'

'No.'

'You should. You're sure there is nothing else you wish to tell me?'

'I don't think so, I put everything I remembered in my statement.'

'I see from your passport that you're a writer.'

'Yes.'

'What sort of books do you write?'

'Thrillers mostly.'

'Are they translated and published here?'

'Some of them have been.'

'I must seek them out '

'Allow me to send you a copy.'

'That would be kind. Thrillers, you say? I imagine murders in novels are easier to solve than the real ones, aren't they?'

'Don't you believe it.'

'The trick is, I believe, to surprise your readers. What is the expression – to put in red herrings?' He paused, looking me straight in the eye. 'Perhaps I should tell you that the victim had also been sexually violated.'

'Poor girl,' I said. 'How hideous '

'Yes. But that's the red herring, you see. Real life occasionally imitates art.' He took his time before continuing, then savoured each subsequent word, his eyes all the time searching my face. 'You have made your own contribution to this mystery, did you know that?'

'No. How so?'

'You constantly refer to the victim as "she". But the victim was not a girl, he was a teenage boy. A very pretty boy, I grant you, so perhaps your error is understandable.' He closed his notebook. 'So it would appear, Mr Weaver, we both have something more to think about.'

Before leaving the police station I was warned that, being the only material witness, I would be recalled to give evidence at a later date, once the players had been identified.

I walked back to the Gritti Palace utterly confused. I was conscious that there had been several opportunities for me to elaborate on my possible sighting of Henry, but I had held back because I had no wish to invite further suspicion by introducing the idea that a man certified as dead could suddenly materialise, especially when there was a possible connection to a murder. The more I thought about it the more I convinced myself it must have been something prompted by the subconscious – the association of Sophie and Venice. If it had been Henry, what possible explanation could there be for him keeping company with the murdered boy? Nothing made any sense.

I gave less than my full attention to the rest of the conference, for I could not rid myself of haunting images: Sophie, Henry, the old man and the dead boy were more real to me than the subject under discussion. As I had predicted to Bill, the sessions produced ponderous resolutions, but I cynically doubted their ultimate value to those who needed more than brave words. The final statement expressed our solidarity and, amongst other things, called upon the Iranian government to renounce the death sentence on Salman Rushdie. No doubt all concerned departed home in the odour of sanctity. I exchanged addresses with the German lady and promised to do what I could to help find her a publisher for her biography.

Bill and I took the same plane to Heathrow and during the

flight he produced a packet of photographs he had had developed overnight.

'Some of these are half-way decent. I haven't quite mastered how the bloody thing works, but some of them have come out OK, don't you think?' He handed them to me. Most of them were the usual, inexpertly framed, tourist views that have made Kodak rich, but as I politely scanned his efforts I suddenly came across a shot of the dead boy on the deck of the water-taxi. Looking again at his poor, drained face, a face that even in death had certain similarities to Sophie when young, I was transported back into the country of the past and other images came to mind, images that time had not blurred.

3

THE PAST

Although it was not given great prominence at the time most of the dailies had covered the story of Henry's supposed suicide. The *Sun*, predictably, had coupled my name with Sophie's – *Lifelong friend, thriller writer Martin Weaver, who at one time was romantically linked with Blagden's wife, expressed shock that such a potentially brilliant career had ended so tragically, describing Blagden as a diligent Member of Parliament who had been shamefully passed over for a Cabinet post.*

The *Mail* had unearthed a picture of the three of us taken on a holiday we had once shared in the South of France – Sophie delectably young and attractive in a bikini, and Henry and I looking like a pair of owlish sex deviants. I read every paper carefully. Most reports relied on CNN news, giving the basic facts and stating that Henry had been in Moscow as a Parliamentary observer. A post-mortem was to be carried out and according to *The Times* his political agent was intending to arrange a memorial service at a later date, but it was a small item in the *Telegraph* that caught my eye. Their man in Moscow had managed to interview the hotel maid who had discovered the body in the bedroom closet.

Whatever anybody thinks of my efforts, I have a professional pride in getting my facts right when writing a novel (readers latch on to any mistakes with irritating regularity I have found) and mention of the closet immediately triggered a response. Henry stood just over six feet and the last time I had seen him he must have been carrying 180 lbs. Suicide by hanging is an imperfect art and it would have been nigh impossible for a man of his height and weight to suspend himself inside a closet little higher than himself. I went to one of my own closets and carried out an experiment. I am only 160 lbs and shorter than Henry, but the hanger bar immediately started to buckle the moment I put any weight on it. Nor could I get my feet off the ground. Hanging by such a method was not only improbable, I concluded, but impossible.

On an impulse I tracked down Henry's political agent to try and get a current telephone number for Sophie and probe him for further details. He proved to be a real smoothie, with one of those moustaches that look like a smudge, and volunteered little. Yes, it was definitely suicide (this given a little too glibly); Henry had used electric flex and according to the preliminary report he had been dead several hours before his body was discovered.

'Did he give the impression he was depressed when he took off?'

'Not to me.'

'And how about Mrs Blagden? How has she taken it?'

There was a pause before he answered.

'I haven't been able to contact her yet,' he said in an offhand sort of way. 'She's out of the country, in the States I believe. Abroad anyway, and moving around. Hell of a time to fight a by-election,' he said, gliding effortlessly into a *non sequitur*. 'Between you and me Central Office think it bloody tiresome of him to top himself when we're trailing seven points in the opinion polls. The word is to play it down, though naturally I feel the loss very keenly.'

I ignored his crocodile sorrow. 'Well, as and when you do locate his wife, please ask her to ring me. I'd like to help if I can.'

'They've thrown the whole mess at me. I'm supposed to fly to Moscow and attend to the formalities,' he continued as though I had never spoken. 'Imagine what a hassle that's going to be, with all those ex-Commies running around like headless chickens.'

'I shouldn't worry. One thing they're good at is dealing with dead bodies,' I said. 'You won't forget about Sophie?'

'Forget who?'

'Mrs Blagden. Please, when you make contact, do ask her to ring me.'

'Oh, yes, that. Well, I'll do my best, but I can't promise.'

I had deliberately made no mention of my doubts about the maid's account. For all I knew she had been misquoted in translation.

The following day I made an appointment to see Henry's solicitor, a pompous character I had a passing acquaintance with; at Henry's insistence he had once handled a house purchase for me, but I found his general air of superiority too big a pill to swallow twice. He operated out of one of those superb town houses bordering the precincts of Westminster that nowadays only the legal profession can afford.

'This business seems inexplicable to me,' I began when seated across from his partner's desk. 'I just can't take it in.'

'One never knows, does one? It makes three I've had to pick up the pieces for this year. Always a sign that the economy is shot. I had a word with the Under Secretary at the Treasury only last week and told him it's time they got their act together.' One could almost taste the lemon juice in his voice.

'Did Henry have money problems then?'

I knew that would immediately put him on his professional dignity. 'I don't think I can discuss that with you at this time. We must wait for probate. As it happens I had you down to call sooner or later.'

'Really? Why was that?'

'I naturally acted for Henry in drawing up his Will and although I can't divulge the contents I think it's in order for me to tell you that he appointed you his literary executor.'

'You surprise me. He never mentioned it to me.'

I had a sudden horror at being asked to edit and attempt to

publish a collection of his ghosted political speeches, some of which I had had a hand in, since I was well aware that Henry lacked any natural literary bent.

'You're a writer, aren't you?' There was an offensive hint of query in his voice. 'I imagine he felt you'd be best able to deal with such side issues. As soon as probate is granted I'll arrange for all his private papers to be made available to you.'

'Is there a lot of material?'

'I wouldn't know. I imagine his widow is the person to ask about that.'

'You don't know where she is by any chance? His agent seemed to think she was travelling in the States and couldn't be contacted.'

'No. I spoke to her this morning.'

'This morning?'

'Yes.'

'Is she in the country then?'

'I believe she's staying with friends somewhere.'

'Oh, well when you speak to her again, could you be kind enough to ask her to ring me, or else give me a number if that's possible.'

'I'll pass on the message. I daresay if she wants to speak to you, she will.' His condescension festered in my ear

'Thank you. You'll be in touch then?'

'Yes. When the dust has settled. Suicides always create so much extra work one could well do without.'

And an extra large account at the end of it, I thought.

It was odd that Henry had never broached the question of my being his literary executor to me during his lifetime. God knows he was seldom shy when it came to asking me favours. The title has such a noble ring about it, implying as it does that the deceased has left behind an unknown master-work, but to the best of my knowledge Henry had seldom written anything worth preserving. In a moment of candour he once told me he had never written Sophie a letter and even now that memory causes a momentary enlargement of the heart for I wrote her so many love letters. Did she keep them

29

after their marriage, I wonder, tied with ribbon in the manner of the Victorians? Probably not; she was not a sentimentalist and had no feeling for places or possessions. Nor did she care where or how she lived. To her, houses were just empty spaces that had been bricked up. Sophie's idea of bliss was to live permanently in hotels with room service and the beds and towels changed every day. Whenever we went away on holiday she took a childish delight in collecting the free soap, shampoos and bookmatches; she had drawers full of them. I'm quite the reverse, I need to have a secure base, everything in place – my books, paintings and favourite records – somewhere to return to that never changes. Prolonged stays in hotels which from time to time I am compelled to endure eventually fill me with angst. I inevitably find myself reduced to striking up immediately- regretted conversations with strangers in coffee shops, and always at the end of the day one has to take the elevator to the anonymous room. Sophie and Henry were forever on the move; in many ways I envied them that carelessness, that refusal to conform to convention. They had one house in Amersham I would willingly have killed for, but they left it within a year and without apparent regret.

If he did write, Henry confined himself to postcards. In the days when we three were inseparable he used to send me the type that once festooned every seaside novelty shop – depicting women with enormous bottoms and boobs, the men skinny and henpecked and wearing old-fashioned bathing costumes, the captions vaguely scatological. I came across one the other day used as a bookmark, on which he had written: 'This reminded me of you,' though there were many times when I doubted Henry ever thought of me unless he wanted something. He kept a store of such cards, for he liked buying things in quantity – shirts, postage stamps, pencils, notepads – everything, now I come to think of it, except my own books. 'Why don't you give me one, you get them free, you mean bugger?' he would say, and in that he was no different from the rest of my circle of friends, all of whom shared the same misconception. Even when I did bestow a copy upon him I have the suspicion that it went straight on to his bookshelves, unread. Certainly he never commented on anything I wrote except to ask what advance I had received. Henry equated success with money. I suspect that this was his motivation for entering politics. He had what appeared to be an overnight conversion, going from being a venomous critic of successive governments straight to the bosom of the Tory Party. To my astonishment he was quickly adopted in a marginal seat winning it with an increased majority, for he was personable on the hustings and could get his tongue around most of the platitudes that never fail to lull the electorate. I mentioned earlier that I always expected his political star to soar, but curiously he did little to curry favour in Downing Street or with the whips, it was as if all he really wanted was the status of an MP without any of the in-fighting and intrigue so necessary for advancement. It was, for him, merely a means to an end. He was, as I said to the *Sun* reporter, diligent in the sense that he kept his nose clean and talked a lot about how the important thing was not power but an opportunity to serve your fellow men, though I was left with the feeling that the person he served best was himself.

I badgered his appalling solicitor later the same week for any further news of Sophie and the funeral arrangements, only to be told that the Foreign Office had decided that because of the crisis in Russia his body should be buried there. Following a post-mortem the embassy would be taking care of all the arrangements. He let slip that Sophie was content to let such arrangements go forward.

'Did you give her my message?'

'Yes, I passed it on.'

I waited. 'And?'

'She asked me to thank you for your sympathy.'

'Nothing else?'

'Not that I recall.'

'And you're not at liberty to tell me where I can call her personally?'

'No, I'm afraid not.' It is so very British to employ the word 'afraid' when the speaker is anything but.

'Then can you tell me when you expect the post-mortem findings?'

'No, I can't. Communications from there are completely snarled at the moment,' he replied, his voice growing more distant as though, while talking to me, he was dealing with other more vital matters.

'Do they work through a coroner in such cases?'

'I believe they have some sort of system. Inferior to ours, I imagine.'

'And how long after that before they release the body?'

'Mr Weaver, I have no knowledge of Russian judicial procedures. If you want more detailed information I suggest you contact the Foreign Office.'

I was shunted to three separate departments in the Foreign Office before an obviously junior official was produced.

'Are you family?'

'No,' I said, 'just a very old friend.'

'One doesn't usually give out information of this kind except to family.'

'Information of what kind?'

He fingered his tie and adjusted his cuffs. 'Personal details,' he said.

'Well, I'm not asking for those. What I'm asking is whether the post-mortem has been conducted and the date of the funeral. Mr Blagden's death has been reported on television and in the papers, so it's not classified, surely?'

'Well, one can't rely on the media, can one?'

'No, that's why I'm here.'

Although a junior he was well schooled in evasive tactics.

'I think your best course would be to put your request formally, in writing, and we'll forward it to the embassy in Moscow.'

'Couldn't you fax it to save time, otherwise the funeral will be over before it gets there? You do have fax machines, I take it, or perhaps you're still using the bush telegraph?'

My sarcasm produced no crease in his features.

'Yes, we could do that for you, sir, but whether they'll supply the answers, given the current situation, is not something I can pronounce on. I'm sure you're aware they have more pressing matters to deal with right now.'

'Are you saying that the suicide of a British Member of Parliament in a foreign country is of no concern to Her Majesty's First Secretary of State? Is that what I should take away?'

This ruffled him for the first time and there was a change of colour in his close-shaven cheeks.

'No. I was merely stating that the situation in Moscow is very fluid. It's all a question of priorities.'

'Yes, well thank you for all your help,' was my parting shot, delivered with loaded emphasis, but it was wasted on him.

Leaving there I could not make up my mind whether my persistence had goaded him to be deliberately evasive, or whether he was under orders to withhold a more sinister explanation. I determined not to let it rest there and decided to tackle somebody at Tory Central Office.

For the headquarters of a major political party the premises in Smith Square are fairly unimpressive. The entrance hall has the appearance of a provincial hotel going through hard times. These days they maintain high profile security for good reason, but having passed scrutiny and given my reason for my visit, I was handed an adhesive visitor's pass and left to cool my heels for a good twenty minutes. I studied the large coloured photograph of the current leader which was prominently displayed, then scanned the various brochures offering the faithful package tours of an England that existed only in the imagination of the Party hacks who wrote them.

Eventually somebody descended to see me – an immensely tall character wearing the regulation dark blue pinstripe suit and a shirt which suggested it had been bought for him by his wife, a size too small. It doubtless helped to give him his strangulated voice; he addressed me with vowels so clipped that I often missed the odd word. He introduced himself purely by his surname, which probably meant he had a title, but again his mouthful-of-marbles-diction scrambled it.

'Weaver, is it? I understan' you're enquiring about poor old Blaggers.'

'Yes. I was shocked to hear of his death.'

'Sad end, yes. Greatly missed. You're a friend, are you?'

'Yes, I'd known him thirty years.'

'Have to ask, one can't be too careful these days, the Press being what they are. Good, get that out of the way. You're not related to Cecil, by any chance?'

'Cecil?'

'Lord Lanchberry. He was a Weaver before he was sent upstairs.'

'No,' I said. 'I don't think there's any family connection.'

'Well, now, how can we help you?'

'I find I've been made Henry's literary executor, and I'm anxious to get in touch with his widow, but I don't have a current address for her.'

'Literary executor, eh,' he said, looking past me as somebody else entered the lobby. 'Excuse me.' He went to greet the new arrival. I heard him say, 'They're ready for you in the studio, Minister. I think you'll be happy with the new draft, I worked it over myself.'

When he rejoined me he continued as though there had been no interruption: 'I hope it doesn't mean we're going to be faced with the publication of his diaries one day. What with the Royals shooting themselves in the foot and those characters on the other side of the House constantly churning them out, I think we all need a rest, don't you?' He gave a short, barking laugh. 'On the whole, best not to copy their example. Save the rain forests and all that.' Again the same disconcerting laugh.

'I've no idea whether Henry actually kept a diary. His papers haven't been released to me yet.'

'Well, perhaps you'll let us have sight of anything that

touches upon matters of public interest.' His blandness seemed to congeal his face.

Trying to take him off guard, I said: 'Do you have any idea why Henry took his own life? Did anybody here suspect he was in that frame of mind?'

His expression remained the same. 'Didn't really know him myself. Can't know them all, though one does one's best. The word around was he was a thoroughly decent chap. Good constituency man.'

'I believe his wife was a great help there,' I said, edging the conversation back to Sophie.

'Was she? You, well makes all the difference to have the little woman by your side, lending support. Looks good at election time.'

'So, could I ask you, do you have an address for her on file?'

'Daresay we can turn up something. Must have sent condolences. Let me go back upstairs and make a few enquiries.'

He was away about ten minutes. When he rejoined me his manner had changed.

'Look, Weaver, this could prove a little tricky. *Entre nous*, it would appear that he and the wife were separated. Surprised you didn't know that. In the circumstances, it's felt that perhaps we shouldn't give out any address. Sure you understand. Very good of you to call, I'll pass your regards to Cecil when next I see him,' was his parting remark, as though he had never registered my disclaimer.

I left Smith Square thinking that those who make up what is known as the Establishment are unique. MI5, the CIA and the KGB have all been pierced, but our permanent mandarins have perfected the art of concealment. Their attributes may provide the material for successful television sitcoms, but in real life their obsession with secrecy rots our society. Whenever their position is threatened, a whistle is blown, emitting a sound that cannot be heard by ordinary mortals but which is immediately detected by those in the know. We should never underestimate the vindictive hostility of the Establishment when one of its members breaks rank.

Having been fobbed off three times I was now convinced that, following Henry's death, somewhere between Moscow and Whitehall, a decision had been taken to batten down the hatches. Yet, despite the fact that nobody I had spoken to was prepared to help, I still could not reconcile the Henry I had known with somebody embroiled in a situation that major scandals are made of. It made me all the more determined to discover why he was being brushed under the carpet. I have to confess to a further, less altruistic motive: the disclosure that Sophie and Henry had separated prior to his death gave me the hope that she would be grateful for a familiar shoulder to cry on.

Perhaps I never understood Sophie. To love somebody is remote from actually knowing them and I think I have always lacked sophistication in matters of the heart. Perhaps there is some buried, Freudian reason that has yet to surface, but I have always laid myself open to deception, taking everything at face value. I never seem to learn from experience, clinging to trust until it is too late. When, after an enforced interval of a year following their marriage, I met Henry and Sophie again, I handled the situation badly. To socialise and make small talk with a girl whom I had loved, now married to somebody I had once considered my best friend was a scene I would rather have written than acted out. Irrationally, I assumed most of the guilt for having lost her. I could not purge myself of the conviction that she had left me for Henry because of my own stupidity. Every day I could think of new reasons – I had taken her for granted, I had become a careless lover, I had been too wrapped up in my own career.

In the immediate aftermath of Sophie's departure, my normal routine had been shattered. When one is content (or in my case I should more honestly say 'complacent') one can embrace any sort of discipline in one's work. Over the years I had schooled myself to produce a certain number of words every day of the week, come what may. I have a dim recollection that this stemmed from something I had read about Trollope's ability to write against the clock. It seemed to me that this was the way a true professional tackled the job. When Sophie left me my creative adrenalin dried up, it was as if, with the end of love, a tap had been turned off. Writers are often credited with being able to use every emotion to their own advantage and thrashing about for means of revenge, I began a novel with Henry as the Baron Samedi of my subconscious, but salvation refused to transfer itself to the page. After three chapters my anguish proved a fire that refused to flame.

If their marriage changed the whole thrust of my life, it also changed Sophie. I could not help noting she had picked up Henry's manner of speech and many of his attitudes. Often their dialogue overlapped, one echoing the other. Whereas, before, Sophie had never hesitated to have her own opinions and to express them wittily, now she readily agreed with Henry's reactionary views. And it dulled her in my eyes. I was prepared for cruelty but not for an obedient *hausfrau*: she was no longer the scatterbrained, divine creature who had once rumpled my sheets. Perhaps, being the loser, I was deliberately looking for defects.

Nothing is left of all that now. I've moved on, moved backwards, forwards, slept with other girls, told them different lies, the loss is like an empty room in an abandoned house: you lived in it once and now you can't remember exactly why you left it.

4

THE PRESENT

As it turned out there was no memorial service for Henry, nor did I manage quickly to discover Sophie's whereabouts. Some six months after his death his solicitor contacted me about his papers, but when I collected them they proved of little value or interest; Tory Central Office had no need to fear that he had left behind any embarrassing material. His diaries contained nothing but faithful notes of all his social engagements – weekends spent as a house guest in the Shires, some starred alongside names that I took to be conquests of one sort or another, but on the whole sparse and dull accounts: Henry was hardly a diarist in the Harold Nicolson class. I also inherited a quantity of books, some going back to his university days but, in the main these, too, proved worthless. I packed them up, intending to dispose of them to a secondhand dealer, but somehow never got around to it. Amongst the bundles of correspondence and old receipts I found nothing relating to Sophie; it was as if she had never existed in his life. It would have been a hard task for anybody attempting to write his biography. The enigma of his life, like the mystery surrounding his death, remained hidden.

After my return from Venice I constantly found I was haunted by the incidents there. I could not rid myself of the memory of the murdered boy's face. I made no progress on a new novel and for the first time in ages suffered from insomnia.

There are some deaths, even of friends, that recede from memory, only recalled when one goes through the Christmas card lists, or revises old telephone books, but Henry's true fate continued to obsess me. Nothing changed after I awoke from yet another disturbed night: Henry young and the Henry I knew I had glimpsed in Venice was still there. I say *I knew*, but perhaps it would be more accurate to say that I could not admit I was wrong. Lying in bed one morning in that twilight area between sleeping and waking, I came to the decision that one way or another I had to lay his ghost once and for all: I resolved to go to Moscow. The act of making up my mind brought a calmness laced with chill.

Common sense dictated that I had to go prepared. I didn't speak Russian and apart from a pen-friend in Leningrad whom I had never met, I had no Russian contacts. Despite the fact that I had often depicted Moscow in my fictions, I had never been drawn to visit Russia, not even when certain restrictions for Westerners were relaxed. Like so many others of my generation I knew only as much as we had been told. We had all been indoctrinated to the fearfulness of the Russia of the Gulags and despite the recent newsreel footage it remained a country as remote to the ordinary individual as the interiors of our own prisons.

The closest I had ever been was in 1968 when I made a trip to Berlin, courtesy of a film company. I had written the original story for a small black and white British movie which, doubtless because of its obscurity, had been entered for the Berlin Film Festival – its sole moment of glory, for it emptied cinemas everywhere else. This was during the halcyon days when Sophie was living with me and I splashed out for a second air ticket and took her with me.

By this time, of course, Honecker's NVA units had refined the original barbed wire of the Wall. We all made the statutory visit to the now elaborate fortifications, standing numbly before the faded wreaths marking the spots where the first escapees had fallen. Sophie cried, I remember, and the publicity man took shots of us all – though our displayed emotions were somehow bogus: we were merely transients, there for a good time, the Wall was spectator sport for those who could come and go as they pleased. To be in Berlin during that period gave one a feeling of living on the edge, close to the cusp, of being part of a different kind of decadence from the earlier Berlin depicted by Isherwood, more brittle, the brittleness covered with a veneer of imported charm, as though along with the food and supplies flown in by the great airlift, the allies had included a high-voltage, supercharged energy.

During that first visit, I was introduced to an engaging villain called Herr Otto Grubel who had made his fortune in black-market coal immediately post-war, and had then convinced himself that his destiny lay in being a film producer. German movies of that period were collectors' items of ineptitude, with abysmal plots, indifferent direction and acting of the lowest order. I was invited to Grubel's garish house in Grünewald where all the new German money was concentrated and he invited me to do some revisions on a script he had purchased during the festival. That was the start of my on-off movie career as an occasional screenwriter, employed by a series of Grubels over the years, all of them masters of the broken promise.

Thus when I decided to fly to Moscow my first move was to phone an old contact, Rainer Mauritz, an ex-production manager for Grubel. Like many who perform that function in the film industry Rainer knew how to circumvent all the normal channels and on two occasions had been instrumental in ferreting bits of classified information for me that I needed to give authenticity to my spy novels.

'Rainer,' I said after we had exchanged greetings, 'I need a favour. Do you have any contacts in Moscow?'

'Don't tell me you're going there. Wait five years until they learn how to cook. You want excitement, come back to Berlin. This is where the action is now.'

'I'm not looking for excitement, just information and I need somebody who knows his way around.'

'Something to do with one of your books?'

'No. This is personal.'

'A girlfriend you want to get out?'

'Don't be so bloody one-track. A friend of mine died there. The official version is he committed suicide, which I don't believe. I'd like to find out the truth, and I need someone who knows his way around.'

There was a pause before Rainer answered. 'This friend, was he Russian?'

For some reason I lied, I'm not sure why except that I had begun to believe in a conspiracy. 'Yes,' I said.

Again he paused. 'Maybe it's not the best time to be asking those sorts of questions. The coup's over, but from what I hear everybody's still very nervous.'

'Really? Our papers say it's the new age of freedom.'

'This isn't the movies, my friend. Forty years of fear don't evaporate overnight.'

'So, you can't think of anybody?'

'I didn't say that. I was just suggesting you should tread carefully. I do know somebody who did my job in their state film industry. I got to know him when we worked on a co-production a couple of years back.'

'Would he help me?'

'He might. I can't promise, but he might. Living all your life in a police state does nothing for friendships.'

'Can you give me his name?'

'Vasily Golitsin.'

'Spell it.'

I copied it down carefully. 'Do you have a telephone number or address?'

'Wait a minute. I'll have to look it up.'

I waited. He was gone from the phone for a full two minutes. 'I'll give you the last one I have,' he said on his return. I took it down and checked it back with him.

'Course, it may be out of date.'

'You're a pal. I won't forget.'

'Listen, when you get through, make a stop over here.

There's even more action since the Wall came down. If you thought it was jumping before, you're in for a pleasant surprise. Come and stay with me, I promise you a good time.'

'I may do that. Thanks again.'

'Good luck,' he said. 'Proceed with caution, my friend.'

5

THE PRESENT

When I took the Aeroflot flight for Moscow I had the feeling that, like the fable of Zero's arrow, I might never arrive at my destination. From the outset I found myself prey to spurts of paranoia – was it merely imagination or was my passport subjected to a more thorough scrutiny than usual? When I boarded the plane I studied my fellow passengers closely; most of them were doubtless businessmen keen to cash in on a new market for Western goods and know-how, yet in my nervous state it was easy for me to read something more sinister into their faces.

I bought two cartons of cigarettes in duty free, together with a bottle of Scotch, and some perfume in case I needed bribes. Apart from these, I went armed with little other than a guide book and the name and address of Rainer's contact.

In many ways I was a captive of my own previous inventions. Like most people during the week of the failed putsch I had been glued, day and night, to CNN news, unable to believe that these plastic figures we had all feared for so many years could have been so inept. Their incompetence at doing the very thing we had all imagined was their major talent was perhaps the most surprising aspect of those extraordinary few days. We had been conditioned to think that, whatever else, the Politburo knew how to survive, that the KGB had a terminal stranglehold on hope. I had not been alone in thinking that the reforms, if they ever came, would come slowly; that the same aged, clockwork robots perched high on the Kremlin walls reviewing the long-range nuclear warheads and the high-strutting ranks of the Red Army were a permanent fixture, come rain, come *glasnost*. And then, like the Berlin Wall a year previously, the whole edifice crumbled. It was like being taken backstage having witnessed an amazing drama from the stalls and finding that the actors who had frightened us were just ordinary mortals with masks, that the forbidding sets were one-dimensional and made of canvas. These and other conjectures went through my mind as I sampled Aeroflot's sparse hospitality for the first time.

The first Russians I encountered on arrival still seemed like people wandering around in the aftermath of an earthquake, relieved that they had come out alive but knowing that their lives would still be an unceasing battle. And old. There seemed to be a preponderance of old women doing menial tasks. I had the impression I was watching everything in slow motion, that the clocks as well as the failing economy had been put on hold. The officials who examined my passport behaved as though they had come second in a long race and could not believe their misfortune, though the Customs guard took one carton of cigarettes without a blink, presumably as a reminder that the old regime was not completely dead. I was allowed to retain the rest.

Forewarned by my travel agent, I was prepared when the taxi-driver who took me to my hotel immediately asked if I had foreign currency to exchange at the black-market rate. I offered him some pounds. He looked disappointed.

'No dollars?'

'No dollars, I'm afraid.'

He spoke reasonable English and confided he had once been a medical student, but had incurred the displeasure of a Party member, been denounced and forced to leave his training hospital.

'Will the revolution succeed?'

'Until the bread runs out,' he said. 'But after a lifetime we can live with a few bad months.'

'No more KGB?' I asked, testing him.

He crossed himself. 'Who knows? Maybe they crawl back with another name. Nothing changes forever in Russia.'

I had booked myself into the hotel where Henry was found. It was ornately hideous and I had the feeling of *déjà vu*; having often described such buildings, now, as I stepped into the crowded lobby, everything seemed curiously familiar. A babel of voices echoed around the scruffy marble foyer and I took it that most of the people milling about were from the world's media. There were several obvious television crews with earnest Russian interpreters in attendance working out the itineraries for the next day. As I went to the desk to register I heard an English voice say, 'Don't take that shit. Just tell them we have to get satellite time tonight. To-morrow's too late.' It took a good twenty minutes to get my room sorted out and the paperwork completed. The pro-cedure was more akin to completing an application for life insurance than being granted permission to stay a few nights at the inn.

I was escorted to the seventh floor by an elderly bellhop wearing a quasi uniform that had seen better days. As he unlocked the door I noticed that he was wearing odd shoes. The room itself was clean, but spartan, the furniture a motley collection of leftovers from a bygone age. It was like stepping through the looking-glass into a faded world: a film in Technicolor suddenly reverting to monotones.

I tipped the old boy heavily and at the sight of money he came to life, thanking me profusely and then demonstrating the mysteries of the ancient bathroom. Had I been describing it in a novel, I would have made much of the smell of the place, for there was a mustiness mixed, it seemed, with the odour of cooking such as I remembered from childhood holidays spent with an old aunt whose staple diet was cabbage. The associations with my fictions were such that without feeling foolish I actually examined the room for bugs, taking the only framed print from the wall to see if anything was hidden behind it. I paid special attention to the closet,

45

remembering the real object of my visit. A few metal hangers banged together as I opened the door. It was immediately apparent to the eye that suicide in such a confined space was a remote probability, but all the same I repeated the experiment I had carried out in London. Stepping inside to check the height, I found my head touched the flimsy wooden bar and any elevation was impossible.

Having unpacked my few belongings, I put several packets of cigarettes in my pockets and pondered my first moves. Rainer had said that his friend was reliable, but I did not take that as gospel; a country ruled by fear for nearly five decades would not make the transition easily. Carefully memorising my opening question from the phrase book, I picked up the ancient phone and passed Golitsin's number to the hotel operator. After a long wait I was put through. A girl's voice answered in Russian.

'Can I speak to Mr Golitsin?' I asked in what was doubtless an execrable attempt at the real thing.

'Who wants him?' I took her to say, again in Russian.

I reverted to my own tongue. 'Do you speak English?'

'Yes, of a kind.' Her accent was, in fact, extremely good. It is always shaming how many foreigners have mastered our difficult language, while few of us make the effort to learn theirs.

'My name is Weaver. I'm British and just over here for a few days. Mr Golitsin doesn't know me, but we have a mutual friend in Berlin, Rainer Mauritz, who gave me this number and suggested we might meet and discuss a film project.' Instinctively caution dictated the lie.

'My father isn't in at the moment,' the girl said, 'but I will give him the message when he returns. Are you a film producer?'

'Sort of, I'm a writer. Nothing to do with the Press,' I added in case she became nervous.

'Where is it you can be found?'

I gave her the name of my hotel and my room number.

'I'm sure he will contact you later this evening,' she said.

46

The rest of the afternoon I spent walking around observing. The first thing that struck me was that the shops seemed to be stocked with remnants from a garage sale. There were queues outside all the 'gastronomes', the Orwellian name for the empty food shops and I came to understand as never before the surreal nightmare of the daily struggle by the average Russian to survive. There were no smiling faces in the queues, just expressions of anger. It occurred to me that I had been brainwashed by those early propaganda films of happy tractor drivers bringing in what had now become the non-existent harvest. It was an odd experience for me to be walking streets I had often described in my fictions. I mingled with the crowds gathered in front of the KGB headquarters; somebody was shouting incomprehensible announcements over a loudhailer. In front of me a man was suddenly, liquidly sick. Then I was surrounded by half a dozen young girls – Romanies – holding small children, their free hands outstretched for alms. I distributed a few English pounds and fled as they pursued me.

Later that afternoon I retraced my steps and went back to the hotel to enquire whether I had a message. The answer was no and my query seemed to evoke suspicion. I thought of calling Golitsin again, then decided against it; to appear too anxious might worry him. I had no idea what sort of man he was, whether he was running scared or elated. Rainer had said he was reliable, but even Rainer had no true conception of what existence in Russia was like. Rainer had lived his life in West Berlin, just an onlooker on the outside, like me. How could we know, we who took freedom for granted?

I was crossing the lobby on my way out again when I was confronted by a middle-aged man wearing a reasonably well cut sports-jacket and carrying a topcoat over his arm. He stopped in front of me. We stared at each other.

'Mr Weaver?'

'Yes.'

'I am Golitsin.'

We shook hands. 'It was good of you to come,' I said. 'I hope I'm not inconveniencing you?'

'No, I'm sorry I couldn't get here sooner.' Like Rainer there were traces of an American accent in his speech, but his English was fluent.

'Can we go somewhere and have a drink?'

'Yes, but not here. The prices here are for foreigners.'

'That's all right. I'm a foreigner and I'm paying.'

'No, please, I think better we go to my home.'

'I'd have met you there and saved you the journey if you'd phoned me.'

'Hotel phones were always tapped, maybe they still are.' He led the way outside.

'Isn't that all over now?'

'That's what we're now told.'

'You don't believe it?'

He didn't answer the question immediately. We walked to a side street where he unlocked his small, home-produced car, a Zhiguli, a rip-off of a Sixties' Fiat. It reminded me of the jokes which used to circulate, like the one where the Russian boasted, 'I've got my first car. In ten years' time I'm getting the wheels.'

'Do I believe them?' he said when he had rattled the gear shift into place. 'I want to believe them, but I also want to be sure that I'll stay believing them. The papers also say that vegetables will be in the shops soon. We shall see, we shall see. How long have you known our friend Rainer?'

'Oh, we go back many years, but I haven't seen him in a long time. He told me you're in the same line of business.'

'I have the same job, yes. But making films in Russia is, or rather was, different from Hollywood or Berlin. Here you had to sign a dozen forms every time you wanted an extra piece of equipment. They didn't count our schedules in weeks, but in years. I'm not complaining, don't think that, I have been one of the privileged, my daughter and I have an apartment to ourselves and as you see I have a car, such as it is. But work, work vanished with the old order. Maybe it will return, maybe not.'

'You don't have a wife?'

'My wife is dead,' he replied in a matter of fact way, then changed the subject. 'This jacket I'm wearing, that came from Rainer. It was worn by George Segal in *The Quiller Memorandum*. That was a good film, I'm told.'

'You didn't see it? No, of course you wouldn't have. Stupid of me.'

He made small talk about the films he had worked on until we drew up outside one of the many flaking mansions I had quickly learned were characteristic of Moscow I imagined that once upon a time they had been elegant town houses, occupied by wealthy families, not too dissimilar from parts of London during the Forsyte era, but now, like their counterparts at home, divided up into rabbit warrens of apartments. The entrance hall to Golitsin's house was dimly lit and again, as in the hotel, was permeated with old cooking smells. Somewhere above us a Beatles number was playing.

Golitsin led the way to the second floor. In contrast to my hotel room his apartment immediately conveyed a feeling of friendliness. I was shown into a cramped, combined living room and kitchen. Golitsin's daughter, a girl I took to be in her twenties, was seated at a table covered with a patterned plastic cloth such as my grandmother had used. A ginger cat on the window-sill was trying to catch a fly.

'This is Luibava, my daughter.'

His daughter tidied some papers she had been working on and stood up as we were introduced. She brought to mind one of those haunting heroines H. E. Bates often described: tousled, abundant hair, china-blue eyes, fresh complexion devoid of make-up, the sort of face to make the heart leap.

'We spoke on the phone. How do you do?'

Luibava wore jeans and a sweater with BANANA RE-PUBLIC stencilled on it which I guessed had been another gift from Rainer, stretched tightly across her soft breasts.

'A drink?' Golitsin asked. 'Do you like lemon vodka, Mr Weaver?'

'I've never tried it.'

'Perhaps Mr Weaver would prefer coffee?'

'No, the vodka sounds intriguing. And please call me Martin.'

The vodka was poured and we toasted each other. His daughter did not drink with us. Although more than anxious to bring the conversation round to the reason for my visit, from politeness I asked her what she did.

'I work with my father, as his assistant.'

'When I work,' Golitsin interjected. 'She is a trained designer. Show him some of your sketches.'

'Don't embarrass me, Father. They're not good enough.'

'The trouble here is, Martin, you have to know somebody who knows somebody who knows somebody else higher up who can pull the necessary strings to get you where you want to be – *blat*, as we call it. What's your word?'

'At a guess, influence?'

'Stronger than that. Influence accompanied by a bribe. That hasn't changed.'

I thought I detected a slight hesitation as he said this, and he glanced towards the door as though still expecting somebody to break in and denounce him. 'Maybe that too will change now. My baby is too talented to waste her life playing assistant to me. Too talented and too modest.'

The moment I had savaged my throat with the first glass of vodka he poured another. 'So,' he said, 'you are here for what? To set up a film?'

'Not exactly, no.'

I looked from one to the other, searching for the right words to preface my case. 'You must forgive me for not being completely frank when I first phoned. I don't know the ropes here and I was being cautious for your sake.'

Golitsin put his glass back on the table.

'What do you have to be cautious about?'

As briefly as I could I outlined some of the background to my long friendship with Henry and then told them of my suspicions and concern about the circumstances of his death. I was not surprised that they knew nothing of the event for the suicide of a little known British MP had probably not even been mentioned in the Moscow papers. When I had finished my halting explanation neither Golitsin nor his daughter made any comment.

'You're the only contacts I have, I know nobody else here, I don't speak your language, and I've no idea how to go about this thing, so I'm completely in your hands. If you feel you can't help, I quite understand.'

'In what way would we be able to help you?'

I produced the cutting from the *Telegraph* which gave the name of the hotel maid who had discovered Henry's body.

'This woman. Is there any way you could arrange for me to meet her?'

He exchanged a look with his daughter. 'Why would you wish to do that?'

I told them my thoughts regarding the improbability of a man of Henry's weight and build being able to hang himself in a small closet, but made no mention of the sighting at Venice airport. I sensed them pulling back.

'Are you saying that your friend could have met his death in another way?'

'I think there is something that doesn't add up.'

'But in that case, wouldn't your embassy be the place to go to?'

'Well, yes, I suppose that would be the right procedure, but from enquiries I made in London, it seems that the authorities there have accepted the official version of suicide and washed their hands of it. I don't imagine they would welcome somebody like me reopening the issue just on a whim.'

'So what is the purpose of tracing this hotel maid?'

'I've brought a photograph of Henry with me. All I want is for her to confirm that he was the man she found. Just to set my mind at rest. And to do that I need somebody like yourself to locate her and interpret for me.'

Golitsin stared at me, then moved his eyes to his daughter before answering. 'That's all?'

'Yes. If she confirms it was Henry, then that's the end of the matter.'

'What if she is no longer employed at the hotel?'

'Then I'll have put you to a lot of trouble for nothing.'

'Or what,' he said, 'if she is there and says it was not your friend?'

'I haven't really thought past that,' I confessed.

'Perhaps you should,' he said and again I sensed that I was losing him. It was Luibava who came to my rescue. She spoke rapidly to her father in Russian, and he appeared to be arguing with her. When they had finished she turned to me.

'I was saying there is nothing foolish in trying to find this woman and asking such a question, but that I think she is more likely to speak to me than you or my father. That might make it appear too important, it might scare her.'

'Yes, I can see that. But is that something you would be prepared to do?'

'Why not? I just take the photograph and say your friend's family wish to thank her and have sent her some money.'

'You don't think giving her money would make her suspicious?'

'No, it would make her very happy, I'm sure. Especially foreign money. That makes most people in Moscow happy.'

I looked at Golitsin. 'How d'you feel about that?'

'I've long since given up arguing with my daughter,' he said. 'She goes her own way in most things.'

After a further exchange between them in Russian, he agreed to let Luibava go. Between us we decided that twenty pounds would be a proper sum to offer the maid.

'That's plenty,' Golitsin said.

'Will you contact me at the hotel when you have any news?' I asked.

They spoke again in Russian before she answered. 'My father thinks it best you come here again. One never knows, even though everything's changing for the better. Old habits die hard in Russia.'

'How did you tolerate it all those years?' I said.

She shrugged. 'You think we had a choice? There was no choice.'

'And now?'

'Now we have to learn how to live from the beginning. This is part of it, you being here asking us for favours. That in itself is a new found luxury.'

In return for their kindness, I gave her the bottle of perfume, and the cigarettes to her father.

'Not *blat*,' I said, 'just returning your kindness and hospitality.'

They seemed overwhelmed by such meagre gifts.

6

THE PRESENT

'I will drive you back to your hotel,' Golitsin said.

'Please,' I said. 'You don't want to turn out again, I'll get a taxi.'

'This isn't London, my friend, taxis are few and far between. Besides, though I am ashamed to say so, our streets are not safe any more.'

'Well, I have to tell you, London isn't that safe either.'

Although he had accepted his daughter's decision, I sensed he remained uneasy about it on our return journey. As his Zhiguli hiccuped its way through the deserted, wet streets I tried to draw him out. 'What are the main differences now?'

'Differences?'

'Yes, what has changed most since perestroika?'

He laughed. 'Perestroika is just a new word for the old chaos. Before we had bread and fear. Now we still have fear, but no bread. A hundred years ago one of our great writers, Lermontov, wrote, "Farewell, unwashed Russia, country of slaves, country of lords." Now we say, "Welcome unwashed Russia, country of poverty, country of crime." '

'But it has to be better than before, surely? No more secret police. At least I'm here and we're talking about it.'

Before answering he glanced into his rear-view mirror. 'I once saw a programme on television about a species of beetle who exist by living off dung. They survive the winter underground until the time is ripe for them to emerge and begin the cycle once again. We have always had secret police. You think they won't emerge again? Yes, we're talking, but we're alone in a car.'

I made no comment when he automatically dropped me off in a side street close to the hotel; some of his uneasiness had rubbed off on me. When I collected my key I found that I had been moved to a different room. This was odd, but not unexpected. I once spent a few days in Prague and there the hotel instructed me to keep my bags packed 'in case we have to move you while you are absent.' That night when I examined my suitcase I found two packets of cigarettes had been pilfered but my spare shirts and socks left undisturbed.

I spent the following day killing time with some desultory sightseeing. Twice I had the impression that I was being tailed, but perhaps this stemmed more from my anxiety over the success or failure of Luibava's mission than from any real threat. By the end of the day, with no word from her, I began to doubt my original motive. Henry was dead, my finding out the truth wouldn't bring him back and maybe there was nothing more sinister in the cover-up than a desire on the part of the Establishment not to further rock the boat at a time when things were going wrong for them. Over the years that Henry and I had drifted apart God knows what his private life had become. There were many reasons why people decided to commit suicide and many could be prevented if only a friend was close at hand. Come to that, my new hotel room was certainly a place for terminal melancholy.

Presenting my guest ticket I sampled the hotel restaurant, but the meal, when eventually I was served, was best forgotten though it induced a disturbed night's rest. I woke suddenly believing it was the noise of gunfire in my dream that had disturbed me, but when I stumbled to the window and opened it to look out, I saw rockets bursting in the night sky as, somewhere, Muscovites were celebrating the end of an epoch. The spectacle continued for half an hour. I was still at the window when my phone rang. I was aware that it had been standard practice for Russian hotels to ring the rooms at odd hours to check whether the occupant was there, but I picked it up hoping that it was Luibava.

Instead it was a man's voice.

'Weaver?'

The voice was unmistakably British.

'Yes?'

'Leave Moscow as soon as you can.'

'Who is this?'

'Do as I suggest. Leave Moscow.'

The line went dead. For some reason I had the feeling that the call had come from within the hotel rather than from outside. The voice had been so close and there had been none of the static that seemed a characteristic of the Russian system.

Shaken and unnerved, I sat on the edge of the bed and helped myself to a large shot of whisky, drinking it straight from the bottle since there was no glass available. Only Rainer and the Golitsins knew the true purpose of my visit and I could not believe that any of them had deliberately betrayed me. I retraced what I had done and said to them. Where Rainer was concerned I had only told him the bare details, never revealing Henry's name. Did I trust him? Yes, there was no good reason not to. What was the suicide of an unknown Englishman to him? The Wall was down, the Cold War over, there was no profit to be made out of the betrayal of an individual. It was true that he had led me to the Golitsins, but I trusted my instincts about them: two innocents, the father a reluctant conspirator, the daughter less so, anxious to test a degree of the new freedom. Of course, there was always the chance that contacting the hotel maid had been a mistake, that my bribe had frightened her – it was after all a vast sum in her terms. Had she gone immediately to the authorities? But that did not explain the British voice on the telephone. I cursed myself for having blundered my way into the country of the unknown, the stupid victim of my own dramatic imagination. There was only one constant factor: a great number of people seemed determined to keep me from finding out about Henry's death.

Then, as the whisky hit my empty stomach, I was consumed by something I had never felt so strongly before: a sense of outrage. If they wanted me to leave, then, OK, I'd give them the impression they'd scared me off, but having come this far I wasn't leaving until I had seen Luibava once more. Two could play at their game. I rang down to the desk and pointedly asked for the flight times to London – if my phone was tapped, they would assume I had immediately acted on the warning. The concierge told me the information would not be available until the morning. I also determined to ask the Golitsins if I could stay with them until I departed.

When I checked-out early the following morning I asked for a copy of the British Airways timetable in a loud voice before settling my bill, and although I kept a weather eye open for signs that my departure was under surveillance, I detected nothing untoward. As usual the lobby was buzzing with foreign journalists and television crews discussing the events of the week. Spotting the familiar face of an ITN newscaster I asked him about the latest developments. 'Nothing of any startling importance,' he said, looking past me, weightier things on his mind. Newscasters are all stars now.

'Did you see the fireworks during the night? I thought they were gunfire at first.'

'Really? You must be new here,' he answered in a way that cut me down to size. 'Look, excuse me, I have to find my crew and get to the airport.'

'No chance of bumming a lift, I suppose?' I said on the spur of the moment, seeing a perfect opportunity to give the slip to whoever might be following me. 'I've got to catch a plane in a hurry.'

He looked at me for the first time. 'I'm afraid not.'

'Just that I'm desperate.'

'You're not BBC, are you?'

'No. I'm not Press either. Be a sport.'

'Well, OK,' he said reluctantly. 'Ask my crew. If they say yes, go with them in the camera car, but we're leaving now.'

'That's fine by me.'

We arrived at the airport without incident and I felt reasonably confident I had given anybody on my tail the slip. I helped the crew hump their equipment into the departure building, then announced in a loud voice that I'd catch up with them again when I'd checked in. Instead of going to the British Airways counter I dodged outside and as luck would have it found a waiting taxi, giving the driver Golitsin's address since I felt I must warn them what had happened.

When we arrived outside their apartment building I paid the taxi-driver in hard currency and promised him the same again if he would wait for me, an arrangement entirely to his liking.

I passed nobody on the stairs on my way up and apart from the muffled sound of a radio or television broadcast coming from one of the other flats, the building was silent. The door of their apartment was slightly ajar. I knocked, waited, then knocked again. Nothing. I gently pushed the door open and once inside called their names. Nobody answered. I looked inside the living room first. It appeared to be exactly as I had left it the night before, the vodka glasses and Luibava's papers and sketches were still on the table. Before going to the bedrooms I called their names once more. Then there was a slight bump, as though something in one of the bedrooms had fallen and a few seconds later the cat appeared and rubbed itself against my legs. I bent to stroke it and it was then that I saw the trail of red paw prints on the shabby linoleum. I bent down and touched one of them with the tip of a finger. It was wet, and I knew then what it signified. The prints led me into the first bedroom. Luibava lay just inside the door. She was wearing a nightdress that at one time must have been white. Now it was dyed a dark red with blood. Most of her face had been blown away and her loose hair was matted like seaweed left on the rocks by a receding tide.

Fear brought bile into my mouth and I gagged at the sight, but somehow found the courage to look into the second bedroom. The shot that killed Golitsin must have been fired at close range, possibly while he was asleep, for he was still in his bed but twisted against the brass headboard and the wall behind it was splattered with pieces of skull and brain. The bedclothes were sodden with his blood and I saw where the cat had walked, for there was a criss-cross pattern of paw marks on the counterpane.

I backed away, touching nothing. The cat was purring loudly, the sound intensified in that silent charnel house. Perhaps because I had written descriptions of such scenes many times, I took a kitchen towel and wiped the door-handles free of any prints I might have left. I dropped this on the landing after I had closed the front door, and stood listening for any sound of the neighbours. As I started down the stairs my legs suddenly failed to hold me, and I stumbled to my knees. Now real terror took over. I shall never again have any of my fictional characters walk calmly away when caught in such a situation. I somehow managed to regain control of my limbs and made it to street level. When sure that I could walk normally, I went out to the waiting taxi.

'Back to the airport,' I said in a voice I scarcely recognised. 'My friends weren't at home.'

This time I went straight to the British Airways desk only to be told that all flights were fully booked, with thirty or so wait-listed ahead of me.

'You could try Aeroflot or Lufthansa, but I think you'll find it's the same with them,' the girl said, parrot fashion, obviously tired of repeating the same information. 'London might put on an extra flight tomorrow, but it's not definite. I'll add your name to the standby list, never know, you might be lucky.'

I hate airports at the best of times, they seem to infect everybody who has to use them with a feeling of helplessness. By the time you get there, you are committed, trapped, at the mercy of the elements, traffic controllers and the incomprehensible technology that actually gets the aircraft into the air, if the bloody things take off at the scheduled time, to which can now be added the security checks, X-ray machines, armed patrols, none of them conducive to calm the already uneasy traveller and certainly at variance with the ads extolling the romance of flight.

I queued for nearly half an hour for a substance they were selling as coffee, trying to make up my mind what to do next, all the time expecting to feel the tap on the shoulder. A television monitor was operating outside the men's toilets of all places, surrounded by travellers and Muscovites anxious to keep up with the volatile scenario. I lost myself amongst them, there being security in a crowd, and was peering up at the black and white pictures when I suddenly heard my name spoken.

I swung round to find myself crushed close to a well- dressed young man with a bland, clean-shaven face. At such close range he gave off a strong aura of cologne, not unwelcome in the mass of humanity.

'Mr Weaver, isn't it?' he said, smiling, in a voice that was immediately recognisable as text-book Whitehall.

I nodded.

'I was at the BA desk just now and happened to overhear you were trying to get a ticket. They're like gold-dust I'm afraid, almost as rare as a seat for *Phantom of the Opera*.' Again the smile. 'It so happens I've got a spare for Copenhagen which you're welcome to.'

'I'm trying to get back to London,' I said.

'Aren't we all? I wish these characters could make up their minds who they want in charge, then we could all get on with our own lives. You shouldn't have any difficulty picking up a connection in Copenhagen.'

A certain insistence had crept into his voice, although he kept the smile in place, like an escort asking a reluctant deb to dance.

'It's generous of you, but I think I'll chance my luck for a direct flight.'

His voice hardened perceptibly. 'It's possible, Mr Weaver, your luck may have run out already.'

'Who sent you?' I said.

'Sent me? Nobody. Just trying to help a fellow country-man. Take the ticket, please. There isn't much time, it's already boarding.'

I looked around. There were two other men standing a short distance away staring in our direction.

'I'm giving you good advice,' my man said. 'Things change here so rapidly. Be such a pity if you were delayed for a long period. Especially somebody like yourself with a distin-guished career still to pursue.'

He took hold of my upper arm with a firm grip and steered me through the crowd towards the departure area. I glanced back and saw that the other two men had also moved.

'I've enjoyed your books, Mr Weaver. I think I've read them all. Very much my cup of tea.'

We were at the Departures door now and he put the ticket in my hand. 'I was so sure you'd accept I've already confirmed the booking and had the ticket changed to your name, so you won't have any problems. Enjoy your flight.'

I tried to stall by asking, 'How much do I owe you?'

'On the house,' he said 'Just our contribution to your well-being.'

'I'd like to know who to thank.'

'Just thank your lucky stars,' he said, straight-faced.

As he had said, the ticket was in order and I was waved through. I turned at Passport Control and looked back. All three men were standing at the barrier. I now knew that whatever else was to come, my card had been marked.

7

THE PRESENT

The SAS flight was uneventful though it wasn't until we climbed above the early turbulence into clear skies that I was calm enough to think rationally. I could not believe that my benefactor was a member of the embassy staff, yet everything about him smacked of Foreign Office; he had that snotty confidence of those accustomed to privilege. Probably the other two were MI6 attachments, to be there if needed, and the most presentable had been chosen to front the operation.

Certainly he had his facts, he knew who I was, which in turn pointed to the fact that he knew why I was in Moscow. I thought back to everybody I had contacted in London prior to my departure – Henry's political agent, his solicitor, the reporter from the *Sun*, the pompous cove at Tory Central Office and of course the Foreign Office itself – if my persistence had aroused suspicions there was certainly a choice to pick from. Nursing my free drink in the plastic glass, I finally decided on the Foreign Office as the most obvious candidate; the embassy would have the kind of *blat* to produce an air ticket at a moment's notice. And that opened up a dread can of worms that led straight to the horror of Golitsin and Luibava for which I was directly responsible. I could just about believe that somebody in the embassy had been instructed to get me out of Moscow (instructed by whom?) but to have ordered the murder of the Golitsins? No, that didn't ring true.

I wasn't so naive as to believe that our side never ran a dirty tricks section; my research in the past had uncovered too many shady areas, too many 'economies' with the truth for me to believe that we were always the good guys, detergent white. Somebody had moved quickly to frighten me off, denoting that they wanted to ensure that Henry's secret died with him. Only my small measure of fame had saved me this time: another death in Moscow would have been an embarrassment, so I had had a stay of execution, providing I didn't delve any further. That smooth joker at the airport had spelt it out for me in official double-speak: go home, forget it, it's none of your business. The Golitsins were expendable, just two more to add to the body count of a country in transition.

I realised I had been looking over the wrong shoulder, thinking the danger would come from the left, that it was some Russian faction I had to fear, when all the time the danger was closer to home. Obviously from the moment of my arrival my movements had been tracked, the trail leading them to the Golitsins, and from there to the hotel maid. Had Luibava succeeded in tracing the maid before they killed her and if so what had she found out? Or had the maid already been silenced?

I stared out of the window as we circled for the final approach; like the plexiglass between me and oblivion, the mystery had too many layers for comfort. I was out of my depth.

On landing, I decided that it was more sensible not to leave the airport until I had worked out my next moves. Copenhagen seemed a safe haven for the moment. I had a meal I did not want and two or three stiff schnapps that I badly needed, all the time keeping a weather eye open for anybody who looked in my direction, but most of the other diners were fellow transients killing time. I booked into one of the airport hotels, glad of the slick, modern anonymity of the decor. There was comfort in the neat bed, the sterilised lavatory seat, the complimentary samples of shampoo and bubble bath.

I drank myself to sleep hoping that by morning I'd have thought of a way out of the maze, but when I woke I still didn't have the answers. At breakfast all I could think of was the irony of my situation. On the page, my own pages, on the television screens, violent death is at one remove; the bookmark can be left in the novel, suspense held over for another day; the actors will get up once the scene is over, wash off the fake blood, go home to their families. But there was nothing fake about the cat's footprints.

I was scared all right. I had none of the fortitude I gave to my fictional heroes, nor could I bring my usual expertise to work out what lay ahead. Everything stopped in those blood-splattered bedrooms where Golitsin and Luibava met their end. Panic loosened my bowels and it was only when sitting on the toilet that a plan of action came to me. I've often done some of my best plotting while in the john. In the past I had several times consulted an acquaintance in Scotland Yard's Anti-Terrorist Squad, a Superintendent Albert Clempson, who had helped correct the more blatant factual errors in my thrillers. He had been a career cop, starting in Traffic and working his way through the ranks to his present position: cynical in the most positive way about the world he moved in, straight, uncompli-cated, with his quota of disillusionment about the battle that could never be won. He seemed my best bet, I had to take the risk.

I phoned him immediately after breakfast and with a fragment of good fortune that had eluded me of late, he was in his office when I called.

'Albert,' I said, 'it's Martin Weaver, remember me?'

'Of course. How are you, got a new book on the way?'

'Not exactly, but I need your help. I'm in trouble.'

He was somebody conditioned to receive such blunt openings calmly. No doubt most of his calls betokened a crisis of one sort or another.

'When you say trouble – personal?'

'Yes.'

There was a slight pause. 'And you think I can help?'

'Yes. I haven't broken the law or anything, I just need advice.'

'Can you talk? Where are you?'

'Copenhagen.'

'Copenhagen!?'

'Yes, I'll tell you why if we can meet. I know it sounds far-fetched but I think I have to have some sort of protection.'

'From whom? Or should I say from what?'

'I don't know, I wish I did.'

'When are you coming back?'

'Today, if you can see me. Is that possible?'

'Yes, at the moment all's quiet, though we never know what those brave Irish bastards will throw at us.'

'I'll catch the first plane out and ring you the moment I get in.'

'Fine. Sure there's nothing else you want to tell me now?'

'No, I'd better save it.'

'OK, well I'll be here, and if I'm not I'll leave word where I can be found.'

The moment I hung up I set about getting a flight to London. It was late afternoon when I landed at Heathrow and I phoned him immediately I had cleared Immigration. He picked up on the second ring.

'I've been thinking on the flight,' I said, 'can we meet somewhere before I go home? It's possible that my place could have been visited in my absence.'

'Sure. Meet in the bar opposite the news-stand on Victoria station. I'll be there in an hour, and don't worry if you're late I'll wait.'

I took the Underground rather than a taxi – already I had fallen into the habit of believing in safety in numbers – but my luck ran out again. Victoria was closed, roped off by police lines: there had been another bomb scare. The latest IRA ploy on the mainland was to swamp the switchboards with hoax calls then, when police resources were stretched to the limit, slip in the real one. They usually timed it for the commuter rush-hours, thus ensuring maximum confusion. That day they scored a double, tying up both Victoria and Waterloo stations for two hours.

When my train was finally allowed to disgorge its passengers I was miles from where I wanted to be. I rang Albert's office, but of course he was involved with the latest incident. I was still chary of going back to my apartment, but in the end decided to risk it. Before letting myself in I rang my neighbour's doorbell. She was a pleasant, middle-aged soul, a spinster in need of comforts I couldn't provide and inclined to gush over me. It was her misguided belief that authors are what they write. Normally I kept our relationship at a polite arm's length.

'Oh, you're back, Mr Weaver! How nice, do come in.'

'No, I won't come in, Ethel, thank you. I've just got off a plane and need to freshen up. I was just checking you're OK.'

'I'm fine, never better. Well, I did have a touch of flu last week, but I don't think I'm contagious. How caring of you to think of me. Where has your wonderful life taken you this time?'

She gave off a faint scent of Vicks vapour rub. Beads of sweat appeared on her upper lip; she tended to glow when excited.

'Oh, nowhere special. Just the South of France.'

'Just the South of France he says! All right for some people! You sure you won't come in?'

'I'd better not, but thanks again. Just one thing, I was expecting an urgent package. I don't suppose you took it in?'

'No. Nobody knocked here. And I'd have noticed, because I haven't been out all week on account of the flu.'

'It'll probably come later. Good to see you again.'

'Good to have you back.'

At first glance, apart from the usual collection of junk mail on the mat, my apartment seemed just as I had left it. When I had checked all the rooms, I phoned Albert again. This time he was back in his office.

'I sure picked a great place for a rendezvous, didn't I?' he said.

'Was it a bomb?'

'Not at either station, but we found one close to the British Museum. Luckily we managed to defuse it. So that's one up to us . . . Now, look, your problem, sorry I can't make this evening.'

'No, I understand.'

He detected the note of disappointment in my voice.

'It's my son's birthday and I promised to take him to *Starlight Express*. How about tomorrow?'

'Whatever's convenient for you.'

'Let me just check.'

He left the phone for a minute. 'I've got a briefing at nine. How about eleven?'

'Fine. Where d'you suggest this time?'

'Let's avoid railway stations. D'you know Neal's Yard in Chelsea? The one in Sydney Street in the garden centre. There's a café there where you can get a good cup of coffee and a healthy Danish.'

'We all need to keep healthy,' I said with a joviality I did not feel. 'I'll be there. Thanks a lot Albert. Enjoy the show.'

'It's his fourth visit,' Albert said. 'If he could roller-skate he could take over.'

For the first time since Moscow and in the familiar comfort of my own home I began to relax. I disposed of the junk mail (how many forests are sacrificed in the name of *Reader's Digest*?), took a shower, opened a bottle of claret, put a frozen pizza in the microwave and switched on my computer to resume where I left off. I have always found work to be a panacea and I was hoping to dispel recent horrors with a creative session.

It was in this frame of mind that I keyed in my software, but instead of my usual menu coming up on the screen a message appeared.

If you are sensible, you will now accept that the events in Moscow are no concern of yours. You have been given examples of what happens to those who meddle, so take heed. Your friend no longer exists.

I stared at the screen and a new attack of panic made the glass of claret shake in my hand. Even with my limited technical knowledge I knew that all computers are open to attack by alien viruses, but this was too personal to be a random invasion. I had been expecting my apartment to have been broken into but this was a violation that left no clues, a state-of-the-art, sophisticated means of forcible entry. I had the presence of mind to print the message before deleting it, then checked the contents of my directory to see if anything important had been wiped. All my previous documents were intact.

I left my pizza uneaten as a new set of anxieties began to gnaw.

8

THE PRESENT

As I drove to my delayed meeting with Albert, I found myself thinking that London was fast becoming a city of empty office blocks, a sort of concrete set for an abandoned film. It was some months since I had ventured across London to Chelsea and as I made slow progress through what is now a day-long rush hour, I lost count of vanished landmarks, several times losing my way because once familiar streets had totally changed their personality. While I edged down the Strand towards Trafalgar Square, shoppers were skirting round the bag ladies and other human flotsam who had spent the night wrapped in newspapers in doorways. Only the even red surface of The Mall reintroduced a sense of permanence and the park on either side seemed a world apart from the garbage-strewn thoroughfares behind me. Threading my way around Hyde Park Corner into Belgrave Square I then took Walton Street where an army of traffic wardens were going about their sacred business and used the back streets to cross into the King's Road where most of the shops were selling American imports at five times the original price.

I managed to find a spare meter near to a new hospital that seemed to be catering exclusively for whole tribes of depressed-looking Arabs, and made my way to the agreed rendezvous in Neal's Yard. It was a cold and blustery day but stalwarts were toughing it taking coffee and wodges of carrot cake outside in a sad imitation of Parisian sidewalk café life. Whatever else, the British know how to punish themselves.

Albert was there before me, sensibly sitting inside. I had the impression he had shrunk since I last saw him. Certainly not even a clairvoyant would have guessed at his profession. He looked, if anything, like a bank manager in his neat herring-bone suit and white shirt. It was hard to imagine him going up to a suspect vehicle knowing that at any moment it might explode in his face.

'I beat you to it. This OK?' he said.

'Fine.'

I looked around. Two or three other tables were occupied with matrons surrounded by Peter Jones shopping bags and deep in suburban scandal.

'Let me get you coffee. Want anything to eat?'

'Just coffee,' I said.

'So, what's troubling you?' Albert asked when we had settled.

With half an eye on the adjacent tables I told him everything that had happened, beginning with my probable sighting of Henry at Venice airport, my engineered exit from Moscow and ending with the message on my computer. He did not interrupt or comment until I'd finished.

'Sounds as though you've been taking some of your own medicine. Tell me more about your friend Henry. I met him once, by the way, during one of the IRA campaigns when I gave a briefing to MPs after the assassination of Airey Neave. I remember he wanted to know how he could tell if his phone was bugged.'

'What d'you want to know about him?'

'Well, assuming you were right and it was him at the airport, it's not unknown for people to fake a suicide – they've had their hand in the till, or they just want to leave the missus and go off with some young popsy. If he was in one of those kind of situations, he could have decided to do a Stonehouse.'

This was a reference to an old political scandal.

'Was he in trouble?'

'I've no idea. I hadn't seen him in ages. It's always possible. I often thought he lived too high for a backbencher's salary.'

'I'll dig around for you, see what turns up. Tell you what did strike me. The murdered boy in Venice you took to be a girl. You say you saw them kiss – you did say Blagden kissed the boy, didn't you?'

I nodded.

'Was he bent?'

'Jesus, I don't think so. He had some odd views about sex, a puritanical streak in certain things. I remember the first time we met Sophie he was shocked because she'd posed in the nude. Didn't stop him marrying her though.'

'He might have been your best friend at one time, but you didn't really like him, did you?'

That pulled me up short. 'Why d'you say that?'

'Something in your voice.'

'We were close once,' I said slowly, 'but people can change, can't they?'

Albert shook his head. 'Not really. They may sublimate certain things, but if they're bent, they're bent and it'll come out sooner or later. Take my word for it. Anyway, put that aside for later. Let's assume you weren't mistaken, that he faked his death and that by some freak coincidence you spotted him. Others involved now need to throw you off the scent.'

'That's fairly obvious, isn't it?'

'Nothing's ever obvious, otherwise I'd be dead by now. The question is who else is involved and why? You thought chummy at the airport who gave you the ticket to Copenhagen was Foreign Office material?'

'Yes, I did.'

'That would tie in with them handling the post-mortem and cremation. I hate those tight-arsed types as much as you do.'

'Do suicides follow any pattern in your experience?'

'The considerate ones take the trouble not to leave too

much mess for others to clean up. The other types blow their brains out in the kid's bedroom.' He looked straight at me. 'Don't change the subject, what're you holding back? I can't help if you are. You've trodden on somebody's forbidden patch and they've flagged you to stay away with three murders. If three, why not four? They've given you the cue to forget it. If you're right, if your friend is still around, maybe he was the one who arranged the reprieve. It would have been easy enough to dispose of you in Moscow; from what I hear it's the perfect place for disappearing acts right now.'

'It's a long story,' I said finally.

'OK. Let me check with the office and I'll listen. Isn't that what I'm here for?'

He used his portable phone while I ordered two more coffees and sandwiches and wondered where to begin.

'That's a rare comfort,' Albert said. 'All's quiet on the home front.'

There was little of comfort in the story I began to relate, yet in a way going back to the very beginning was a welcome catharsis.

9

THE PAST

One of the many curious aspects of this story is that Henry and I first met Sophie at exactly the same moment.

It was during the summer of 1967 and we were returning home from a weekend house party in Henley early one Sunday evening and, hoping to avoid the traffic, had taken the back roads. The party had ended in some acrimony, our host having lost heavily at what he liked to describe as 'a friendly game of poker.' Henry was driving his pride and joy, a red MG, which had seen better days but which he cherished like a pet bitch (he actually referred to it as 'she' – or 'the old girl' which led to my inventing a code – PFN, standing for Pause For Nausea whenever he launched into a defence of the beast). Eventually, having refused what he considered an insulting trade-in offer from a dealer, he was finally compelled to dispatch it – her – to the breaker's yard, and he actually had tears in his eyes on the day. Years later he was still bemoaning the fact 'It's absolutely typical of this country that the only car we ever made that everybody wanted was junked. Now, they're collectors' items and fetch a fortune whenever one comes on the market. I should never have parted with her.'

'But it didn't go,' I said, 'we were always having to jump-start it.'

'She had character, that car. Not like the piece of German crap you drive.'

That particular Sunday the MG was behaving true to form and I had twice been forced to get out and push before, as Henry put it, she 'cleared her throat' and coughed into life. We had just passed through Datchet village and were crossing the humped Albert Bridge that forms part of the Windsor Castle estate when we spotted a girl thumbing a lift.

'God!' Henry said, 'did you see that?'

'Did I ever! Pull up!'

The MG not only had problems starting, it also did not stop on a penny. We slid forward another twenty yards before coming to a halt.

By now the girl was running towards us. I always have difficulty describing heroines in my novels; give me a villain and I can usually paint him vividly in a few sentences, but compelling descriptions of beauty often defeat me. Sophie – for the girl by the roadside was she – could not have been more than seventeen the first time we saw her. She had that throat-stopping bloom peculiar to young English girls who have never fried their skins in the sun and who take walks in the rain. In those days most of her contemporaries aped the Mary Quant/Jean Shrimpton look, but Sophie was an original, she did not fit the current mould. Against the then fashion there was nothing even vaguely anorexic about her; she wore a figure-clinging dress of startling whiteness – as if she had just stepped off a tennis court, although I later discovered she was incapable of returning a ball over the net. Whatever other stunning attributes she possessed, skill at games was not amongst them.

Arriving by the car, she switched on a searchlight smile. 'Oh, thanks. You've saved my life. I don't suppose you're going to London by any chance?'

In close proximity, she seemed to be flawless: even teeth, shining hair, the faintest blonde down on her upper lip. At that period our joint sex lives, athough varied, had a high failure rate and owed more to fantasy than fact. Sophie was fantasy in the living flesh.

'Yes, that's where we're headed,' I stuttered. Had she said

Land's End there is no doubt Henry would have driven through the night.

'Where're you making for?'

'Anywhere I can pick up a taxi. Don't go out of your way.'

Henry had not uttered so far. He sulked if ever I took the lead.

'See, I got dumped,' Sophie said.

'Dumped?'

'Yeah, I've been on a houseboat all weekend and the jerks I was with were all smashed, so I cut – didn't fancy a scary drive home late at night.'

'No, who needs that?' I agreed.

'You made the right decision,' Henry said, finally joining the conversation. I noticed his neck was red.

Her physical attributes became more disturbing by the minute. I got out of the car and offered her my seat. 'I'll hunch up in the back.'

'No, that's not fair, I can sit there.'

'He wouldn't hear of it,' Henry said. 'You're travelling with two gentlemen.'

'I'm Sophie,' she said, as she slid in beside him.

'Henry, and this is Martin.'

'Well, thanks again. I did get another offer, about a mile back, but the driver's eyes were too close together.'

Henry and I both filed this piece of feminine character analysis for future reference. After a few sooty coughs from the cracked exhaust, we got under way and Henry put his foot down.

'This is a fab car. It's an MG, right?'

She could not have said anything more guaranteed to steal Henry's affections. I watched with envy as his left hand brushed against her thigh when he shifted through the gears

'On a houseboat, eh?' Henry said, taking his eyes off the road too many times for comfort. 'Do you do that often?'

'No, I've never been on one before. Just happened I met this character at a session last week and he invited me down. He turned out to be a real turd.'

'Sounds like you're well out of it. You said "session", what sort of session?'

'I do modelling. That's not my real profession. I'm a dancer really, but in between jobs, which is most of the time, you know, have to pay the gas bills.'

'Don't we all? Are you a ballet dancer?'

'Modern, not classical. I've done classical, but I wasn't good enough. The competition is really heavy in classical. What do you two do?'

I got in first this time. 'I'm a writer, and Henry works in the City.'

'I forgot to ask where you want dropping off,' Henry said, but his voice was lost as a 707 screamed in over the road with its wheels and flaps down. Sophie turned to watch it land.

'Wow! Me and a friend, the girl I room with, we went to Majorca last year. Not on one of those. It was a charter cheapie, just two engines, least I think it had two, but it sounded like it was falling apart.'

'Still the safest way to travel,' I said as Henry overtook a Porsche on the inside. 'So you share a flat, do you?'

'Yes. In Bayswater.'

'Bayswater? That's a nice area.'

'Not where we live. We live under a Chinese chiropractor and next door to a takeaway kebab joint. Well, he says he's a chiropractor, we think he runs a massage parlour, the kind that gives French lessons.'

'Is your friend a dancer?' Henry asked, giving me a wink in the mirror.

'No, she works in a restaurant, she's an actress.'

The *non sequitur* made her more vulnerable in my eyes.

'Are we going to have the pleasure of meeting her when we drop you off?' I knew the way Henry's mind was working. He would charm the delectable Sophie and I would be left with the friend, who was doubtless not in the same league.

'She went home for the weekend.'

'Well maybe we could take you both out for dinner next week?'

76

'That'd be great.' For the first time I detected a note of caution in her voice. Henry always pushed too hard.

'Want to fix a date now?'

'I'll have to ask Melanie first. She works shifts.'

'Lunch, then, if you like. We're easy, aren't we Martin?'

'Yes, we're easy.' How free we were with our favours in those days. No inhibitions, no premonitions of disaster or rejection.

'I don't eat lunch,' Sophie said. 'And I have class every day.'

'Why don't we call you when you've worked it out with Melanie?'

Arriving outside her door she thanked us for the lift, but did not volunteer her phone number. Henry gave her his business card. 'Call me. Martin and I can make any evening.'

We watched her walk down the basement stairs. She walked like a dancer. As she disappeared from view a man rang the chiropractor's doorbell and looked around furtively. He did not look as though he needed conventional treatment. The nameless meats turning slowly on the spit in the kebab shop smelt like burning tyres.

Henry could hardly contain himself. 'How could we get that lucky?'

'Amazing,' I said. 'But don't get too excited, any girl who looks like her has got to have some great hunk of a boyfriend.'

'Not necessarily. I bet all she meets are a lot of limp-wristed dancers who pad their jock straps with cotton wool.'

'My friend the ballet critic,' I said. 'Anyway I think you blew it by pushing too hard.'

'I did not.'

'Very unsubtle. Notice she didn't give us her number.'

'I gave her mine though.'

'The funny thing is I've got the feeling I've seen her before.'

'Oh, sure!'

'Yes, I'm convinced I've seen her picture in a magazine. It struck me the moment she got into the car.'

'Crap!'

'You wait.'

'For what?'

'Just wait.'

At that time I was staying in a pad off the Fulham Road, one of a row of semi-derelict Victorian studios tucked away in a mews which had so far escaped the attention of the property speculators. It belonged to a painter friend of mine who found it difficult to make a living in England and had gone off to decorate some rich Arab's villa in Tangier with murals. He had given it to me rent-free in return for babysitting his Russian Blue cat. It suited my meagre requirements. I had just published my first novel which hadn't exactly seared the pages of the *Times Literary Supplement* and I was now sweating through a second. This was before the day of Monopoly money advances – I seem to remember I got four hundred, half on signature and half on publication, but in 1967, with no rent to pay, I could scratch along on that doing occasional reviews and the odd bit of journalism. Henry was the affluent one, making his mark with a merchant bank, the officers of which eventually ended up in the dock of the Old Bailey.

The moment we got inside I started to sort through my collection of old magazines.

'What're you looking for?'

'If I'm right, you'll see.'

I finally waved one at him in triumph. 'How about this for total recall?'

'That's a girlie magazine,' Henry said.

'Wrong. It's a serious photographic publication. It's got whole sections on Bailey and Norman Parkinson.'

I handed him the magazine at the open page which featured a nude study of Sophie. It was an 'artistic' shot, with the pubic area in shadow, since this was still the air-brush age of innocence. Whatever our fevered imaginations might have dreamed was underneath Sophie's white dress, we could not have come anywhere near the real thing. Henry stared at it, dazzled: I had impressed him for once.

'Well?' I said finally. 'Aren't I right? Something clicked the moment I saw her.'

'Amazing. Bloody amazing.'

'Don't drool. How is she allowed to roam the streets? No wonder she didn't make Covent Garden. Ballet dancers aren't allowed to have tits like that.'

Henry studied it like a diamond salesman calculating the carats.

'God, just my luck,' he said finally with real sorrow in his voice.

'What?'

'There's always a snag.'

'What're you talking about?'

'There was I thinking I had stumbled across the perfect girl and now this ruins it.'

'We both "stumbled" across her as you put it, and what are you rambling on about?'

'This. Lives in Bayswater, well known red-light district, poses nude, it all fits.'

'What fits?'

'Another dream shattered,' Henry said.

'What fits?'

'It's obvious. The evidence speaks for itself. Any girl who does this sort of thing has to be on the game.'

'Oh, give me a break,' I said, snatching the magazine away from him.

'Listen, if you want to be naive, go ahead. I'm telling you.'

'If I'm naive you're a sexual fascist. Why does one photograph automatically make her into a tart?'

'This is probably only the tip of the iceberg. I bet she's posed more than once. I happen to know they always take two sets of prints. One for magazines like this and one for the pornos.'

'The photographer is Walter Bird, can't you read? He doesn't go in for that sort of stuff. And how d'you happen to know they always take two sets?'

'I just do.'

'You're warped. Look what happened with that last conquest of yours – what was her name – Maggie?'

'What about Maggie?'

'You were crazy about her, then the moment she went to bed with you you went off her.'

'I prefer my women to be innocent.'

'How can they be innocent when you can't wait to get them between the sheets?'

He didn't answer that.

'But, OK,' I said. 'If this turns you off, that's fine by me. I think she preferred me in any case.'

'I don't think so. She was very impressed with my car.'

'Well, we'll put it to the test. If you can't bring yourself to date her I will.'

The wrangle went on for another twenty minutes, until we had both exhausted our prejudices. I daresay we were a comical pair at such moments, crass to a degree. Henry finally compromised.

'All right, I'll go this far: we take her on one date just to establish her true character.'

Despite all that has been written about the sexual Sixties, Henry and I were curiously removed from the mainstream. I was out of it from lack of funds and Henry was too picky to plunge in without analysing his motives. He liked the thought of promiscuity, but he wanted life insurance to go with it: Casanova with his flies tightly buttoned at all times. Me? I was forever the romantic. I was never quite sure what charged Henry's emotional batteries, but I needed to fall in love before I could operate.

10

THE PAST

'Memories,' I said to Albert. 'Don't you find they're like movies shot out of continuity? They never surface in strict order.'

I was trying to put those first months with Sophie into perspective. The late Sixties were the years when they gunned down Martin Luther King and Robert Kennedy and a Czech student publicly burnt himself to death in Prague in protest at the Russian occupation, when Mylai happened and the body bags were shipped home from Vietnam in their hundreds, when Walt Disney, Oppenheimer, Ike, Waugh, Jack Ruby and Oscar Wilde's son died, when closer to home France flirted with revolution, British troops went into Belfast, the Shah of Iran crowned himself à la Napoleon and our future king was created Prince of Wales in a mock Camelot and Tynan said the F-word on BBC television, when a place called Chappaquiddick wrote itself into the history books, M.A.S.H. hit our screens, Rosemary's Baby frightened us, Fassbinder told us Love is Colder Than Death, the first heart transplant was achieved and we were all singing 'Hey Jude' while intellectuals encouraged us to tolerate violence and accept the social engineering being practised by dictatorships of the Left.

It was also a time when, against all the odds, Sophie and I set up house together. There were other people who entered my life that first summer, for with the publication of my second novel I had my brief quota of fame, but now I cannot recall their faces or what influence they transiently wielded; the only image which has not faded is Sophie. Bailey photographed me for *Vogue* where I was described as 'going places', though I had no maps to guide me, and I hoped I wasn't going to the same places as the bored socialites who adorned the pages of the same issue.

In many ways we led a life untouched by world events, caught up in the unjustified euphoria that gripped swinging Britain during that period. I don't think Sophie was ever conscious that she was one of the shock troops of the new order, she lived a day at a time, taking whatever came.

The first date we all had together began hesitantly. We took Sophie and Melanie to San Lorenzo, in Beauchamp Place, then an unpretentious Italian restaurant, but very much in. Girls as pretty as Sophie usually take the precaution of choosing a room-mate who poses no threat, but Melanie was attractive in her own right with the slowest smile I have ever come across. Henry visibly thawed the moment they were introduced and rather to my amazement I found that I was paired with Sophie. In those days San Lorenzo was small and cramped, you ate cheek by jowl with your neighbour, and I could feel the heat of Sophie's body whenever our legs touched beneath the table. Blinded by instant lust in the smoke-filled, noisy atmosphere I fell into the trap of talking too much, immediately pulling the conversation around to the only subject I felt confident to discuss – my own work.

'Do you read a lot?' was my fairly obvious opener.

'Some.'

'What sort of books do you like?'

'He's hoping you've read his book,' Henry interrupted. 'He's dying to meet just one person who's actually bought his masterpiece.'

'Thanks, Henry.' I turned back to Sophie, 'I'd be happy to give you a copy.'

'What's it about?' Melanie asked politely.

'Thinly disguised autobiography,' Henry said. 'Very turgid stuff.'

'He wouldn't know,' I countered. 'Henry's reading is confined to balance sheets.'

'I'd like to read it,' Melanie said. 'What's the title?'

'*Prayers and Promises*.' For the first time the title struck me as grotesquely gauche.

'I shall buy it,' Melanie volunteered. 'As soon as I get paid.' In those days the average novel cost one pound ten shillings in the old money, giving me a three shilling royalty on the few copies sold. I had no idea what Melanie earned as a waitress except that it couldn't have been much and books were a luxury that probably she could ill afford. I warmed towards her.

'I shall give you both a copy,' I said grandly.

'I don't know how anybody writes a whole book,' Sophie said, 'it takes me an age to write a postcard.'

All the time I was looking at her I could not get the memory of that magazine photograph out of my mind. I had undressed other girls, but being with a girl who had actually stripped for the camera had never before entered my reckoning. It gave Sophie a special, dark mystery and, unlike Henry, did not cheapen her in my eyes, rather it made her infinitely more desirable, like crossing the frontier of a country which held nothing but danger. The damning perfection of her breasts at such close quarters unnerved me.

Leaving the restaurant in exuberant mood we piled into Henry's MG, but only got as far as Knightsbridge before ominous clouds of steam issued from under the bonnet. Henry jumped out, ignoring the snarled traffic behind us. He sprang the bonnet catches and as it opened the radiator exploded, shooting the cap into the air, followed by a hissing stream of rusty water. We all scrambled on to the pavement, fearful the whole engine was going to self-destruct.

'I don't believe this,' Henry said, close to tears. 'I'm going to sue that bloody garage, this is criminal neglect. Look at her, she's ruined!' His distress was painful to see. 'It means a tow job. God, *quelle* bloody nightmare. Anybody got change for the phone?'

I produced some coins and he sped off down the road.

'I feel so sorry for him,' Melanie said.

'Men really relate to cars, don't they?' Sophie observed.

We made small talk until Henry came panting back to us. 'Thank God for the RAC. They said they'd get somebody here in about an hour, apparently all their breakdown trucks are out at the moment, there's been a ten car pile-up on the Chiswick Road.'

Callously, I seized my moment. 'Look, if it's going to be an hour, I'd better take Sophie home, she's got an early class in the morning.' Before Henry could raise an objection I had grabbed a passing taxi. With more than a touch of masochism I did not suggest a nightcap at my place, but gave the taxi-driver Sophie's address.

'D'you want to come in?' she said when we arrived.

'I wouldn't say no to a quick cup of coffee, but I mustn't keep you up if you have to work tomorrow.'

'Don't you?'

'I'm not too hot in the mornings, I usually write at night.'

Her basement flat allowed little natural light to filter through the front and rear windows so she and Melanie had to have lights burning all day. There were posters of James Dean and the Stones on the painted walls, a lot of scatter cushions, piles of those magazines young girls favour containing ponderous articles which ask such mind-blowing questions as *Can you hold a conversation with your eyes*?

'Not exactly *House and Garden* is it? We bought most of the furniture in junk shops, gives it a sort of homespun eclectic look, don't you think?'

'Good description. I like it.'

I discovered that 'eclectic' was one of her buzz words that year.

'How d'you take your coffee?'

'Black with no sugar.'

'That's good because we're out of milk.'

'Can I use your bathroom?'

'Go ahead.'

I ducked under a line of washed smalls strung across the bath.

'That was fun tonight,' she shouted.

'Glad you enjoyed it.'

People's bathrooms fascinate me. The girls' looked like the annexe to a chemist's shop – I had never seen so many bottles of shampoo, make-up, colognes and deodorants. It was a serious display. I helped myself to a splash of one of the colognes. That was a mistake. The scent was pungent and sickly. I went to wash my hands only to find a solitary goldfish swimming in the basin.

'Did you know there's a goldfish in the basin?' I said on my return.

'Oh, God! It was Melanie's turn to change his water.'

She came out of the kitchen carrying a glass bowl with a sprig of coral in it.

'Poor old Fred, he must be freaked out.'

'A goldfish named Fred?'

'Yeah. Different, huh? We won him at a fun fair.'

Returning with the replenished bowl she placed it on a rickety bookshelf then sprinkled some fish food into it. Fred immediately rose to the surface and sucked down the tiny flakes. Sophie suddenly turned to me. 'What're you wearing?'

'I rudely helped myself to some of your cologne.'

'That's a freebie I got when I did a commercial. No wonder they give it away, I mean who would buy it?' she said, unoffended. 'Excuse the odd china. We seem to have had a spate of breakages recently. That's tea, by the way,' she added without pause, 'we're out of coffee too, so don't drink it if it's filthy. Isn't housekeeping a bore?'

She sprawled in an armchair, first removing an aged teddy bear who seemed to have undergone a limb transplant. She cradled him while we talked.

'Will you really give me a copy of your novel?'

'Sure.'

'I promise I'll read it.'

'I can't ask for more than that,' I said. I was keeping myself under hair-trigger control. She stretched herself in the chair in a recognisable dancer's pose, the legs splayed forward, the feet turned outwards. I shifted my own position to conceal the old priapic giveaway. It wasn't just desire she aroused in me, but the fear that my luck would not hold.

'Are you rehearsing for something right now? Is that what you do at class? I'm ignorant about these things.'

'No, you don't really rehearse at class, you just do warm-ups and practise routines for auditions. That's all I give, auditions.'

'Why is that? I'm sure you're good.'

'I'm OK. But dancers are two a penny and there isn't any decent work around. A lot of girls take jobs abroad, mostly the Middle East, but I don't fancy going topless in some Beirut nightclub. I might be up for something next week though – a shampoo commercial.'

Mention of the word 'topless' evoked the damning photograph again.

'Are your parents theatrical?'

'They're both dead. No, they weren't anything to do with the business. Daddy was a bank clerk.'

'No brothers or sisters?'

'Nope.'

The conversation had reached that stilted stage which always occurs when the unspoken thought is more potent than what is being discussed. I had no idea what the house rules were or whether she and Melanie had contingency plans for such situations. Knowing Henry as I did, the agony over his beloved MG would have driven all thoughts of a quick bonk out of his head. The chances were that once the bloody thing had been towed away he would bring Melanie home in a taxi and call it a night. Having made this much progress I did not want to blow it with some clumsy pass which, even if not rejected, could hardly lead to consummation.

86

I lingered another fifteen minutes, probing her for scraps of information I could utilise to my advantage at a later date: what she liked eating, which day she didn't go to her class, what pop music she favoured et cetera. With that conceit that comes so easily, I took it for granted that my exemplary behaviour now would pay off handsomely. A girl like Sophie must have been slavered over by a legion of lecherous men, therefore I would be the intriguing exception.

'Look, I must let you get to bed,' I said. 'Do you sleep with teddy?'

'Always.'

'Why do girls have such a fixation about bears? I mean it's not as if they're friendly creatures in the wild.'

'I don't know,' Sophie said. 'What's your theory?'

'I haven't got one, but I envy him.'

That was the only piece of innuendo I permitted myself. I did not kiss her, I did not attempt to kiss her. Powerfully eroticised though I was, I was not prepared to risk anything by a premature move.

Henry rang me much later.

'You asleep?'

'Yes.' I wasn't, but I wanted him to feel bad.

'Oh, sorry about that. You alone?'

'Yes,' I said. 'How did you get on?'

'Well, I think she's going to be OK. It was a bit touch and go, but all the signs are good.'

'Are you talking about Melanie or that lousy car?'

'The car of course. They don't think it's anything serious.'

'Terrific. How about Melanie, did you tow her back to your place?'

'Oh, very droll.'

'What did you think of her?'

'She's OK.'

'What does that mean?'

'She's OK.'

'Nothing more? You going to see her again?'

'Probably.'

87

'Don't sound too enthusiastic. I thought she was very attractive. Intelligent too.'

'Yeah.'

'But?'

'Do you think she's Jewish?'

'No, but so what if she is?'

'Jewish girls are always a big problem. It's a well known fact.'

'Is it? What is?'

'They want marriage.'

'Well, not necessarily to a good Gentile boy like you.'

'You know what I mean. Unless you promise them marriage they keep their legs closed.'

'Where d'you get all this shit?'

'I've got a lot of Jewish friends, and that's the story they put out.'

'They're just trying to keep it all for themselves.'

'We shall see,' Henry said darkly.

'How about Sophie, what's your opinion now?'

'Did you see what she was wearing? You could see her nipples through her blouse.'

'So?'

'Proves my point. It all adds up with the photo.'

'Get back to you. Assuming Melanie proves to be a certified grade A pasteurised Gentile, and her legs open wide enough for your much vaunted pecker to gain entry, are you saying you'll refuse to perform if she's shameful enough to remove a stitch of clothing?'

'What's that meant to mean?'

'I'm talking about what's the difference between a real live bird naked in your bed and a bloody photograph in a magazine?'

'A world of difference,' Henry said. 'Other people share the photograph. I couldn't go out with a girl knowing that the rest of the world is wanking over her.'

'You're full of crap, know that?'

'Well, we agree to disagree,' Henry said. 'I'll talk to you when you're in a better mood.'

'I was in a great mood, until you woke me up to listen to your racist sexual phobias. I hope your car survives surgery. Is she in a private ward?'

'Goodnight,' Henry said.

It was two months before I bedded Sophie, two months of frantic uncertainty when my work was neglected and my every waking moment was like being in training for a title fight I might never win. She proved a virgin, something which shot Henry's theory down in flames and which he refused to believe.

11

THE PAST

At the start of an affair there is usually a compulsion to find out as much as we can about the other person. Later, we become more wary, for what we have learned we use as weapons.

Sophie and I followed the same pattern. As our relationship deepened we felt the need to bury ourselves in the trivia of our pasts. She made me unearth snapshots of my childhood, ghastly reminders of past seaside holidays: a small boy with a prison haircut, pinched of face, bucket and spade in hand, braving the freezing waters of the English Channel; then the adolescent in cricket clothes, the features partly formed under the still-hideous haircut. Sophie pored over them, claiming several of the more nauseating to keep in her purse. For my part I questioned her closely as to where she had been brought up, what schools she attended. She was a convent girl I discovered, which gave her an added mystery in my eyes, for it had been a schooldays myth, never tested but steadfastly believed, that once beyond the clutches of the nuns, convent girls were in a perpetual state of sexual arousal.

'Show me your early photographs,' I said, 'otherwise it's not a fair exchange.'

'Mine are revolting, you'd go right off me.'

'Try me.'

'I had braces on my teeth and we had to wear a hideous uniform.'

When, reluctantly, she brought them to light, I found them enchanting. 'How old were you when this was taken?'

'Fourteen.'

'A well developed fourteen.'

'Oh, sure. I've always had these. The nuns used to make me bind them up. Boobs were a no-no at St Teresa's.'

'Barbaric. Were your parents Catholic?'

'No. Aftr they died I was farmed out to a distant cousin and his wife. They didn't have children of their own and couldn't cope, so they boarded me at the convent.'

'What about now? D'you go to Mass?'

'Never.'

'Just as well,' I said, 'for you have entered the house of the Great Unbeliever.'

By now she had moved in with me, bringing with her all her worldly goods: several suitcases of clothes, her record player and a box of pop singles, the teddy bear of course, a couple of posters, a small, self-painted chest of drawers and her manic store of cosmetics. My small bathroom was immediately transformed, as indeed was my whole existence.

I wondered how Melanie would fare with no room-mate to share the rent.

'Oh, she's fine, she'll find somebody else.' Sophie, like most people in love, betrayed a streak of callousness. I knew that Melanie and Henry were still seeing each other periodically, but so far he had shown no sign of wanting to emulate my new domestic arrangement. On the contrary, he had been shocked. 'Lunatic. What will happen when it all turns sour, how will you get her out?'

'Give me a break, she's only just moved in.'

'Does she have her own key?'

'Yes.'

'The thin end of the wedge, chum. Well, you can always change the locks, I suppose. Is she tidy?'

'What's that got to do with it?'

'You won't be able to write if she's untidy. You won't be

able to write, period. You'll be too busy fucking your brains out.'

'Thus spake Zarathustra.'

'Watch this space. Remember where you heard it first.'

He was certainly wrong at the beginning. The fact that Sophie went to her dance class most mornings meant that I was force-weaned away from my old slothful habits. I now went to my desk the moment she left the house. She was untidy, sometimes the bedroom looked as though it had been trashed, but in the first flush of love I turned a blind eye. A waste-paper basket is a writer's best friend and my work area was no better than the bedroom most of the time. She was extraordinarily easy to live with and to wake every morning and find her pliable warmth pressed against my anxious tumescence was bliss beyond compare.

Despite being denied her main ambition, the classical ballet remained her passion. I feigned an interest whenever she took me to a performance at Covent Garden since although I can appreciate the formalised beauty of the standard repertoire, I guess the ballet has never been emotional enough for my taste. Not that I ever let on to Sophie and her own pleasure – tinged I am sure with regret – was touching to watch.

I had never mentioned having seen the nude photograph. Perhaps I feared Sophie would take such an admission the wrong way and assume that I had baser motives from the start. I hid the magazine at the bottom of a box file, but sometimes when she was out of the house, I would take it out and study it. Although it might strike others as ridiculous, it became more real than the actual body I slept beside every night.

I remember one occasion when I took her to see a revival of *The Life and Death of Colonel Blimp*, at The Cinema on The Green, and we came away humming the rippling polonaise from *Mignon*. All my life anything sad and romantic reduces me to tears. Seeing that film in the company of somebody as desirable as Sophie who had that lethal combination of innocence and sensuality, scarred my memory. That night we made love like two frenzied people about to part forever. There is a theory, I believe, that contends that sound never disappears but floats for eternity in the stratosphere like the debris from an exhausted satellite. If true, then those wrenching cries she gave when the moment came for her still exist somewhere, not just as dream echoes that now return to fragment my nights.

Sometimes, after rehearsal, she would bring back some of her friends from a world I could never inhabit – wiry, earnest girls with dancers' calf muscles, all dressed in layers of shapeless woollen sweaters and leg warmers which to my eye made them almost sexless, for they were scarcely distinguishable from the young men who accompanied them. They chattered like starlings at nightfall, bitching about the ballet mistress, the fact that there was never enough work to go around, that so and so who could not put one leg in front of the other had somehow managed to land a West End job. I don't know what they made of me. I was a 'civilian' in theatre parlance, Sophie's friend, provider of instant coffee and biscuits, old by their standards and unable to translate much of their camp. I sat on the sidelines ignored and content to be ignored, happily observing a writer is always storing material – proud that the most ravishing amongst them, whose beauty could not be hidden by the oddments of clothing she sported, belonged exclusively to me. They did not drink or do drugs, at least never under my roof – they were only concerned with the vagaries and petty intrigues of their chosen, unfair profession.

'Was it very boring for you?' Sophie would ask when they had departed.

'No, I think they're all fascinating. Especially Freddie.'

'Isn't he too much? So naughty. He just says the wildest things. Brilliant dancer, though.'

'Who was he referring to when he kept talking about Mother Lloyd? Is she your ballet mistress? He didn't seem over fond of her.'

'Him. "Mother" Lloyd is a him. I think he once made a pass at Freddie and got his wrists slapped. He's not Freddie's type.'

'What is Freddie's type?'

'He likes rough trade. You would tell me, wouldn't you, if they get in your hair?'

'I would tell you,' I said.

'I mean, I won't bring them here again if all that silly talk bothers you.'

'This is your home, and they're your friends, you can bring who you like.'

'But you don't see your friends any more.'

'Course I do, I see Henry. I saw him this week.'

'Oh, Henry,' she said. 'I didn't mean Henry, Henry doesn't speak your language, I meant your other friends, your writer friends. People you must have seen before you met me.'

'Writers don't hunt in packs or get together much, they're too jealous of each other. What d'you mean, Henry doesn't speak my language?'

'Well, he doesn't. Henry's only interested in money.'

'Don't you like Henry?'

'He's all right. But you shouldn't trust him.'

'Henry? He's my oldest friend and harmless enough, just ambitious that's all.'

'Melanie's told me some things he's said.'

'Such as?'

'He doesn't think I'm good for you. That I'll ruin your life.'

'What's he know about it? Do they go to bed together?'

'Not often. He told her all actresses are basically whores and then complained because she didn't act like one. Melanie says she's had it.'

Never before having lived with a girl for any length of time, I had no idea how complicated they could be, or to be fair how complicated life was made for them. I came back from shopping one afternoon to find her lying on the floor with her legs propped against the side of the sofa.

'Doing your exercises?'

'No, I'm bleeding badly,' she said.

'God! Shall I call a doctor?'

'No, I'm just bleeding. I get one bad month out of two. This happens to be the one.'

'Well, what can I do?'

'Nothing. You can make me a cup of tea if you like.'

I was suddenly conscious of her bruised and battered feet.

'And what's happened to your feet?'

'You've seen them like that before.'

'Not as bad as that.'

'All dancers wreck their feet.'

'I'll bathe them for you,' I said.

'I'm fine, don't fuss.'

'Come on, it'll make you feel better, help the other thing, relax you.'

'I'm not dying. I'm just having a period.'

Despite her protests I insisted, but I had no sooner begun when she pulled her feet from the bowl.

'Don't! It spooks me.'

'Spooks you? You mean I'm tickling?'

'No, it reminds me of the convent.'

'I remind you of the convent?'

'Not you. That's all they ever drummed into us. Washed in the blood of the lamb. Mary washing Jesus' feet. Stuff like that. Blood was a big thing with them. Everywhere you looked there He was on the cross, painted blood dripping down his side, bleeding hearts, a piece of the patron Saint's finger under glass. Then you were supposed to believe you were drinking His blood and eating His flesh before breakfast. The cup was always cold, I remember, and tasted of metal polish. They were big on blood, except you weren't supposed to know about it happening to you. That was dirty, you didn't mention that. We weren't told about the curse. The first time it happened to me I really believed God had singled me out for punishment. I thought I was bleeding to death.'

'You make it sound like the Middle Ages. You mean nobody told you beforehand?'

'It wasn't something nice girls talked about.'

'Are you kidding me?'

She shook her head violently. 'It was all so phoney, you can't imagine.'

'But how long ago was this? Can't have been more than, what? – six years?'

She nodded.

'What did you do? You must have been scared out of your wits.'

'I just sat there in the loo for ages until one of the nuns came and found me, because I was late for class.'

'And she told you?'

'Oh, sure. She wrapped it up in a lot of bullshit about original sin and a week later she came to my room and made a pass. I woke up to find her bending over me with her hand down here.'

'Did that go on a lot?'

'I don't know, that was the only time it happened to me, and shortly after she left the order. A lot of the girls had crushes.'

'Did you?'

'No, I didn't make many friends.'

'Sounds like hell,' I said.

'Did you go through anything like that?'

'No, I had the dullest childhood imaginable – came through it unblemished, never had a single scout master lay hands on me. You poor darling.'

Although Sophie had her share of black moods, she was mostly optimistic: the big break was always just around the corner, the next audition would be the one, there was a chance that a friend of a friend would put her up for a television special. It worried her that she did not contribute her fair share of the housekeeping, for the few odd engagements that came her way – usually a day here or there on commercials – scarcely paid for her basic outgoings.

Once, in the aftermath of lovemaking she asked: 'Supposing I was offered something in a show like *Oh, Calcutta* . . . would that upset you?'

I hesitated a fraction too long.

'No, it's your life, what you've worked for, if it helps your career you should do it.'

That was the moment when I should have mentioned the photograph, but I funked it. 'Have you been offered it?'

'I did the first audition and I've had a call back.'

'That's terrific.'

'You don't really like the idea, do you?'

'Darling, you must do what's best for you. Why don't you try and get yourself an agent?'

'Agents aren't interested if you're just a dancer. They want people who earn big money.'

'It's the money, isn't it, that's what's really worrying you?'

'Well, I can't expect you to pay for everything.'

'What's everything? I'd be living here anyway, so the mortgage is the same. You don't eat much because you're always dieting. What else do you cost me? Nothing. How did you manage when you were sharing with Melanie?'

'It's different with two girls.'

'How is it different?'

'It just is.'

'Look, the day I start worrying about it, you can start worrying about it. Do I seem worried?'

I put on a good act, but I remember that, even as I smiled, I saw with terrible clarity the time when I would lose her.

12

THE PRESENT

'And you lost her to your good friend Henry,' Albert said.

'Yes.'

'How long did the affair last?'

'Long enough to destroy me when it ended.'

Albert stared into his empty cup. 'I often wonder if I missed out.'

'On what?'

'A grand passion. Don't misunderstand me, I've got a good marriage, better than I deserve, because most of the time my job has been rough on Liz. She's spent the best part of her life waiting for the phone to ring telling her I'm in the morgue.'

'No affairs?' I asked.

'A few. But not affairs like yours. They were way back when I was pounding the beat, so long ago I've forgotten their faces. Isn't that a shocking admission? In those days the Old Bill wasn't the enemy. On the night shift you got invited in for a cup of tea and maybe a bit of the other if you were lucky. A bit of the other, that says it all, doesn't it? Not the love of my life, not even the love of their lives.' He looked me straight in the face. 'Tell me, is it worth all the pain? I'd like to know.'

'Yes,' I lied.

'But you said it destroyed you?'

'A writer's hyperbole.'

'When Sophie left you was Henry already an MP?'

'No. But he was bored with banking by then and thinking about changing direction. It would be convenient to think of him as a monster, but he wasn't. Not then, anyway. Driven, yes. Ambitious, always needing more money, and not too choosy how he obtained it. All that. Yet at the same time, there was something about him which perhaps he only allowed me to see.'

'You're very generous,' Albert said. 'I don't know that I'd feel the same in your place.'

'Friends don't have to be perfect,' I said. 'He never got into a rut like me. And if you must know I don't think he seduced Sophie away from me, I think she went to him. I was careless. I thought I was giving Sophie domestic bliss when all the time I was giving her domestic boredom. Henry held promise of more excitement than me. And of course, if I'm right, she made her move at the right time for him. Tory Selection Committees prefer married men.'

'Did you see much of them after they married?'

'Not for a long time. Henry waved the first olive branch. And by then I was more or less over it . . . More or less, not completely. I had somebody else by then, anyway, a nice girl, quite different from Sophie. But it didn't quite click. I only saw them together half a dozen times, and then usually by chance, getting invited to the same parties, although I didn't really mix in the same circles as Henry. When he got elected, his whole lifestyle changed. They went in for country weekends and all that. You pulled me up earlier when you said I didn't like him. That isn't true. Until the split we were inseparable, even though we were chalk and cheese, close friends often are. He had qualities that I lacked – an ease with strangers – and he was funny even if his humour was often sardonic.'

'Did they have children?'

'No.'

At that moment his portable phone rang. He listened for a moment, then said: 'OK. They've got him, right? Was he armed? . . . Boy, heads are going to roll for this one. Are the Press on to it? Well, tell everybody to seal their lips. I'll be back in half an hour.'

He gave me a sheepish grin. 'Sorry, I've got to go. Some fucking lunatic climbed the wall at Buckingham Palace. I'd rather deal with a bomb. Something like that is really explosive.'

I got up and paid the bill.

'Don't leave with me,' he said. 'Start being careful.'

'You think I'm still in danger?'

'You wandered into something but, so far, you've been let off the hook. I believe you did see your friend in Venice that day, and I believe that's one reason why you're still alive. So you could be right, friendship must still count.'

'What should I do?'

'Do nothing until I've had a dig around. It's not really my scene.' He smiled for reassurance. 'But . . . I've got contacts in low places. Let me get back to you. Act normally, keep a low profile. Do you have to stay in London?'

'Not really.'

'Have you got a friend you could go and stay with?'

'Yes, probably.'

'Well, do that. Just let me know where you are.'

'I can't tell you how grateful I am.'

'I enjoyed listening. Reminded me of the old days when I just went after ordinary crooks.'

With that he walked out. I lingered, bought some organic vegetables and bread, then went to my car. A parking ticket was stuck behind the wiper blade. For once I didn't resent a fine.

I took Albert's suggestion seriously and it was while trying to decide where to go that I suddenly thought of Roger Marwood, my old university English language tutor. A Cornishman, when he retired he used his savings to buy a fisherman's cottage overlooking the harbour in Porthleven, choosing to return to his origins and somewhere as remote from the glades of academe as was possible. He had always stayed in touch, always wrote when a new novel came out – not always admiringly, I must add – long handwritten letters that often betrayed a basic loneliness. In many ways he was on my conscience, for I owed him much. He had been the first person to discern that I had a talent and given me the fillip to stretch myself. It had been Roger who had sent my first manuscript to a publisher he knew, accompanied by a forceful recommendation that paid off. Although I always answered his letters and sent him a bottle of his favourite malt at Christmas, I had never made a real effort to supply the sort of friendship he craved. He was gay, though the colloquialism was even more of a misnomer than most when applied to Roger; few would ever have suspected his inclinations, for he had an owlish appearance, peering at life and his beloved books through pebble spectacles, the very antithesis of camp. 'Dour' would have been more accurate. His comments on the passing scene had always had a vinegar flavour.

'Given a more generous stipend I would have preferred Greece,' he once confessed, 'but at least I have the sea in front of me. Not as blue as the Adriatic, but better than nothing.'

I had never visited him since his retirement despite many invitations but he had always taken my thin excuses without rancour, though I am sure he realised they were fabricated.

Now, the more I thought about it, his cottage seemed the perfect answer. I rang him that same night.

'Roger, I know this is out of the blue, but would I be welcome as a house guest for a week or so? I'll quite understand if it's not convenient, but as the years roll by I'm very conscious that we don't see enough of each other.'

I felt slightly ashamed putting it to him that way, especially since his reaction was so immediate and genuine.

'What a lovely surprise to hear from you, dear boy. Yes, of course, come whenever you like and stay as long as you can.'

'Really, you're sure you're not just being your usual polite self?'

'I'm not polite,' he said. 'I never was. If I didn't mean it, I'd say so. Don't expect anything grand.' Then, with some of his old insight he added: 'Nothing wrong, is there?'

'No.'

'Good. That's wonderful news, dear boy. When shall I expect you?'

'I'll catch the train tomorrow.'

'You get off at Helston, you know. Then take a taxi here. Can't meet you myself because it was a choice between giving up drink or driving, and that didn't take long to decide – I like my mahoganies too much.'

This was his pet name for the Scotch he poured for himself, never diluted by water or ice.

Armed with a new laptop computer loaded with my software and work in progress, I made my way to Waterloo the following morning.

Before nationalisation, the *Cornish Riviera* had been one of the crack trains on the old Great Western line. Now it was just another route on the Inter City network, the grubby carriages bearing little resemblance to the glories of the old train's brown and white livery. The day I caught it I discovered all too late that there was no dining car; staff shortages were blamed, an explanation that struck me as unconvincing in view of the three million unemployed. Instead, passengers were expected to make a perilous excursion to the snack bar, where scarcely-edible plastic fare was on sale for the foolhardy. I had more or less resigned myself to a long and hungry journey when, just after we left Reading, a cheerful Pakistani opened my compartment door and exhibited a suitcase full of fresh and delicious sandwiches. He confided he always sold out by the time he left the train at Exeter, and was a welcome, if rare, example of Thatcherite private enterprise in an otherwise barren landscape.

Thus fortified I settled down with my laptop and passed

the remaining hours attempting to salvage some parts of my aborted novel.

There is always the feeling of entering a foreign country when one crosses the border from Devon to Cornwall. It is Brittany without the cuisine; the houses have bleak, stone faces, the trees have been blown into twisted shapes by centuries of unfriendly winds, only those remaining areas of coastline as yet unsullied by camping sites retain the grandeur and mystery of bygone smuggling days. Helston, where I alighted from the train, owes its fame to the Maytime Floral Dance when lads and lassies, suitably bedecked with flowers, dance in and out of the houses and down the streets – an arcane ritual similar to Morris dancing, which always brings to mind a sketch from the Monty Python show.

It was raining when I arrived and I waited twenty minutes or so for a taxi to complete the journey to Porthleven. Roger's cottage, scarcely distinguishable on the outside from its immediate neighbours, was perched half-way up the cliff overlooking the harbour. There was no garden and the front door opened straight into the cosy living room. I guessed he had added some basic creature comforts such as central heating when he converted it to his needs, for a welcome blast of warm air greeted me, together with an immediate glass of whisky.

'It's so good to see you, dear boy,' Roger said. 'Such an age, how long is it?'

'Much too long, though the fault's entirely mine.'

He appeared more stooped than I remembered, although to my undergraduate eyes he had always seemed old. Streaked, greying hair which I noticed he kept brilliantined, bad teeth when he smiled, a shirt with a frayed collar, the college tie loosely knotted, a loose-fitting cardigan fluffed with age. Now he fussed about me, taking me to my room and apologising for the deficiencies.

'Only one bathroom, I'm afraid, but my woman came in this morning and aired your bed. If you're not warm enough, I think there's an electric blanket somewhere my sister gave me one Christmas. I don't use the thing, it terrifies me.'

'It'll be fine. Looks very comfy.'

'Not what you're used to, I'm sure. You'll have to suffer my cooking tonight. Well, hardly cooking. Fresh cold lobster and salad.'

'Sounds splendid.'

'I fend for myself most of the time, but. we'll go out for some meals while you're here.'

I told him about my experience on the train.

'Thank God I stay put these days,' he said. 'I know this is a backwater, but at least it's reasonably unpolluted except for the tourist season.' His lips tightened and I remembered that look from tutorials when I had turned in something he felt was below par. 'But it's you I want to hear about. Are you working on a new novel?'

'Yes and no.'

'What does that mean?' Again I caught sacred and profane remains of his old self – 'be precise' had always been his catchword at college.

'I started something, but then it went sour on me. I'm trying to pick up the pieces again. Hence that,' – I indicated the laptop – 'which I brought with me in case I suddenly got an idea.'

'You can use one of those, can you?'

'Yes, couldn't operate without it now.'

'Frightening. Of course, your life's changed, which is what I want to hear about.'

Over dinner, which proved excellent despite his renewed excuses, we began by retracing the past, reminding each other of old acquaintances, and it wasn't until we reached the coffee and brandy stage that I casually mentioned Henry.

'Henry?'

'Henry Blagden,' I said, 'he was up the same year as me, but I don't think he was one of yours.'

'Oh, yes, I remember. Good-looking boy in a saturnine sort of way. Became a Tory MP, or am I confusing him with Meldrum?'

'No, that's him.'

There was something about the way in which he had immediately pinpointed Henry that surprised me.

'Did you keep in touch with him?'

'After a fashion,' I said. 'We were very close for years, then for one reason or another our lives separated.'

'Not surprising. Last person I'd have thought would want to go into politics.'

'You knew he died, did you?'

'No.'

'Yes. They say he committed suicide.'

He stared at me. 'Good God! What was it, a woman, money?'

'Nobody quite knows,' I said. 'It's all a bit of a mystery, which somehow I got involved in.'

He offered me another brandy which I refused, wanting to keep my wits about me. Roger's capacity for drink had always been a college legend.

'What d'you mean, mystery?'

I hadn't intended to unburden myself on my first night, but recent events had so troubled and confused me that I grasped the opening, choosing to ignore the fact that Roger might tumble to the true purpose of my visit. As with Albert, I took him through the whole episode from the encounter in Venice.

'What an extraordinary sequence of events,' he said when I had finished. 'Sounds more like one of your own plots than something from real life. The business in Moscow is the most sinister development. Quite chilling.'

'Very.'

'No wonder you wanted to get out of London. Brings to mind that plot of Buchan's.'

'Buchan?'

'Yes, *The Thirty Nine Steps*.'

'Or perhaps *The Man Who Knew Too Much*, except that I know next to nothing.'

'What an extraordinary story,' Roger ruminated, staring into the dying fire. 'I can quite understand why you wanted to get away. Still, my gain,' his eyes coming back to me.

'That wasn't the only reason,' I said a shade too quickly.

'And that message that appeared on your computer thing, that's beyond me. How is that possible?'

'It's beyond me, too. But apparently computers can be attacked by viruses just like the human body. I read a case not so long ago where a kid created havoc, put hundreds of mainframe machines out of action. They call them "hackers". It's apparently quite simple if you know how.'

'A sort of mechanical HIV,' Roger said.

'Yes, that's one way of putting it. A dirty needle inserted from afar.'

'So what're you doing about it?'

'What can I do?'

'You say you haven't been able to get in touch with his wife?'

'Not so far. Though I doubt whether she could tell me much. I gather they were separated.'

'Perhaps you shouldn't do anything. Just let it die.'

'If I'm allowed to,' I said.

We didn't discuss it further that first night, and it was past midnight when we went to bed. Brushing my teeth in Roger's uninviting bathroom, I couldn't help thinking how our respective lives had changed. At the university he had been a figure we all respected and at times feared, for his caustic evaluations of our talents pierced us all. Now, looking at the collection of medicine bottles and preparations associated with old age, the ragged toothbrush, the cracked wooden bowl of shaving soap and denture steriliser, I suddenly saw him as somebody marking time towards the grave.

I was touched the following morning when he woke me with breakfast, bringing it to my room on a tray. For the first time since Venice, I had a feeling of peace. The rain had cleared and thin sunlight cast slanting cathedral shafts on a calm sea. Once dressed, Roger suggested a walk. There was a fresh bite to the air and, in contrast to London, an absence of noise. We ambled around the harbour, bought the morning papers, then continued to the serpentine, pebbled beach. The tide was out, leaving behind the inevitable man-made flotsam at the high watermark. Oil slicks darkened the rock pools and ravening gulls strutted and fought over the decaying carcass of a drowned dog. Their cries reawakened my unease.

We spent several pleasant days following the same routine: a walk in the mornings when we visited the fish market and bought the evening meal, then in the afternoons, I would do some work on my novel while Roger took a nap. I began to feel human again, relaxed and invigorated by the sea air and convivial company. The subject of Henry was not mentioned again between us until on the fourth night after we had both retired, Roger suddenly appeared in my bedroom. He wore a faded silk dressing-gown of Paisley design which gaped open as he sat on the foot of my bed, partially exposing his flaccid belly.

'I haven't been quite honest with you,' he began, hesitantly. I put aside the book I had been reading.

'Oh, in what way?'

'Your friend Henry . . .' In the shadows cast by the dim light from my bedside lamp it was difficult to discern his expression. 'I knew him rather better than I let on. You know about me, of course, or I'm sure you've guessed, there are few secrets from undergraduates.'

I said nothing.

'You both caught my eye the moment you came up, but I sensed you were a lost cause, don't ask me why or how . . . people like me always know . . . and I was content to make you one of my specials, having discerned your talents. I settled for friendship in your case, a friendship I have always valued, as I hope I have shown – a love from afar.'

107

He paused as though the confession had cost him dear. 'Henry was something else . . . It'll shock you, I know, but he and I were lovers. No, that's not quite true. It would be more accurate to say I was the lover, Henry was an acquiescent partner. I seduced him and afterwards he merely used me . . . I settled for that even when he blackmailed me.'

'Blackmailed you?'

'Emotionally. I allowed myself to give him better marks than he deserved. You earned yours, Henry claimed his between the sheets. Are you shocked?'

'No. Not shocked exactly. Amazed perhaps. You're telling me something I never suspected.'

'He didn't return my . . . affections . . . he wasn't smitten in that way, to him I was just a useful old poof who provided an easy passage. I had no illusions, I was just besotted by him. It's only happened three times in my life, always with disastrous results I might add. I never went in for cruising, rough trade never held any fascination for me, unlike some . . . It was my lot always to believe in a *grande amour* which meant, of course, I invariably fell for the wrong type . . . and laid myself open to certain disappointments.'

He suddenly became conscious that his voice had become husky with emotion. Recovering, he gave a short laugh. 'I don't know why I'm telling you all this, except I felt I had to. I've lived with the pretence for so long that I felt I owed it to you. Times change and as one gets older it seems to matter less and less.'

'Did . . . did the relationship continue after Henry left Cambridge?'

'We saw each other less frequently, always at my instigation. I used to give him money, you see – money I sometimes couldn't afford but had to – in the end I was reduced to buying his affections, isn't that a shameful admission?'

'No,' I said. 'I suppose we all do it in one way or another.' We were both silent for a while, then I said: 'Presumably you knew what happened after Sophie left me?'

'Oh, yes. He kept me up to date with that, he enjoyed giving me a blow by blow account, using it as a weapon, a very effective weapon. Despite his attractions, he was always devious, even evil wouldn't be too strong a word. Whatever else, Henry looked after number one. It all ended between us when he became an MP. I went to their wedding,' he added, giving a small, self-deprecating laugh. 'In fact I paid for the reception, a last noble gesture on my part, the bride having no father. I think Henry enjoyed the irony of that. You two had come to a parting of the ways by then, hadn't you?'

'Yes.'

'Understandably.'

'What did you think of Sophie?'

He chose his reply carefully. 'She had very obvious physical charms,' he answered, 'but I'm the last person to pronounce on such things. I felt so sorry for you. Well, for both of us.'

'Can I ask you something?' I said, interrupting his flow.

'Of course, dear boy.'

'Have you never been to bed with a girl?'

'Once. Hardly a girl. A friend of my mother's, older than me, the classic syndrome. I went through the motions, did what was required, but I can't say I enjoyed it and I never tried it again.'

He drew his dressing-gown together and smiled at me. 'So there you have it. A chapter ended for both of us.'

'You don't think he is alive?'

'Oh, on the contrary, I think it's highly probable you weren't mistaken. I never thought of Henry as a suicide. He might drive others to it, but not himself.'

I moved my foot from under him as he shifted his weight. 'Why do you think he had such a hold over people – you, me, Sophie presumably?'

'Most of us never choose wisely, do we, in matters of the heart? Such a complicated business, sex. They say even condemned men think about it in their last hours.' He got up abruptly. 'I must let you go to sleep. I hope I haven't shocked you too much. See you in the morning.'

As he turned away from me and left the room the light caught his face and I saw that he was crying.

13

THE PRESENT

The next morning I was up and about before Roger. He shuffled into the kitchen while I was making breakfast. Normally he was the early riser, appearing shaved and spruced, but that day he was without his dentures and looked his age. It was as if the effort of confessing to me had taken its toll for his face was grey like an under-exposed negative. I felt guilty at having surprised him and made no immediate mention of the previous night's events. Seeing that I had progressed the coffee and toast, he went to the bathroom to retrieve the dentures. Only then did he make the effort to be his old self.

'Do you mind if I use the telephone after breakfast?'

'Of course, dear boy. You'll find it's a bit temperamental, like its owner.'

I waited until he was having his bath, then called Albert.

'I was wondering when you'd check in. Getting worried. Where are you?' Albert said.

'Cornwall. Take down this number.'

'Is that a hotel?'

'No, a private house. I'm staying with an old friend.'

'OK, let me call you straight back. Our phones here are marginally safer. No harm in being extra cautious.'

I waited, conscious of the melodramatic element, then picked up again.

'Are you on your own?' Albert asked.

111

'Yes. Have you made any progress?'

'Not a great deal. As you told me, there seems to be a reluctance on everybody's part to say anything. But I did find out something about his wife. Did you know she'd been busted twice for drugs? Once for cocaine and the second time for heroin? She got a suspended sentence for the last offence.'

'No. That's news to me.'

'You never saw that side of her while you were together?'

'Once. But I thought she'd just been talked into it on a holiday we spent with a strange group.'

'Well, I'll go on searching, but it could be deeper than you first thought.'

'In what way?'

'Just a hunch I have. It's possible the Century House boys could be involved, though so far I haven't been able to figure out why.'

The reference to Century House startled me. This was the headquarters of MI6 and until quite recently its very existence had always been officially denied; a pathetic subterfuge but, as with Royal scandals, like ostriches the Establishment believed that if you buried the head the rest of the body was invisible.

'Why d'you think that?'

'Call it experience. When I draw blanks from all normal sources, it usually points in that direction. The place where he is alleged to have met his Maker is also a positive clue. Anyway, leave it with me, I'll go on digging around. How long do you intend staying where you are?'

'At least another week.'

'I should have something more before then. Let me know if you move, but otherwise I'll ring you.'

Roger came back into the room at that moment and I finished the call with some non-committal pleasantries.

'My publisher,' I said to Roger. 'Worrying about my delivery date. They paid quite a hefty advance for this one. Have you ever thought of writing a book?'

'I've had one on the stocks for years, but somehow I can never get around to finishing it.'

'What's the subject?'

'Rousseau and the cult of the divine genius in the 1770s and 80s, hardly likely to be an automatic Book Society choice.'

'Can I read it?'

'If you're that masochistic. I'll think about it.'

It wasn't until we were half-way through our customary morning walk that Roger returned to the subject of Henry. Tight-lipped, avoiding my eye, staring at the flecked waves, he suddenly said: 'Thinking about your problem, I wonder if an acquaintance of mine might be able to throw some light on the matter.'

'Really, who's that?'

'Nobody you'd know. An ex-policeman. Well, I suppose you'd call him a policeman – he was a member of the Vice Squad who once did me a good turn.' Again he did not look at me when he spoke.

'Why d'you think he'd be able to help me?'

'We birds of a feather tend to nest in the same places,' Roger said slowly. 'He also knew Henry at one time.'

'Would Henry have ever mentioned him to me?'

'I doubt it. The curious thing is, and it kept me awake most of the night thinking about it – the truth of the matter is that although in many ways you thought you knew Henry better than anybody, you probably knew less than me. You had the best of Henry, I had the worst, and that's really what counts when it comes to judging character. He led a double life, as you must now realise. A life that, like so many of us, was a lie.'

We walked another short distance in silence, then he said: 'Let me contact this man and see if he's agreeable to meet you. That is, only if you want to pursue it further.'

'I've come this far,' I said.

He didn't mention the man again until the day I was leaving. I had decided that after two weeks I was probably outstaying my welcome. Although too polite to mention it, Roger, like many accustomed to living on their own, was very set in his ways and I sensed that certain things about his house guest were beginning to irritate. A shared single bathroom must be a major factor in many a domestic upheaval. He made a show of protest when I announced my departure, but I detected an underlying note of relief. Albert had phoned once again though without having made any further progress and it was difficult to press him with Roger in the room. The fortnight away from London devoid of any menace had lulled my original panic and in truth I was anxious to progress my novel in familiar surroundings. As a parting gift for Roger's hospitality I left half a dozen bottles of malt. It wasn't until the last breakfast together that he pushed a note across the table.

'That's the name and address of that man I talked about. He said he'd be happy to see you if you want to follow it up.'

When my taxi arrived he did something he had never done before. He put his arms around me, clumsily, and kissed me on the cheek. The gesture embarrassed us both. It was the first time I had ever thought of him as a sentimentalist.

'Take care of yourself, and don't leave it so long next time. It's been wonderful having you, I can't tell you what a difference it's been to me. Talking of old times. Well, just having somebody to talk to. Pleasant though they are, I can't pretend the locals are very stimulating.'

'It was good of you to have me, I've had a really relaxing time. You look after yourself, too. Finish your book. It sounds fascinating.'

'Not really. Doubtless as boring and pedantic as I am.'

I didn't open his note until I was on the train. The name on it was George Pearson and the address was somewhere in Wembley. I folded it carefully and put it in my wallet. I should have left it at that. I wish to God I had left it, heeded the warnings, been content to let the unexplained, the unthinkable, sleep undisturbed and resumed my old, tranquil life. A lot of pain would have been saved.

Happily there was a restaurant car this time and I lingered over my meal, pondering Roger's revelations anew. As he had said, it was difficult for me to reconcile the Henry I had known with somebody granting sexual favours to Roger. When our trio broke up I had been forced to come to terms with Sophie leaving me and the mental pictures of her making love with Henry but I could not easily visualise Henry and Roger in bed together. I have always closed my mind to the physical aspects of homosexuality. Perhaps that's a typical heterosexual attitude or merely peculiar to me, I wouldn't know. For most of the journey I searched my memory for other incidents that should have given clues to Henry's true identity. With hindsight I realised how naive I must have been. I had always suspected that lying was the thing Henry did best. He did it with total cool and confidence, as though every move he made in life was pure revenge for something. Albert's revelation that Sophie had done the drug scene made me realise I had been hopelessly wrong about her too.

The closer I got to London, the more old concerns resurfaced. I reminded myself that the Venice police were liable to call me back as a material witness, something I did not relish. Once home I satisfied myself that nothing had been disturbed and was relieved to find no further messages on my computer. The danger seemed to have passed and I relaxed.

During the following week I thought several times about the friend Roger had suggested, wondering whether I should follow up or not. On the face of it contacting him seemed reasonably safe; coming from a source like Roger, whom I trusted, it was extremely unlikely that this man Pearson could have had any connection with what had gone before. From what Roger had hinted I guessed that he would prove to be another closet skeleton from Henry's past. There was always the faint chance that he could throw some more light on why Henry had chosen to take himself out of circulation, and it was a chance that I decided I would take.

Before ringing Pearson something drew me to inspect the boxes of Henry's papers again, hoping that I might find a clue I had hitherto overlooked. The single new item that came to light was a curious reference to *Walter, My Secret Life*, that dreary account of monotonous, cheerless fucking by the anonymous, apparently inexhaustible, Victorian lecher. Henry had noted: *Came across a copy in New York where it is now freely available. Found it very exciting reading, and must pass it on to S.*

Did the 'S' signify Sophie, I wondered, or somebody else with the same initial? In public Henry had always liked to occupy the high moral plateau, but this entry hinted at a grubby fascination with the sexual underworld, in keeping with Roger's revelation.

I remembered that after he reluctantly accepted that my relationship with Sophie was not just a passing fancy, we resumed the old pattern of our lives, often going out on double dates. Henry invariably showed up with one of those angular girls who remind me of fashion dummies in Harrods windows: leggy, flat-chested, and incredibly bored. Most of them were rich and passing the time before marriage by taking part-time jobs as estate agents, or else serving in one of those chintzy little boutiques that come and go in Belgravia selling expensive kitsch like fart cushions with oh so witty jokes embroidered on them, musical toilet rolls and other toys for the tasteless. They drove Mercedes SLs or hotted-up Minis with personalised number plates and flashed Louis Vuitton purses, desperately trying to camouflage their arid lives until, sufficiently plastered in Annabel's, they managed to land Mr Right by giving him a quick hand job under the table.

Henry's response to any criticism of his choices was, 'You only go for the obvious,' to which I replied that I didn't fancy bedding ice maidens.

All the while he was deliberately moving up the social ladder. His next acquisition was a young Chilean girl who lived part of the year in London with her mother and twin brother.

'They're seriously rich,' Henry told me. 'Private plane and a permanent suite at Claridges. That's rich, rich.'

He was anxious to introduce me to the twins and fixed a dinner date. 'And you don't have to go Dutch, it'll be on me.'

'My God!' I said. 'It must be love. What are their names?'

'Eva and Victor.'

He booked the private dining room at Les Ambassadeurs, in those days the high rollers' favourite eatery which boasted the most elegant gambling room in London.

I sometimes think that God put rich people on this earth to give us lesser mortals the satisfaction of detesting them. From that very first evening I thought Eva and Victor were a poisonous pair. They brought to mind the brother and sister in Thomas Mann's short story, *The Blood of the Walsungs*, for they shared the same effete, pampered mannerisms of children who had never been young, though at the time I first met them they were both eighteen. Eva wore too much expensive jewellery for somebody of her tender years and whereas to my eyes Sophie looked streamlined and spiffy, Eva was more like a child decked out for a fancy dress party in borrowed adult clothes. Her brother had one of those perfect, all-the-year-round tans that can only be acquired from fashionable winter and summer resorts. Both of them seemed to have been the recipients of a million dollars' worth of dental care: I had never seen such perfect teeth. Henry was obviously captivated and in awe of their life-style. I must be fair and say that they shared good manners, but there was a certain distance to their smiles, a certain condescension in their reaction to anything Sophie said. Small talk proved difficult.

'What d'you do, Eva?' Sophie asked early in the evening. 'Are you at university?'

'No. I hated school, couldn't wait to leave. I shop and play tennis. We just follow where our mother goes.'

'And where does she go?' I asked.

'Where we have houses. Madrid, Tangier, Bermuda. And Chile, of course.'

There was no adequate response to that and I tried my luck with Victor. 'Is tennis your game, too?'

'He trains with Arthur Ashe,' Henry interjected, and that ended that topic.

Both of them spoke excellent English, though Victor's accent was a shade more pronounced. I noticed Henry's growing concern that neither of them really ate anything. They pushed the superb food around on their plates with their forks, but little of it touched their lips. As a first course Henry had ordered one of the house specialities, caviar blinis, but he had yet to learn that you cannot impress the rich with what they are used to. The exotic has already bored them, the mundane hardly holds their attention, it is only when one takes them slumming that they summon up a passing interest.

Several times during the meal I noted that Victor reached for his sister's hand and stroked it, more like a lover than a brother. Thomas Mann's story ended, I recalled, in incest.

I was proud of Sophie because, although out of her depth, she held her own. The meal only came to life when Victor found his voice for once and said to Sophie, 'I've been studying you. I have the strongest feeling that you should be in films. You have the sort of face they are looking for. Have you ever acted?'

'Not really. I'm a dancer.'

'The ballet?'

'No, modern mostly.'

'No films?'

'No. I do modelling sometimes.'

Henry said: 'Sometimes nude modelling.'

It would have been charitable to believe that he said it without thinking, but now I realise it must have been deliberate.

'Really?' Victor remarked. 'How interesting.' His eyes flickered towards his sister and for a moment the boredom left their faces. 'You mean you pose for artists?'

'No, just photographs.'

'Aren't you embarrassed?' Eva asked.

'I'm more embarrassed if I don't have the money to pay the

rent. You see, unfortunately, I don't have a mother to pay it for me,' Sophie said sweetly.

After that brief interlude the conversation reverted to its previous desultory mode until Henry suggested they might like to gamble. The twins visibly brightened.

'How do you play?' Sophie asked as we mounted the curved staircase to the gaming room. It crossed my mind that, because of their ages, we might be denied entry, forgetting that money always talks.

'Well, it depends what you play,' Victor answered, taking out his wallet and handing his sister a wad of notes. 'I usually start on roulette, then when I've lost at that, I move to Chemmie and hope to recover. The important thing about gambling is not to care either way, otherwise it ruins it.'

The tables were deserted when we walked in, since it was too early for the Arabs. I only had twenty pounds on me which I gave to Sophie and steered her to the low minimum roulette table.

'Now what?' she whispered.

'Back your favourite numbers.'

'You mean birthdays and things?'

'Yes, why not?' I had already mentally kissed goodbye to my money.

Eva and Henry went to the Chemmie table, while Victor bought a pile of fifty-pound chips and sat beside Sophie. 'Play the numbers, *en plein*,' he said. 'Everything else is too boring.'

Sophie did nothing for the first spin, but merely watched what he did, fascinated. Nineteen came up and he wasn't on it.

'Oh, nearly,' she said. 'You were on eighteen.' I nudged her in the back. Next spin she pushed one chip on to number four.

'If you're going low, I shall go high,' Victor said. He bet heavily on the last six. The ball dropped neatly into Sophie's four and I thought she would knock the table flying in her excitement. When she had been given her winnings she offered me half.

'You keep them,' I said. 'They're lucky chips.'

They weren't, of course, and during the next half a dozen spins she had lost most of them. By that time Victor had left us and joined the others at Chemmie, where his sister was holding the bank.

'Quit while you're ahead,' I told Sophie. 'You can then always say you walked out a winner the first time you tried it.'

'Wasn't it fun! I could become addicted.'

Cashing in, she pocketed six pounds and gave me back my original stake. We stood and watched the other three for a while, but then the room started to fill up and we decided to cut and run. Henry and the twins scarcely looked up when we said our goodbyes. He was sweating and I guessed he was paying dearly for his social climbing.

That night when we were in bed together Sophie said: 'Did you know before?'

'Know what?'

'About my modelling?'

'No,' I lied.

'Were you shocked?'

'Why would I be shocked?'

'I know Henry disapproved. That's why he said it.'

'Henry always says things for effect.'

'You were a bit shocked, weren't you? Be honest.'

'No. Don't be stupid. Show them to me.'

'Really?'

'Really.'

She got out of bed and took down her suitcase from the top of the wardrobe. Opening it, she handed me an envelope, then went into the bathroom. There were half a dozen ten by eight prints including the same shot I had seen reproduced in the magazine. In each the pubic hair had been skilfully airbrushed out.

'They're terrific,' I said.

She stood naked in the bathroom door. 'Are you just saying that?'

'No, I mean it.'

'Well, men are funny. I saw how that Victor character looked at his sister. I think he was disgusted.'

'Course he wasn't disgusted. Anyway, I'm not Victor, nor am I Henry. Nothing you do disgusts me, and certainly not these.'

'If you'd seen them before you met me,' she persisted, 'would they have changed your mind? Men drool over dirty pictures, don't they?'

That was the moment when I could have made my confession, but I funked it.

'These aren't dirty pictures. You know my only regret?'

'What?'

'I didn't take them.'

She took one of the prints and stared at it. 'I suppose they'll be nice to have when I'm fat and old.'

'Can I keep one for when I'm fat and old?'

'You can keep them all. Now that you know, I don't mind.'

In the end I thought I had convinced her that nothing had changed between us, but our lovemaking that night was curiously different, as though a line had been drawn between us, separating reality and fantasy.

Henry's phone call woke us both the next morning.

'What did you think of them?' was his opening remark. Before I could answer he went on: 'You can't believe how much Eva won. Would you believe eleven thousand? Imagine!'

'The rich are different from us, they win at Chemmie,' I said. 'That's a homage-to-Hemingway-joke.'

'Oh, very clever. They're both amazing looking, don't you think?'

'And piss elegant, but listen, whatever turns you on.'

'I'm not going to continue this conversation if you're in that mood.'

'I've only just woken up.'

'Well, I thought they were super and it was a great evening.'

'You paid for it, you're entitled.'

I didn't begrudge him the secondhand snobbery of it all, which in turn infuriated him since he often tried to make me see what I was missing.

Now, going through his papers again, I half expected to come across something linking him to that period in his life, but the only memento he appeared to have saved was a ticket to the bullfights when he accompanied Victor and Eva to Madrid for a holiday.

I turned my attention to the motley collection of books; they were mostly book club editions of past bestsellers mixed with some turgid memoirs of forgotten politicians. The only volume that caused me to take a second glance was a worn copy of Kraft-Ebbing on sexual aberrations. I was just about to throw it back into the packing case when a single sheet of paper fluttered out. Typed on it was a list of some twenty surnames, some with ticks against them, two or three crossed through. None of the names were immediately familiar to me, but at the bottom of the page, written in ink this time, were the words: *To gain entry to SIGOP and CUG use PBBW.*

Although it signified nothing to me at the time, I opened a file on Henry and tucked it inside, for in the course of getting down to work again on my novel I had begun to realise that more and more I was drawing on Henry for one of my main characters.

That night I had a bruising dream where I pursued a nude and unobtainable Sophie.

14

THE PRESENT

When I finally rang Pearson he was extremely guarded. There were remnants of a Cockney accent in his voice which made me think that at some time he had been at some pains to correct it, for it was bogus posh.

'Our mutual friend Roger Marwood gave me your number and suggested I rang you.'

'Ah! yes, dear old Roger. How is he these days? Getting a bit long in the tooth I imagine.'

'He was in good form when I last saw him a week or so back.'

I waited for him to say something, but he remained silent.

'Did Roger mention why I wanted to contact you?'

'Yes, in a roundabout way. A personal matter, I gather.'

'Yes, I'd rather not discuss it over the phone.'

He gave a short laugh. 'Funny things happen to phone calls these days don't they? Especially if you're a Royal.'

'Good God, yes. Isn't all that extraordinary?'

'Big brother,' he said.

There was another pause at his end and I got the feeling that he was not alone. 'Do you think we could meet for a chat?'

'Bit tricky at the moment.'

'Well, to suit you. Perhaps you'd like to come here for a meal?'

'Let me sort out the old diary and get back to you. Got rather a lot on.'

'I understand. Let me give you my number and address, and when you're free let me know. I work at home so I'm usually here.'

I passed the details. 'I would be grateful if you can manage it.'

'We'll do our best,' he said and hung up.

It was some ten days, late at night, before he returned my call.

'Pearson here.' Abruptly.

'Ah, yes, Mr Pearson,' I said after a momentary blank. 'How good of you to call back.'

'I could manage tomorrow.'

'Fine. That's fine by me.'

'Around eight, shall we say?'

'By all means.'

'I'll see you at eight then.'

The line went dead. This time I had the distinct impression that he had been using a call box, for there had been traffic noises in the background.

The following day I shopped at Marks and Spencer having been initiated into the delights of their prepared meals by the girl I employed to handle my correspondence. 'I never cook any more,' she told me. 'Not worth it. Whenever I give a dinner party I just pretend I've been bending over a hot stove all day. Fools everybody.'

Since my culinary skills were non-existent, I have taken her advice ever since, frequently complimented by guests who are none the wiser or, more likely, practise the same deception.

Pearson arrived promptly. In appearance he was totally different from what I had imagined – tall, burly and well preserved, for although probably in his middle fifties he looked younger. His hair was well-groomed and greying; I suspected he had once been a red-head, for his skin had the peculiar whiteness that goes with that hair colouring and which I always associate with dead pig. There was some-thing else, too, which I couldn't put my finger on at first, something odd about his face.

I offered him a glass of wine and he asked for lager.

'I find wine too acid,' he said. He seemed nervous, disinclined to settle, but roamed my sitting room looking at my library and pictures.

'I'm sorry to say I haven't read any of yours. Not a great reader. Roger told me you published quite a few. You knew him at university, I gather.'

'Yes, he was my tutor and in many ways responsible for my becoming a writer.'

We made small talk through dinner, the usual topics: how England was fast becoming a nation of ex-shopkeepers, the decline of manners, the rising tide of violent crime. He passed no comment on the food, but ate what was set before him with a healthy appetite. We swopped anecdotes about Roger and it was as if he was prepared to go to great lengths to avoid the real purpose of his visit. I searched for an opening.

'Roger told me you were a great help to him at one time.'

It was then, as he looked straight at me, that I discovered what it was that was odd about his face. His left eye was much paler than the right and it occurred to me that he might have lost the sight of it.

'From the old days, when you were in the police force.' He said nothing. I passed the Stilton. 'I was hoping you might be able to help me.'

'About Blagden?' he said with that brusqueness I had noted from the initial phone conversation.

'Yes. You knew him too, I believe?'

'I came in contact with him, yes.'

'Professionally?'

'Yes.'

'We're fencing, you and I, aren't we?' I said, deciding to bring matters to a head.

His bad eye had begun to water and he took out a silk handkerchief and wiped it.

'I wouldn't say that. It seems to me we're both being cautious. From what Roger told me you, especially, have good reason to be cautious.'

125

'How much did Roger tell you?'

'As much as was necessary to put me in the picture. You see, Martin – may I call you Martin?'

'I wish you would.'

'I gathered that through no fault of your own, by what seems to have been an unhappy coincidence, you haven't done yourself a favour. Far from it. I might be able to help, and then again you have to ask yourself whether I would be doing you a good turn if I helped.'

'Yes, I accept that.'

'Henry's officially dead and buried. It might be more sensible to leave it that way.'

He spread the Stilton on a cracker and watched my face as he took it to his lips.

'Murders fall into many categories, but in the main you can narrow them down to two. There's your domestic murder – the most popular you might say – and there's the kind that's done for profit or gain. The gain is sometimes survival. For reasons which are still obscure it would appear that your friend Henry has a compelling wish to survive, wouldn't you say?'

I nodded. His way of speaking was stilted, made the more so by the overlaid accent.

'Because of my past job I could venture a guess as to why that is. Call it circumstantial evidence for the moment. But if I'm right the stakes would merit faking a suicide. And if we take it he had a compelling motive to do what he did, what's yours?'

'I don't honestly know,' I said. 'Until the first murder in Venice it was just bewilderment – the shock of suddenly seeing an old friend I thought was dead. When everybody fobbed off my enquiries, I got mad and took matters into my own hands, doubtless stupidly, made that trip to Moscow, which proved a tragic mistake. By then my original motive had become blurred. Perhaps . . . and this has only just occurred to me . . . perhaps my original motive had less to do with Henry than with his wife. I was in love with her once and I wanted to find her again. I knew she had come back into this country shortly after his supposed death. Not that I had any illusions about the possible outcome if we did meet again – I don't believe in happy endings, as most of my novels demonstrate – but the urge to see her again became a compulsion. Maybe that compulsion is still with me. I never found anyone to take her place, you see.'

He heard me out before replying. 'You want me to find her, is that it?'

'Yes. Yes, I do.'

'In spite of putting yourself at risk again? Have you considered that carefully enough?'

'They were separated before all this happened. I can't believe Sophie's involved in whatever Henry's mixed up in.'

'Can't or won't?'

'Don't want to, put it that way,' I said, then it was my turn to ask Pearson a question. 'You said you'd had some dealings with Henry in the past. What were they?'

'Not dealings. I met him in the course of my job. Did Roger tell you how that came about?'

'He didn't go into details.'

'I used to be in the Met's Vice Squad. We were having one of our periodic purges, more a public relations exercise than anything else. I caught Roger *in flagrante delicto* in a public urinal with a young rent boy.' He paused and wiped some crumbs from his mouth. 'The kid was the usual slag and Roger swore blind it was the first time he had succumbed to the temptation. I didn't believe him because they all say that, but I felt sorry for the poor old sod and let him off with a caution. In return he gave me some useful names and addresses. Now there's a funny thing: the majority of sex deviants have a compulsion to keep lists of their contacts. Strange that, isn't it? Anyway, amongst the names in his little black book was your friend Henry.'

'Was Henry an MP by then?'

'Yes. So I checked on all the names, including Henry, and paid him a friendly call. I can't say he was intimidated by it. He maintained there was a perfectly valid and innocent reason why his old tutor should have his name in an address book. He was very forceful, very convincing.'

'You don't still have the book, do you?'

'No. Why?'

I got up and fetched the file. 'I came across this amongst Henry's papers the other evening. I was named as literary executor in his Will.' I handed Pearson the list of names. 'D'you think this could have any significance?'

Pearson studied the scrap of paper.

'Mean anything to you?'

'Not at first glance,' he said, 'but you never know. May I hang on to it for a bit?'

'Please. Tell me, do you still have any connections with your old job?'

'Oh, no, that's long finished. I trod on the wrong toes once too often,' he replied in a way that implied he was not going to elaborate. He looked at his watch. 'Well, if you're really sure you want to track down the wife, I'll do what I can. Are you sure?'

'I would like to write finish to that particular chapter in my life, yes.'

'Right.'

He got up. 'Well, thank you for a pleasant meal.'

'I'll obviously pay you for your time and any expenses. Just tell me what you want.'

'Let's leave it until I come up with something. If I come up against the same dead ends, it won't cost you anything.'

His bad eye was watering again as he left.

15

THE PRESENT

It was an evening, a week later, when Pearson arrived, unannounced, on my doorstep.

'Well, some progress,' he said, when we'd both settled down with a drink.. 'Thanks to plastic money.'

I looked blank.

'I remembered you telling me his wife came back into the country after his death, so using a chum who can hack into anything, I had him take a look at all the major car rental companies – everybody's credit ratings are on computer database. They sell lists, you know, that's why all that junk mail shit keeps coming through the letter-box. Your Sophie hired a Mercedes 300SL at that time, charging it to American Express, still using her married name of Blagden and giving this address in Buckinghamshire a house called 'Inglewood', in Penn. Mean anything to you?'

The village of Penn is the habitat of upwardly-mobile gentry. I had once been summoned there by a somewhat grand film executive – so grand in fact that his pretensions eventually led to bankruptcy – but whether this 'Inglewood' had been one of Henry's and Sophie's many homes, I had no idea. The last I heard they had a place in Oxfordshire.

'It's apparently a listed building, stands in ten-acre grounds. Designed by Lutyens, the original garden laid out by Miss Jekyll – quite a pedigree.'

'No, I've never heard of it in connection with either of them.'

'Next I checked Directory Enquiries. The telephone is under the name of Seymour.'

'Again, doesn't click, but let me take a look at *Who's Who*.' I went to my shelves and checked all the Seymours, and for good measure, the Seymors, but nobody fitted the bill.

'Pity,' Pearson said, dabbing at his gammy eye. 'Well, that's about it so far. Even so, might be worth following up.'

'How would we do that?'

'Take a drive down there and spy out the land. It's a small place, you might even bump into her, you'd be surprised how often that happens when you're searching for somebody. You look dubious.'

'Now I'm faced with it, I've got cold feet.'

'Up to you.'

'I don't suppose there's anything to lose. There haven't been any other developments, no more sinister messages on my computer or midnight phone calls. Which reminds me, did that bit of paper I gave you produce anything?'

'I'm working on it.'

'Yes, well, OK, let's do that. When shall we go?'

'To suit you. Tomorrow as far as I'm concerned. Perhaps the sooner the better.'

'Right. Tomorrow then.'

'I'll pick you up at, say, ten? We might miss the worst of the rush hour.'

'I'll be ready,' I said.

It wasn't until he had gone that the full realisation hit me. I had wanted to see Sophie again for so long but now the risk of reopening an old wound terrified me more than I had bargained for. The jumbled emotions I felt stayed with me the following morning during the journey.

We found the house without much difficulty. It stood about a mile out of the village, off the road, surrounded by park-like grounds. There was an entry-phone let into the brick pillar on one side of elaborate wrought-iron gates. From what I could see of the house, it was a typical Lutyens design, gabled under red brick with parts of the façade covered in Virginia creeper. There were no signs of life.

Using the number Pearson supplied, I rang on his car-phone. A male voice answered.

'I wonder if I could speak to Mrs Blagden, please.' My voice was strangely hoarse.

There was a pause.

'Mrs Blagden?'

'Yes, is she there?'

'Who shall I say wants her?'

I took the plunge and gave my name.

Again a pause.

'Weaver?'

'Yes.'

'I'll see if she's available.'

While I waited I heard two people talking in the background, and then, finally, Sophie came on the line. I found I was sweating.

'Martin?'

'Yes . . . Sophie? . . . I've been trying to reach you for over a year. Did you ever get a message from your solicitor?'

'I may have done, it was a very confusing time.'

'Of course . . . I was very sad about the news. It must have been hideous for you.'

'Yes,' she said. 'Yes, it was.' Her reply strangely lacked conviction.

'Henry was the last person I imagined would do something like that.'

'One never knows about anybody really,' she said.

'Your solicitor told me you were out of the country when it happened.'

'Yes.'

The conversation was decidedly one-sided. 'Look,' I said, 'it's difficult to discuss these things on the phone. Can I see you? You're staying with friends, I gather. I'm phoning locally, happened to be in the vicinity. Would it be convenient?'

'Not today,' she said.

'Well, any time. What's tomorrow like?'

'Tomorrow's Wednesday, isn't it? No, Wednesday's no good. Nor is Thursday, but Friday's OK.'

'How about lunch? Do you want to come into town or should we meet down here?'

'No, I'll meet you in London.'

'Great! I'll book at San Lorenzo for old times' sake. One o'clock suit you?'

'Fine. I'll be there.'

I started to say, 'Will you remember what I look like?' but before I could finish the line went dead.

'So, journey's end?' Pearson said.

'Seems like it. Listen, thanks, I can't thank you enough.'

'A great weight lifted, eh?'

'Yes. I still can't take it in. Hearing her voice again like that. It's been years.'

'Did she explain Seymour?'

'No.'

'Well, I wouldn't read a great deal into that.'

It was only later that his answer struck me as odd. I didn't talk much on the way back to London. I thought of all manner of explanations for her coldness: she had been stunned by my turning up out of the blue, or there had been other people in the room listening to the conversation, or she knew that Henry's death had been faked. The elation I had at first felt at speaking to her again gradually receded.

Before we parted Pearson promised to be in touch if he traced the names on the scrap of paper.

'I must pay you,' I said.

'All in good time. I hope your reunion goes well.'

I made the restaurant booking immediately, insisting that I must have a quiet table. Accomplishing this, I was left feeling strangely elated, an emotion more suited to an adolescent who has finally summoned the courage to clinch a first date. Going to my bedroom I opened the drawer in an old leather stud box and took out the folded and creased nude photograph of Sophie I had masochisticly preserved. Looking at it I knew again the madness that had once reduced me to a state of unreason. I remembered love in the afternoons, baths taken together, the wonder of waking to find her curled beside me in the narrow bed. I wish I had the ability to recapture the intensity of love, as Joyce did in that great *Ulysses* monologue, to be able to put it down with just an echo of his genius.

I was awake long before my usual hour on Friday morning, like somebody waiting to be taken down to the operating theatre for major surgery. Arriving at the restaurant twenty minutes before our agreed time, I ordered the wine, shirking the obvious ostentation of champagne and settling on a good Italian white.

I did not expect Sophie to be on time – punctuality had never been her strong point – and I remained reasonably sanguine until half-past one. By two o'clock I knew she wasn't coming. Nobody is that late without telephoning an explanation. In order to pass off my embarrassment I picked at a plate of pasta then, as casually as I could, I paid the bill and left. The busy street outside seemed strangely alien and I walked home feeling like somebody who had just been told he had a terminal condition. My expectations had been so high; I had been prepared for all manner of things except total rejection.

Gradually disappointment gave way to anger. After I had brooded over it for half an hour, I got into my car and drove back to Penn, intending to face her with it. This time I did not phone ahead. When I arrived outside the Seymour house I used the entry-phone. After a pause a distorted voice answered.

'Yes?'

'Martin Weaver,' I said. 'I've come to see Mrs Blagden.'

133

'Of course, Mr Weaver.'

There was a slight delay and then the large iron gates creaked open. The drive curved slightly, bordered on either side by plane trees, with large plantings of hydrangeas in the gaps. Everything smacked of wealth – the manicured lawns, with not a daisy or a weed in sight, the sort of perfection that indicated an army of gardeners. Miss Jekyll could rest easy in her grave as far as Inglewood was concerned.

I parked in front of the main entrance, throwing up a shower of gravel. As I arrived the door was opened and I was greeted by a short man, who I guessed was in his middle forties, wearing those casually elegant clothes you only see in Ralph Lauren advertisements.

'Elliot Seymour,' he said. I shook his outstretched hand which was cold and limp to the touch. When he smiled I noticed he had a hare lip.

'You've come to see Sophie?'

'Yes. We had arranged to have lunch in town today, and whether she got the day wrong – today is Friday, isn't it? – she didn't arrive. She isn't ill, is she?'

'No, she's not ill. Blooming, in fact. Look, do come inside.'

I followed him into the entrance hall and immediately slipped on the highly polished tiled floor. Seymour put out a hand and saved me.

'They will polish these tiles like glass,' he said. 'One of these days somebody's going to break a leg. I'm always worried about Mummy. Poor old darling, she's so ancient and her bones are so brittle.'

And at your age, I thought, you should stop calling her Mummy.

He led the way into a panelled study that smelled of stale cigar smoke, and was furnished like a club room with large leather sofas and arm chairs. There were also various display cabinets along one wall, such as one finds in museums.

'Can I offer you some coffee?'

'Well, I don't want to take up too much of your time.'

'My dear Mr Weaver, yours is a welcome intrusion. I lead a very lazy life, one might almost say a useless life down here. London appals me, all that Euro trash walking around in frightful clothes taking snaps of Guardsmen. Daddy used to say Guardsmen are only useful for wars and buggery.'

He waited for my reaction, but I gave nothing.

'How do you take your coffee?'

'Just black, thank you.'

He went to a desk and pressed an intercom button. 'Edith, bring coffee for two to the study, will you?' He turned back to me. 'Do take a seat. I can't think what could have happened to make her forget your lunch date. Very unlike her.'

'I'm sure she's had a lot on her mind recently. Is she here?'

'Not at the moment. You're an old friend, I believe?'

'Yes. But we've been out of touch for some time. Henry was a close friend, too, and of course I was shocked by the news.'

'Weren't we all?' He opened a humidor containing a variety of Davidoffs and offered it to me. 'Do you?'

'No, I'll stick to cigarettes.'

'I gave those up and now I spend a fortune on cigars. But one can't live without at least one vice, can one?' He selected a large cigar and bit off the end.

'Did Sophie take Henry's death very badly?'

'She was remarkable in the circumstances. It's the aftermath, isn't it? All the boring legal things somebody has to sort out. I've been able to help her there. She's not very good at coping with lawyers and so forth.'

'Are any of us?' I said.

'You're a writer, so Sophie tells me.'

'Yes.'

'Fiction?'

'Yes.'

135

'I'm ashamed to say it's years since I opened a novel, so you'll have to forgive me if I'm not familiar with your work. I do read, of course, but only about my specialised subject.'

'What is that?'

'Butterflies.'

'Butterflies? Really? Like Nabokov,' I added in an effort to show an interest I did not feel. I was desperate to get the conversation back to Sophie, and there was something unreal about him. He was being too nice, smiling too much, but the smile was stiff, like something painted on a Venetian carnival mask.

'Well, I'm not in his class. And I don't wear those ridiculous clothes he was always photographed in. Of course he was foreign, that explains a lot. I had a butterfly garden planted two years ago. I don't know whether Miss Jekyll would have approved.'

'What's the particular attraction of butterflies?' I was still trying to be polite.

'Their beauty lasts such a little while. So I preserve it. In my cabinets they become sleeping beauties. I met Nabokov once,' he continued without pause, 'in Montreux. I gather his novels were odd to say the least. All about pubescent girls, weren't they?'

'One of them was,' I said. 'It became notorious for a time. They made a film from it.'

'Still, in character with his major hobby.'

He must have caught my puzzled expression, for he added: 'Butterflies. The beauty that so quickly fades.'

At that moment a maid in a starched and formal uniform came in with the coffee. She placed the silver tray on a side table by Seymour's armchair.

'Will that be all, Mr Elliot?'

'Yes, thank you, Edith.'

When she had left the room, I said: 'When are you expecting Sophie back?'

'She didn't really say, just left it vague.'

I became fascinated by a piece of wet cigar leaf that had attached itself to the furrow on his lip.

'Do you know if Henry left her properly provided for in his Will?'

'Oh, I think she's taken care of,' Seymour said.

I was waiting for him to ask me how I had traced her to Inglewood, but the question never came.

'He appointed me his literary executor.'

'Really? What a chore. Would you excuse me for a moment? I have to tell Mummy to take her pills. She always forgets if I don't remind her.'

When he left the room I walked to one of the cabinets housing his collection of butterflies. The preservation of dead things has never appealed to me; stuffed animals, hunting trophies, fish in glass cases and the like have a sinister feeling to them. Seymour's museum of motionless beauty was no exception. I was repulsed by it.

Returning, he said, 'Would you like to see my garden when you've finished your coffee?'

'By all means. You're sure I'm not inconveniencing you?'

'Not at all. I'm always delighted to meet friends of Sophie's. And Henry's, of course.'

He led the way out of the room. As we crossed the hallway I saw an elderly woman slowly mounting the oak staircase. She was carrying what seemed to be an Army dress uniform. Hearing us, she paused and looked back.

'It's all right, Mummy,' Seymour said. 'I've got a visitor. We're just going to take a walk around the garden.'

'Is he from the War Office?'

'No, Mummy.'

Her expression did not change as she looked me over then continued up the stairs and out of sight.

'Anything out of her normal routine always disturbs her,' Seymour remarked. 'My younger brother was killed in the Falklands, and she's never got over it. Keeps his room exactly as he left it, lays out his dress uniform every night, convinced he'll come back. Poor old darling, sad when they go like that.'

He first led me through a sitting room, which in turn opened into a vaulted Victorian conservatory heated to almost tropical temperature. It was crammed with palms and exotic plants, many of them heavily scented. As we entered a brilliantly plumed macaw flew down to land on Seymour's proffered arm and strutted up to his neck. He allowed it to press its beak against his lips.

'What d'you think a bird like this costs?'

'I've no idea. Twenty pounds?'

'Oh, we're much more expensive than that, aren't we, my darling? We cost Daddy two thousand, didn't we? Most of them have to be smuggled in now,' he informed me. 'You're an illegal immigrant, my beauty, aren't you? Off you go.' He kissed the bird again and allowed it to fly off.

'Is this another hobby?' I asked after I had admired the flowering profusion.

'Not so much a hobby, just a reminder of hotter climes. I have another house in Arizona. Do you know Arizona?'

'No, I confess I don't.'

We continued the tour. The garden at the rear of the house was vast. I later borrowed a biography of Miss Jekyll from the library which included a plan of the original layout of Inglewood. From memory it appeared that, apart from Seymour's butterfly garden which he had created from an old vegetable plot, little had been altered from the original plan.

'Of course we lost a great number of trees in the '87 hurricane,' Seymour told me. 'Luckily none of them fell on the house. They were plucked out like rotten teeth. I have replanted, but I won't live to see them grow to maturity.'

'If you hadn't told me, I wouldn't have known. It still looks spectacular to me. Are the flowers specially chosen to attract butterflies?'

'Oh, yes. That's the whole point.'

Nothing about him tied in with the Sophie I had known in

the past and I could only imagine that he had originally been one of Henry's acquaintances. After he became an M.P. Henry had collected a strange bag of friends, though for the life of me I could not recall him ever mentioning Seymour. That in itself was odd, for Henry had seldom been shy to boast of his social acquisitions.

'What time are you expecting Sophie back?' I asked casually.

'I think she said she was going to be gone until Christmas.'

The reply was so unexpected and startling that I stood and gaped at him.

'Christmas?'

'Yes, that's what she said. I think all the business with Henry was too much for her and she felt she had to get away. Didn't she mention her plans to you?'

'No,' I said

'Oh, dear, naughty girl. She flew back today.'

'Back?'

'To Arizona,' Seymour said. 'I shall join her there later. Sophie and I are living together. I thought perhaps you guessed that?'

I shook my head, unable to speak.

'Nearly two years, but because of Mummy we've been at some pains to be discreet when at home.' Then his whole manner changed and for the first time the painted smile left his lips. 'But I see I've upset you with that news. Unfortunately, Mr Weaver, that's one of the penalties for snooping. And you have been snooping, haven't you? Wasting your time and money on travel, going from place to place, though I'm sure you thought you were acting out of true concern. Was Moscow fascinating, by the way?'

'How did you know I've been to Moscow?' My own voice had also changed.

'Let's just say that one of my little birds told me. I think your trouble, Mr Weaver, is that you let your imagination run riot. Admirable in your chosen profession, I'm sure, but perhaps a mistake in real life. Much better to keep your illusions, like Mummy. Then one is saved so much distress.'

'What I choose to do, where I choose to go, is my business.'

'Of course, but it's never a good idea to go where we're not welcome. Mummy always drummed that into me. Such good advice, I really think you should start taking it . . . Henry was your friend, was he not? And I know that, as a friend, he would echo my words. He would never want you to take risks on his account.'

'Why don't you start living in the real world?' I said. 'Or is it like Mummy, like son?'

'If you're looking to annoy me, you won't succeed. I'm very content with my life. The world I live in is full of influential people, people who don't want the status quo preserved. They have the muscle and the means to ensure that it's not threatened in any way. You're out of your league, Mr Weaver.'

He led me to a side gate opening on to the drive and walked me to my car. The fragment of cigar leaf still dancing on his scarred upper lip as he turned away, dismissing me as one would a canvasser.

I had no sooner gone through the automatic gates when another car pulled right in front of me, forcing me to jam on my brakes. Two men got out and sauntered towards me. One I immediately recognised as the smooth type who had provided me with the plane ticket in Moscow. His companion, who appeared younger, had his hair tied in a pigtail, was dressed in jeans and a leather jacket and wore a single gold earring.

My reactions were slow. I went to activate the central locking device, but he wrenched the door open before I could act. Then the youth in the leather jacket reached in and pulled me out of the car and twisted my left arm in a half nelson. He thrust my face down on to the bonnet.

'My, we do get around, don't we?' my Moscow benefactor said. 'A proper little world traveller, always turning up in the wrong places, bothering my friends.'

The first blow was expertly delivered to the kidney; the shock and force of the blow slammed my head on to the metalwork and I immediately gagged from the pain. The pigtailed youth knew exactly where to place his punches for maximum effect and after the third blow had no need to keep the armlock on me. I slid to the ground and this time he put the boot in. It was all done with appalling casualness, like a bored small boy kicking a tin can on a vacant lot. I was retching from the pain, and the next blow landed on an ankle. I passed out.

When I came to they were nowhere to be seen. My first sensation was that I was suspended in mid-air rather than on the ground, for I could not place myself – the landscape above me was not part of the world I normally inhabited: I could see long, unmoving clouds through gaps in the birch trees. The feeling was not unlike waking in a hammock on a hot summer's day; only the ache from my ankle and ribs had any reality. I lay there for at least another five minutes before daring to test whether my ankle was broken. There was something sticky on my face which at first I took to be blood, but closer examination showed that it was merely tar from the road. I reached for the car door handle and started to lever myself up, coming face to face with my reflection in the side mirror. The streak of tar gave me a lopsided look and there were grazes on my chin.

At that moment a trousered lady cyclist came into view and, spotting me as she passed, executed a wide and somewhat unsteady circle which brought her back to me.

'Have you had an accident?' she asked in a voice that was pure Joyce Grenfell.

'Yes. I twisted my ankle and fell over,' I lied, for something urged caution.

'Oh, dear, how unfortunate. Sprained ankles are the

worst, I always find. Much better to have a fracture.' It came out as 'frecture.' 'Try not to put any weight on it. Then bags of ice as soon as you can. I know about these things because I do an awful lot of it myself. Have you got far to go?'

'Not too far, no.'

'Now let me think. The nearest hospital, if you're going to a hospital that is, would be Uxbridge, possibly. Or could it be Amersham? One of the two anyway. I could recommend my doctor, but he happens to be away on holiday and the locum is, quite frankly, a bit dodgy. You could risk it if you like.'

'Please don't bother. I'll see my own doctor when I get home.'

'Well, do take care. Nasty things, sprains. But don't forget ice. Bags of ice and a good stiff drink. Always works wonders. Ice in the drink and ice on the ankle. Personally I'd go for the drinky first.'

'Thank you, I'll remember that. And thank you for stopping.'

'Well, one can't pass a fellow human being in distress.'

She wobbled away and for a moment I thought she might take a tumble herself. I leaned against the side of the car. It still hurt me when I took a deep breath, but fortunately the damaged ankle was my left one and since the car was an automatic I felt that I could trust myself to drive. After wiping the tar from my face and removing my left shoe, I got back into the car and drove off very slowly. Only then did it occur to me that Seymour must have phoned the two characters when he pretended to be seeing to Mummy's pills. They must have been close at hand which meant I had been followed. The realisation brought on delayed shock; my whole body suddenly began to tremble so that I had difficulty holding the car on the road. I pulled into a layby and lit a cigarette. By now my ankle was monstrously swollen. More than fear, a wave of anger swept over me and when I resumed my slow journey back to London it was thoughts of getting even rather than the steady throb of pain that concentrated my mind.

16

THE PRESENT

Real life seldom lends itself to logic, so discarding common sense which, in my fictions, would certainly have dictated reporting the incident to the police, I convinced myself that I would be safer if I did nothing.

The visit to Inglewood had scared me as much as the actual beating. I was haunted by an image of the ghastly Seymour spearing Sophie just as he pinned one of his butterfly specimens; the revelation of her affair with Seymour further polluted memories of the past. It was as though one of my invented characters had suddenly twisted herself out of my imagination, so that when I came down in the morning to read through the previous night's work, some foreign hand had rearranged the plot in such a way that I recognised nothing on the page.

When next Pearson paid me a visit I stuck to my story about a sprained ankle and volunteered nothing about my meeting with Seymour. I was learning to be more cautious.

'How was your lady friend?'

'She never showed, so I guess that's that. I can take a hint.'

'Too bad.'

'Oh, well. They say you can never go back. Do you have any other news for me?'

"Fraid not. I followed up on that list you gave me, but none of the names I was able to trace meant anything. They were all professional people, couple of them dead, probably just contacts he made as an MP. Sorry, but there it is. I don't seem to have been much help to you.' He gave the paper back to me.

'You did at least find Sophie for me. Talking of which, please let me know what I owe you?'

'Nothing. I'll settle for that nice dinner you gave me.'

'You sure? You must have had some expenses.'

'A few phone calls, that's all. Forget it. If anything else transpires, let me know and maybe next time round. Give my regards to old Roger when next you talk to him.'

Shortly after he left my computer went down, and naturally my own efforts to get it running again proved useless so I was forced to send for Mr Bedford, my computer wizard. I stood behind him in awe as he played the keyboard like a concert pianist, conjuring my lost manuscript out of thin air in a matter of minutes.

'How did you do that? You're brilliant.'

'Yes, but I can't write books, can I? Each man to his own. Known as division of labour.'

'What did I do wrong?'

'Ah, well, that's a trade secret. You teach me how to write a bestseller and I'll teach you the right commands.'

He had the habit of playing pocket billiards while talking to me, making it difficult for me to keep my eyes from straying to his crotch.

'It's all beyond me,' I said. 'Stay and have a drink, Mr Bedford.'

'Never touch it. I'll have a coffee if you like.'

It was while waiting for the kettle to boil that I suddenly thought of trying him with the list of names and the cryptic code.

'Can I pick your brains about something else? I came across this the other day. Must be something I jotted down and now can't make head or tail of. Is it a computer command, d'you think?'

Mr Bedford studied it. 'Well, let's try it,' he said.

He sat down at the keyboard again and ran through a

145

series of arpeggios, producing what to me was an incomprehensible mass of data.

'No. Go another route.' His fingers sped over the keys again. 'Wait a minute, this is interesting. Let me look in my box of tricks.' He fished into his tattered briefcase and took out a floppy disc. After he had installed this in my machine another virtuoso performance on the keyboard followed. 'Now we're getting somewhere,' he claimed. 'I thought as much.'

'What is it?'

'Getting there. Just switch off for a moment.' He dived into the briefcase again, this time producing a microchip and a screwdriver which he used to remove the rear plate and expose the inner workings.

'Don't worry. Just want to install this.'

'I'm not worried, I'm fascinated. What're you putting in?'

'A modem.'

'Why do we need that?'

'It might solve what I think this is all about.'

By the time I came back into the room with the coffee he had completed his task and was ready to operate.

'Let's see if I'm right.' He executed more dazzling strokes on the keyboard and peered at the screen. 'Yes. Thought so.'

'What is a modem?' I asked.

'Stands for Modulate, Demodulate. Which means an electronic process by which words are turned into bleep signals. Course you have to tie it in with the appropriate communications software. That's what I put in your machine. Then you can talk to other machines. Get me so far?'

'Just about.'

'Think of ham radio. It's really an extension of that, except you're talking electronically instead of vocally. You have access to computers all over the world, assuming they have the same facility. You call them up, exchange information, ask questions, get answers.'

'What if their machine is not switched on?'

'The host machine takes care of it,' Bedford said, in his element now.

'Host machine?'

'Robot post office, runs automatically, nobody behind the counter. Most of them are run for people with hobbies or who like to exchange technical info. Others just use it as a chatline, like old women talking over the garden fence. Let me show you, see what we get.'

He consulted the slip of paper. 'The first step is the entry code.'

After the DOS command he typed the letters SIGOP.

'What does that signify?'

'The first three letters stand for Special Interest Group. The OP means operator, or host machine.'

'Let me get a pad and write this down as you go along. I might want to try it myself.'

He waited until I had finished.

'OK, got that? Now then, let's try the next command. It's probably a confidential line.'

'Why d'you say that?'

'CUG. Means Closed User Group. So, put that in, which should get us a little further into the maze.'

He typed the next three letters. After a short pause a prompt appeared, which read: *Supply Identification.*

'Thought so,' Bedford said. 'The last bit is the vital one, the personal password without which you won't get any further. Could be just a combination of letters, or some prefer to use pseudonyms. Let's try what we've got.'

He punched in PBBW.

The prompt, *bad command* appeared, followed by *Abort, Retry.*

'Probably out of date. Closed User Group types frequently change their passwords.'

'Why?' I asked.

'Any number of reasons. Too many people get hold of them, like your telephone number.'

'So, that's as far as we can go, is it?'

'Never say die. Hand me my briefcase.'

He took out a notebook this time.

'I've got a mate who talks to me from Los Angeles, very up in these things. I say "mate", but I've never met him of course. Bit of an oddball from some of the gubbins he tells me, but he knows his way around the CUG network. They use them a lot over there, streets ahead of us, naturally. I want to go one day and take a gander at all their latest gear. Half the price, I'm told. He sends me updates on the passwords, and I sometimes amuse myself. Let me have a go with this little lot.'

He tried several without any success until he used the word RIZKY. After a pause a message started to unscroll on the screen. It read: *Welcome to Lollipop, a service offering an adult noticeboard that allows you to discuss matters of mutual interest. Please wait, then select the specialist section closest to your needs.*

'Now we're cooking!' Bedford said.

This message left the screen and then another menu appeared. As promised it contained a list together with a prompt asking the user to cursor down to the subject of his choice.

SCHOOL
NURSERY TRAINING
PARTY TIME
TAKE YOUR PARTNERS
TRAVEL
FANTASY
VIDEO
PHOTOGRAPHY

'Oh, I see, it's one of those Do-your-shopping-from-home menus. Mail order by computer, the coming thing,' Bedford explained. 'Course you have to open an account with them, give your credit card number, then order what you fancy.'

'Fascinating.'

'You wait, won't be long before we've got computer telephones. See who you're talking to.'

'Not too keen on that,' I said.

'Got to come. Progress.'

He looked at his watch. 'God! Look at the time, I was supposed to be meeting the missus half an hour ago.'

'That's my fault. I'm sorry.'

'She's used to it.'

'What do I do about the new stuff you put in my machine?'

'Keep it. I've got spares. Now you know how you can play around with it.'

'Well, I must pay you.'

After a show of reluctance he accepted a nominal sum and departed to placate a long-suffering wife. The last menu was still on my screen and as an experiment I cursored down to 'Video' and pressed the Enter key. A series of coloured graphics such as one might see any night of the week prefacing ordinary television programmes came and went on the screen. Then a caption appeared: THE VERY BEST IN HOME ENTERTAINMENT. The word 'HOME' was highlighted. When this faded another list of titles scrolled down.

Family Entertainment	(20 minutes)
Uncle Pays a Visit	(25 minutes)
Suckers	(15 minutes)
Babysitters	(45 minutes)
Boy Scouts and Brownies	(20 minutes)
Peter Pan	(20 minutes)
Rear View	(18 minutes)
Alice in Funderland	(40 minutes)
Brothers and Sisters	(30 minutes)
Learning the Breast Stroke	(20 minutes)
A Visit to the Far East	(40 minutes)
Daddy Knows Best	(35 minutes)
Willing Moppets	(30 minutes)

When selecting please specify VHS, Beta or 8mm. and quote membership number. Quality may vary, but contents guaranteed genuine.

I stared at the screen for a long time and it gradually dawned on me what I was looking at. The titles of the videos on offer spoke for themselves. As I sat there the hideous truth suddenly struck me. I realised I had finally found my way to the entrance of the labyrinth.

17

THE PAST

The clues were all there when I had cause to look for them. It was just that I had chosen to ignore them.

Back in the time when Harold Wilson's monetary exchange controls were in force all good, tame citizens had to comply with stringent regulations before being allowed to spend their already over-taxed money. There was a distinctly Orwellian flavour to such demeaning procedures. Being British, nobody took to the barricades, but suffered their package holidays in unfinished hotels, accepting the indignity of being the poor relations on beaches swarming with affluent Germans.

It was Henry who came up with a way around the problem and decided that we three should take a holiday together.

'If the bloody government think I'm going to spend my well-earned vacation in some shitty little hotel sharing the only loo, they've got another think coming,' he announced. 'I've never lived like that and I don't intend to start now.'

'What're you going to do then?' I asked. 'Hollow out the soles of your shoes and stuff them with francs?'

'What an innocent you are! We shall stay at La Résidence du Cap and live it up regardless.'

'How?'

'Sophie, you really must get yourself a boyfriend who knows the ropes. As far as the Gestapo on this side of the water are concerned, we are honest, law-abiding citizens. Our passports will denote that we are travelling with the precise legal amount granted by the parsimonious pricks who rule us – we shall look and behave like model proles. But once we get there adequate funds will be made available. Some of us, Martin, know our way around the world. No wonder your novels are only read by old ladies who subscribe to Harrods lending library. Let me complete your education.'

Then, with the odd smirk in Sophie's direction, he proceeded to reveal how anybody sophisticated in these matters circumvented the regulations. Through his City connections he had a French banking friend who was happy to accommodate him on a quid pro quo basis. 'He provides the wherewithal for us over there, then when he comes to London I pick up the tab for his hotel bill. And nobody's any the wiser.'

'Isn't that brilliant?' Sophie said. 'You are clever, Henry.'

'Yes, I am, as a matter of fact.'

'They're very hot on currency frauds, you know,' I felt compelled to say.

'If you don't want to participate, just say the word. You can stay in a dump and Sophie and I will live it up on our *plage privé*.'

'Yes, don't be chicken,' Sophie said. It was the first time she had openly sided with Henry against me. So I accepted with bad grace and we went and stayed in La Résidence du Cap, which was a pleasant mid-range hotel a short distance from the famed and mega-expensive Eden Roc. Somewhat pointlessly, I remained in a sulk for the first few days and managed to get a severe case of sunburn by neglecting to use a barrier cream. As a result I had to remain on my own in the hotel while Henry and Sophie cavorted on the beach. Perhaps, looking back, that was the moment when I started to lose her. She looked so impossibly full of life and young and the skimpy bikinis she wore would have turned anybody's head. The more they enjoyed themselves the more I withdrew – what self-destructive demon drives us to behave so stupidly when in love?

'Guess who we bumped into today,' Henry announced on the second day.

'Who?'

'Victor and Eva.'

The names did not immediately register with me.

'You can't have forgotten them. The twins! We all had dinner together at Les A.'

'Oh, them.'

'They're here on their chartered yacht and they've invited us to join them on a short cruise.'

'Do we *want* to go on a cruise with them?' I said.

'Well, we certainly do, don't we, Sophie? I accepted like a shot.'

'It's fab,' Sophie said. She always shortened her favourite words that year. 'You should see the cabins. You have to take your shoes off when you step on the deck,' she added, as though this piece of information was likely to impress me.

'You've already been on board, have you?'

'Yes, they came ashore, spotted us on the beach and invited us for lunch. Why're you so crusty?'

'So when are we invited?'

'Now. This evening.'

'I don't have much choice, do I, if you've said yes?' I knew I was behaving childishly but their exuberant mood, far from being infectious, made me all the more disgruntled.

While Henry went to square the hotel bill and make excuses for our early departure, Sophie and I packed.

'You weren't too keen on the twins, I remember, when we first met them.'

'No, well, they seemed nicer this time and I've always wanted to go on a boat, especially a boat like theirs.'

The yacht was anchored off shore at Antibes and we were taken to it in a Riva. Henry and Sophie had not been exaggerating: of a sleek Italian design, it rested like a white dart on the water, slept twenty people in addition to a crew of ten and boasted the latest state-of-the-art navigation equipment. Powered by Mercedes diesels which I was quickly informed gave it a top speed of twenty-eight knots and a range of three thousand miles, it did not seem real. After we had been shown our quarters, the feeling of unreality persisted. I had never seen such tasteless luxury: the fittings throughout the staterooms were gold, the baths marble, the furnishings opulent yet curiously anonymous as though lifted piecemeal from a catalogue for kitsch. I was suddenly aware as never before of the gulf between the very rich and the rest of us. It wasn't envy of their money, but the way in which they used that money, for although the yacht itself was a thing of beauty, it was filled with vulgarity. The holiday that had promised so much now seemed corrupted by affluence.

'Aren't you glad you came?' Sophie said as she tested the bed. 'This is how I'd like to live all the time.'

Once we had dumped our somewhat shoddy suitcases we went on to the main deck where the other guests were already sampling champagne and caviar. They were a strange collection, ranging from the very old to the very young, the majority foreigners, though most spoke good English. They included a blatantly camp Italian couturier and one of his models, a striking girl from Columbia, the ex-wife of a Lebanese arms dealer who seemed to be wearing a fair proportion of Cartier's inventory, an Israeli film producer of gross and unattractive appearance touting his monosyllabic girlfriend, and a 50's American screen siren who had had one too many cosmetic tucks so that now her face did not move at all. The only other Brit was a barrel-chested MP, full of himself, who had held two or three junior ministerial posts before being given a peerage for total incompetence. The twins' parents were absent: Mummy, we found, was undergoing a rest cure in a fashionable American health farm, and Daddy was off making a deal with the Saudis, which figured considering the size of the yacht and what it must cost to run.

Eva and Victor greeted us warmly and seduced by the novelty of the occasion I gradually recovered my good humour. Henry, of course, was in his element and inclined to show off; his voice got louder and his laugh coarser, but since everybody on board was out for a good time, I daresay his behaviour went unremarked. Dinner was served while we were still at anchor. Henry had been seated next to Eva and Sophie was on Victor's left. I found myself sitting between the pretty model and the divorcee who chain-smoked Russian cigarettes and ate nothing. The cigarettes had gold tips, heavily stained by her pillar-box red lipstick.

'Have you any idea why one comes on these trips year after year?' she asked me. She ignored the crystal ashtray and stabbed out yet another cigarette on the side of her plate. 'Don't you find they're always the same? One needs a holiday to get over the holiday. Why do you come?'

'Well, I don't.'

'How sensible of you.'

'I meant this is my first experience.'

'Oh, well, I suppose the first time is tolerable. But it palls. God, how it palls, one longs for the ship to catch fire or something.' She spoke upper-class English with a trace of an accent, which somehow made it a parody of a parody. 'It makes a difference if one is on a large boat, of course.'

'Isn't this a large boat? Seems large to me.'

I had the impression that I was boring her rigid because she didn't look at me when she talked. 'You should have seen my ex-husband's boat. It made this look like a Dinky toy. I thought it might come my way after the divorce, but it didn't. Just as well, really, because one can be bored on one's own boat as easily as on somebody else's. Did somebody say you're a writer?'

'Yes, I am.'

'I once took a poet as a lover, but he was better on the page than he was in bed. He used the most wonderful words to describe what he was going to do to me, but never delivered.' She looked across the table to where Victor and Sophie were laughing about something. 'Who's that girl?'

'Her name's Sophie Campbell. She's a dancer.'

'She came on with you, didn't she?'

'Yes, she's my girlfriend.'

'I hope she doesn't put little Eva's nose out of joint,' she said cryptically. 'Not that that wouldn't be a bad thing.' Then, without lowering her voice appreciably, as though she was determined for the conversation to carry across the table, she told me that she would like to have a love child by Victor.

'How do you think he'd feel about that?' I asked, but by then she had turned away to talk to the Israeli film producer. I tried to make polite conversation with the model but it was hard going. She told me she went everywhere by private jet and seemed genuinely surprised that I didn't do the same. Dressed in one of her boyfriend's bizarre creations, she had the most elaborate eye make-up since Tutankhamun.

As the meal progressed the talk around the table turned to money: what it had bought, what it was going to buy, and where it was safest to keep it. When they weren't talking money they unsheathed their daggers and traded malicious gossip, bitch gabfests that mostly went over my head since I did not know the personalities concerned. The exchanges were conducted in a campy code that outsiders like me could not hope to break – in any case I sensed that nobody wanted me to. It was left to Henry to pretend an intimacy he did not possess, though perhaps I judged him wrongly, perhaps, that evening, he had suddenly found his Xanadu. He and Sophie excepted, everybody around the table had made careers of being exiles from reality and the very rich, I have noted, are tuned in to different sounds from the rest of us. It is not that they avoid ordinary conversations, but they respond in different ways in voices half-way between a bray and a bark. Their accents and appearance allow them to recognise each other and quickly weed out and dispose of would-be intruders to the inner circle. For the most part they inhabit a different country, a glossy place of perpetual summer peopled with micro-celebrities where there is no poverty and everybody and everything is fashionable. Their only token glance towards the rest of the world is to attend a few charity balls. Of course, there are divisions within their ranks separating old money from new money, the old money sticking resolutely together, the new money avid to infiltrate. Most of the money on board that evening was new, and much of it tainted.

Dinner over, we all retired to the main stateroom and shortly afterwards the captain upped anchor and with a scarcely perceptible hum of the powerful engines we moved out into the dark sea.

'Do you know where we're going?' Sophie said. She was flushed and excited.

'No, do you?'

'Victor asked me where I wanted to go and I chose the Greek Islands. When we wake up we shall be half-way there. Isn't it all romantic? He's been really nice to me. Are you having a good time? Please say you are.'

'I am.'

'Wasn't it wonderful at dinner? They're all so witty and knowledgeable. And did you see the jewels?'

'Hard to miss them,' I said.

'Are you in a bad mood about something?'

'No.'

'Good, because I'm having such a good time.'

More drinks were served and then Victor produced what he termed the 'goodies'. It was the first time I had seen hard drugs openly displayed and I tried to analyse whether I was shocked on moral grounds – not very convincing since I drank and had smoked grass at odd intervals – or whether I was reacting from fear of the unknown. The unknown on this occasion was cocaine, which I had never experimented with and *majoun*, a mysterious cannabis confection which Victor announced he had obtained in Tangier and could recommend.

He offered the *majoun* around. 'You'll love this, it produces the most fantastic visions.'

'You going to try?' Sophie said.

'I don't think so.'

'I am.'

'I wouldn't.'

157

'Oh, don't be dreary. It's fun and I'm sure Victor wouldn't give us anything dangerous.'

From the moment we had stepped on the boat she and Henry seemed changed people and now I hardly recognised her.

Henry took a line of coke with the others, anxious to be seen and accepted as one of them. Everybody else helped themselves as though it was candy. When it came to me I made the lame excuse that, sadly, I had OD'd once and had stayed off it ever since.

'Oh, too bad. Have the *majoun* then,' Victor urged, 'it's something else, I promise you.' He demonstrated how to take it with Sophie a willing convert. I accepted the fragment he offered me. Once in my mouth it tasted like fudge that had exceeded its shelf life. I pretended to swallow it and then, at the first opportunity palmed it into my handkerchief.

'Now we're all getting into the right mood, it's film time,' Eva said.

Innocently, I imagined we were going to be treated to one of the latest French hits. The crew member serving drinks was dismissed and Victor first activated a sliding panel on one wall of the saloon to reveal a large projection television.

'Let's have the same one as last night,' somebody said. 'That was so *outré*.'

'And something for everybody,' the Italian observed with a smirk towards his girlfriend. I noticed he had his own silver spoon for the cocaine.

'Are you sure? Because we've got a selection. Victor ordered some real goodies.'

'This is all very jolly,' the MP said and winked at me.

We swivelled our suede-covered armchairs to face the screen.

'Isn't this all a gas?' Sophie said.

As soon as Victor had inserted the cassette the lights were lowered and the screen flickered into life. I had seen a few soft-core films during my university days – there was a character in my last year who ran an underground cinema club to supplement his grant. He ran scratchy prints of unknown origin featuring what was known in the vernacular as 'dry-hump' movies, so called because although the females performed nude, the gents never removed their trousers during the critical stages, a feat that was not only blatantly sexist but also introduced a novel method of contraception. They were too absurd to be truly erotic but seemed daring at the time.

What was shown on board the yacht that night owed nothing to reticence. The film was called *Going Down Slowly* and, from the sparse dialogue, of American origin. The action took place in a coed college and the cast consisted of jocks and very attractive nubile girls, in strict contrast to the weedy actors I remembered from the old Cambridge screenings – they always kept their socks on, I remember. It was also technically far superior. The actors wasted no time in getting down to business and before the credit titles had finished we were witnessing a graphic fellatio – a black girl servicing a well-endowed blond Adonis. I felt Sophie tense beside me and she reached for my hand as the episode ended with a prodigious orgasm which was greeted with applause.

The feeble plot got under way but, in the nature of these things, was not allowed to impede the true purpose of the product. There was something for every taste. Fellatio was followed by the quid pro quo of cunnilingus, followed by full penetration, then a lesbian episode, which in turn led to a *ménage à trois* when the tribades were discovered by a member of the faculty who immediately joined in. There was little attempt at subtlety; all the moves in this game of sexual chess were executed with clinical deliberation.

Several times I looked to see how the others were reacting. Eva and Victor, sitting close together, were staring at the screen with a demonic intensity, the divorcee with bored indifference, but whether it was genuine or affected was impossible to tell. Henry caught my eye and grimaced, pulling his face into an expression I took to mean wasn't it all a splendid lark. It would be a prudish lie to say that I was

159

unaffected by the proceedings, yet equally untrue to say that the images stimulated me. Perhaps, being a writer, the paucity and vacuity of the dialogue had something to do with it. I longed for something human to happen before and during the heroic bouts. It was all so mechanical; as soon as one episode finished, it was dissolved and on to the next. Although Sophie nestled against my shoulder, I sensed that during the forty minutes that the film lasted, something had been irrevocably lost.

When the lights came up at the conclusion there was a predictable, pseudo-intellectual post-mortem. I heard the Israeli remark, 'That's where the real money is in films today. You have no idea what the gross returns are. Out of sight. We should all have a piece of that cake.'

Somebody else made an asinine comment, praising the photography of all things, but it was noticeable that nobody confessed to being aroused; perhaps they were all so sexually jaded that the erotic images no longer had any effect. It was left to the MP to quip, 'Amazing how those chaps manage to keep up their morale,' making what he obviously thought was a stunningly witty joke and which, indeed, was so received.

'Do you think that sometimes leads to the pornographic equivalent of an actor forgetting his lines?' I asked him, but the comparison went over his head. Henry, anxious to be considered as somebody on the inside track, pronounced the film 'really superior', implying he viewed such masterpieces on a regular basis.

There was no camaraderie amongst that group, they were all out for themselves and in the aftermath of the film show they lapsed into an introspective, drug-induced high during which nobody made much sense. They all seemed so fucked up and boring. I watched Sophie closely for signs that the *majoun* was having an effect and at one point I whispered to her, 'Are you OK?'

'Great! Wow! I should have smuggled one of those into the convent.'

The prospect of the trip lasting another four days filled me with despair.

It was an hour or so later before I finally persuaded Sophie we should go to bed. Once inside our cabin she started to hallucinate, by turns hysterical with laughter, then pathetically serious. 'I can't control my thoughts,' she said, 'they keep getting out of the bottle.'

'Bottle?'

'The one green bottle hanging on the wall where I keep them. Catch them for me, they're flying all over the room.'

'Darling, you're just having a bad trip from that stuff.'

'No, I'm not. Don't say that.' Then the laughter again, which doubled her like a rag-doll. When she lifted her face again she stared at me like a stranger. 'How come you turned off the light? You turned it off. I don't want to be in the dark.'

I humoured her and went to the light switch, miming turning it on.

'Don't ever leave me in the dark.'

Then she lapsed into gibberish.

'The music. Hear that? The nuns don't allow that. That's not allowed. It's so tight round my breasts, can't you see? Saint Sophie, the martyr. Say fifty-eight Hail Marys before breakfast. There they go again, they're up on the ceiling now. I can't help these, can I? They're the way I'm made, you stupid, frigid, jealous old cow.'

Now, naked, she flung herself on the bed and writhed there, as though the past had suddenly possessed her.

'Fuck me,' she screamed. 'Fuck me like that man in the film.' I went to her and put my arms round her, cuddling her as one does small children who wake from a bad dream, but her body went rigid like somebody stretched on the rack and it took all my strength to hold her down. 'Don't let me touch the ceiling!' she shouted. With no idea how long a *majoun* trip lasted, I thought of asking Victor for help, but I was terrified to leave her alone. Her spasms gradually subsided and then she lay absolutely still and silent staring at visions I could not guess at, until finally she slipped into sleep. I watched over her all night, chilled by my own fears.

In the morning she had only a dim recollection of what had happened and when I told her, sparing her nothing, her reaction was one of amusement rather than shock. 'Really? Did I talk like that? How bizarre.'

'Promise me you won't try it again.'

'But it doesn't seem to have had any lasting effect.'

'How do you know? Any of that stuff rots your brain.'

'Well, I haven't got much to rot. Anyway, you have to try everything once.'

There was a moment when her flippancy could have led us into a lovers' quarrel. I kissed her without passion because for the first time in our affair I felt no desire for her. It was like kissing a stranger. We showered and smartened ourselves up, hardly talking, then went on deck to have breakfast.

Henry was the next person to surface. He looked ghastly, drank two cups of black coffee in quick succession while at the same time putting on an act of devil-may-care for our benefit.

That was to be the pattern repeated every night during the four-day cruise: drink, drugs and hard-core movies, a diet of depravity, but to the best of my knowledge Sophie never repeated the experiment while I remained on board. I prayed it had scared her.

We anchored off one of the smaller Greek Islands and were taken ashore for a picnic on a deserted beach. It should have been idyllic, a once-in-a-lifetime experience; in different circumstances and with a different set of people I would have surrendered to the magic in the company of the girl I loved, but a distance had opened up between us. In the space of those few days some of the uselessness of that awful group had rubbed off on her. She seemed to prefer Henry's company to mine and I felt hollowed out, presenting a false, smiling mask to the others while concealing a mounting panic.

Some of the guests were due to leave the yacht at Nice on the return trip, the rest remaining for a further cruise to the

West Indies. Victor invited us to stay with them, but I made the excuse that I had to get back to work, assuming Henry would say the same, but I was wrong.

'It's just too good to pass up,' he said.

'Don't you have to work?'

'Well, yes and no. The bank is fairly relaxed about these things. I shall send a cable saying I'm sick. Why don't you do the same?'

'What, send a cable to myself?'

'You know what I mean. You can write at any old time, but it isn't every day that one can make contacts like this. Old Charles,' he added, ("old Charles" being the burnt-out MP) 'has been talking to me about a possible political career.'

'You're not serious?'

'Why d'you say it like that?'

'You've always loathed politics.'

Henry shrugged and looked away. 'Charles has made me see it from another angle. He thinks with my background they could get me selected.'

'The Tories are that desperate, are they?'

'Don't be snide, just because you're out of your depth here.'

'Nice one. See you in Number 11. Enjoy yourself in this scintillating company.'

'I intend to.' There was the slightest of pauses, and then he added: 'So does Sophie. She's staying on, too.'

I walked away before he could see the shock on my face and said nothing to Sophie until we were in bed.

'Henry said you and he were staying on, but he was probably just saying that to annoy me, knowing Henry.'

Sophie remained silent.

'Was he?' I asked.

'No.'

'No, he wasn't trying to annoy me, or what?'

'He thought you'd feel the same way. We both did.'

'So you obviously discussed it without me?' I tried to keep my voice normal.

163

'It just seemed a great idea.'

'To go without me?'

'No, I thought you'd come too. Why can't you?'

'Because unlike these sick creeps I have to work for a living.'

'They're not creeps. I think they're very nice people.'

'I don't know what's come over you. How can you say they're nice? Turn over a stone and you'd find something more attractive than this lot. Jesus, darling, you really come out with them sometimes. Are you forgetting the other evening, you could have died?'

'Well, I didn't, did I?'

'You enjoy their idea of fun – porno movies and drugs?'

'Doesn't do any harm if you don't take it seriously. You're the only one freaked out by it.'

'Can't you see we're just the jokers in their pack? This is just a one-off. You think we're going to be put on their 'A' list from now on? They use people for as long as it amuses them and then they drop them.'

'Maybe.'

'No, not "maybe", believe me. Darling, I know what I'm talking about and I'm not trying to pick a row with you. It's so easy to be generous when you've got their sort of money. They're bored, they have to have periodic fixes of new faces just as they have to have a fix of cocaine. We're just another drug, can't you see that? God! We never row, you and me, what's happening to us?'

'We just don't agree on something, that's all.'

'That's all? I see. My feelings don't matter?'

'It's only a few more days, what's the big deal?'

'And you're going? Nothing I've said makes any difference?'

She didn't answer that. I thought perhaps I might see tears but she remained stony-faced. I resorted to the cheapest kind of jibe in my anger.

'Who's the big attraction? The lovable Victor? Don't tell me you've fallen for Victor?'

164

'Don't be stupid, of course not.'

'I just don't understand you any more.' Seeing the battle was nearly lost I changed my tack and made a last attempt to persuade her. 'Look, darling, I'm not trying to spoil it for you. If the true reason is the lure of the West Indies, I'll take you. The moment I get the advance on my next novel I'll blow it all on a holiday for the two of us.'

It had no effect. She was stubborn and I was stubborn and we had dug a pit for ourselves that neither was willing to climb out of. I left the boat the following morning. Sophie sailed on, tearful at farewell time, but with no last minute change of heart. I left her standing at the rail with Henry beside her and walked away on the quayside without a backward glance. It wasn't the end of the affair, just the end of the peace I had once thought would last forever.

18

THE PRESENT

No matter how well we think we know another human being there are some doors we can never unlock. I thought I knew Henry, I believed I knew how to make Sophie happy, but I was wrong.

Many times after the discovery of the existence of 'Lollipop', I keyed it back on to my monitor screen and sat transfixed, trying to reconcile what I was now seeing to the past. The seemingly-innocent titles on my screen held portents of evil beyond my imagination and I still found it impossible to connect them to Henry.

It was while I sat there one evening searching for the answers that the phone rang and I was drawn further into the maze. Inspector Ghia, he of the Pavarotti proportions, called from Venice to inform me he had finally located somebody whom he believed was the old dandy in the white suit.

'He's been arrested, has he?'

'No,' he said. 'But we do require you to make a positive identification. How soon would it be convenient for you to come? We will, of course, pay your fare and expenses.'

I tried to collect my thoughts. 'Well, I suppose I could get on a plane tomorrow.'

'That would be a great help. The matter is of some urgency, as I'm sure you appreciate. If you let me know your flight I will have you met at the airport and arrange the hotel. I don't wish to put you to any extra trouble.'

I managed to get a single seat on the British Airways flight and Ghia himself was there to meet me and ease me through Immigration and Customs. As the police launch with its distinctive siren set out across the lagoon at high speed I relived the moment when I had spotted the murdered boy.

'Where did you finally pick up the old man?' I asked, raising my voice over the siren. The launch suddenly altered course and I was pitched across the cabin into his lap. Ghia steadied me and I got my first blast of garlic.

'In the apartment of a young male prostitute.'

'Have you got anything out of him about the murder?'

'No, unfortunately. He wasn't able to tell us anything. You see, he was dead when we arrived.'

If he had intended to take me off guard he succeeded. 'Dead? How?'

'A drug overdose, though whether self-administered or injected by somebody else we have no means of telling at the moment.'

'So where are we heading for now?'

'The morgue.'

During the course of research I have visited a few morgues in my time and I guess they are more or less the same the world over, give or take standards of hygiene. They never fail to induce a chill as you enter and, like those who choose to work in abattoirs, I imagine it takes a special kind of indifference towards those who have shuffled off their mortal coils to want to take up employment in such places. The one in Venice was tidy and not all that forbidding once you got inside, although the air reeked of formaldehyde and I was grateful for the odd whiff of garlic as Ghia led us to the cold storage room presided over by an ancient attendant. Following Ghia's order this secretary for the dead shuffled to the oversized filing cabinets and pulled out one of the drawers. After the sheet covering the corpse had been removed I was motioned forward to take a look.

The skin of the upper body was the colour of beeswax scarred with coarsely-stitched post-mortem wounds, like routes drawn on a discarded map. Although the sight was ugly enough to make me give an involuntary shudder, curiously, I couldn't help thinking that the old boy still looked dapper in death. Shrunken, but oddly dapper. His dentures had been removed, sinking the mouth and giving it a crooked look that might have been mistaken for a smile.

'Take your time,' Ghia said. It was the last thing I wanted to do.

'That's him,' I said.

'You're quite certain?'

'Yes, I'm certain.'

Once outside again, the air seemed pure oxygen. Ghia consulted his wristwatch. 'It's lunchtime,' he said. 'Would you care for something to eat?'

We journeyed through narrow waterways until the launch finally tied up outside a small restaurant away from the tourist haunts and where, judging from the effusive greeting he received from the proprietor, Ghia was obviously a regular customer. The menu was small and from the fact that we had to wait half an hour for our main dish to be served, none of the food ever saw a microwave. We cracked a bottle of very smooth Chianti and went on to a second. I warmed to Ghia for not plunging into an immediate discussion of the case. Like most Italians he took eating seriously, and even a corpse was not going to divert him. It wasn't until fortified by the Chianti and the house speciality – *osso buco* cooked with oregano and lemon balm – that I took the plunge and once again told my story.

Ghia had a good memory for immediately I had finished he pounced on a detail from my first interrogation. 'So this Henry Blagden was the man you could not describe when I first asked you?'

'Yes, I know now that was a mistake, but I didn't withhold the information for any sinister reason. At that time I still couldn't believe it was him. Can you blame me? The man was dead and buried from all accounts.'

'Even so, you've had time since.'

'Well, now you know the rest of the story you must realise how confused I've been. In the beginning I was just concerned for an old friend. Then, after the sighting in Venice I admit I did some stupid things, but again I still hoped the whole thing was a ghastly mistake. The deeper I went the more it scared me. Nothing made any sense until I chanced upon those computer codes a few days ago. Then it began to make hideous sense.'

He mopped up the juice on his plate with a piece of bread. 'You didn't go to your own police?'

'Yes and no.'

'What does that mean?'

'I have a friend in the Metropolitan force, he's in the Anti-Terrorist Squad, somebody I've known for a number of years who's often helped me with research for my novels. I did talk to him about it.'

'And what was his view?'

'He said he'd make enquiries.'

'And has he?'

'Well, it's not really his territory, he was doing it more as a friend than officially.'

'Does he know the latest developments?'

'No.'

'You must give me his name before you leave. I will contact him.'

Ghia wiped up the remaining traces of juice on his plate. 'If I may say so, for a writer of thrillers – and I've read one of yours since we first met, by the way – very good – you don't seem to live as logically as you write.'

'No, I can't argue with that.'

'If I had been in your position, the moment I was safely home from Moscow I would have made sure I had protection from the proper authorities.'

'But it was the authorities who appeared to be threatening me. Word had to have come down from high up that I was to be discouraged from taking it any further.'

He nodded. 'British politics and sex scandals seem to go together, or so I read. Not that we can boast. We even elected a porn star to our parliament. Politics are shit. Everything is corrupt. We have the octopus of *Cosa Nostra* with us for life.'

He sipped his double espresso. Mine made my heart thump. It was difficult to gauge his reaction to my story, for his expression gave little away.

'What you've told me . . . a little late in the day . . . begins to make sense of the puzzle I've been trying to solve. I want to show you something else.' He heaved his bulk out of the chair and I noticed he was not presented with a bill for our meal. The proprietor embraced him before we left.

This time the police launch took us across the lagoon to the island of Torcello where for the third and last time I had seen the old man alive. Ghia volunteered nothing as we walked past the tourist stalls and the ruined church until we reached the entrance gates of a large villa. Two weathered stone statues stood sentinel on either side of the gates, the grotesque faces pitted. They seemed more likely to protect the property from intruders than the young uniformed policeman who saluted Ghia and opened the gates. Over the massive front door was a carving such as Ruskin once described – *a head, huge, inhuman and monstrous, leering in bestial degradation.*

'This *palazzo* dates back to the sixteenth century,' Ghia informed me as we entered. 'Venice has always bred eccentrics of one kind or another. And monsters. The romanticism the tourists feed on hides a cruel past. The man you identified, the master of this house, faked affinities with that past. He claimed ancestry with the patrician family Foscari.'

'Was that his name?'

'No, though he used it here. A model citizen, reclusive, hidden away, that is why his death led us to him. He was a German with the given name of Lehmann, Wolfgang Lehmann, born in Celle, which before unification was in West Germany, not too far from Belsen as it happens. The

German authorities were able to give us more information. During the war he served in the Waffen SS. Captured by your troops he escaped standing trial for war crimes and in fact was used by the Americans as an interpreter for a time. Some five years later he surfaced in Hamelin where for a period he was a master in a boy's school, teaching English. According to the records he was asked to resign following an incident with one of the boys. After that he disappeared from view. Nothing else is known until he took up residence here in 1988 using a fake Italian passport under his assumed name.'

'Palaces like this don't come cheap, do they? Where did he get the money to live in this style? This doesn't go with a schoolmaster's salary.'

'Who knows?' Ghia said. 'I have my own theory, but that remains to be proved.'

We were standing in the magnificent marble hallway where the walls were hung with ancient banners, armour and weapons – wicked-looking pikes, crossbows and great bladed swords.

'This house gave up many secrets. We found much he would have been wiser to have destroyed, but like many who share his tastes, he kept careful records of his vice.'

Ghia led the way up the staircase to the first floor and then into the library. A vast glass-topped table divided the room in half. Arranged upon it were a dozen carnival masks, mostly of grinning satyrs, and as we entered the effect was startling, for the direction of the afternoon sunlight caused the faces to be reflected in the surface of the table so that the whole room seemed filled with them. Ornate bookcases with gold mesh fronts lined the room, housing the old man's collection of fine bindings. Ghia gestured towards them.

'Take a look. The first clues.'

I went closer and examined the contents of one of the bookcases. Although each one had an elaborate lock, they had presumably all been opened by the police in the course of their investigation. I took out a volume at random. It was a nineteenth-century German publication, privately printed and profusely illustrated with hand-coloured prints depicting various sexual acts. Like German fairy-tales there was a strong element of sadism in the illustrations.

Ghia went to another bookcase and extracted a much larger, leather-bound volume.

'See this.'

I took it from him. The wording on the spine was in Latin. I opened it, expecting erotica from Pompeii, but instead found the binding held a sickening collection of illustrated pornographic magazines produced for paedophiles with titles such as *Children-Love*, *Lolita* and *Liza, aged ten, and her Father*.

'Jesus!' I exclaimed.

'Most of it originates in Holland and Scandinavia. But let me show you something else.'

To one end of the far wall was a door faced with fake spines so as to appear part of the bookshelves. It opened noiselessly and I followed Ghia into a small, windowless ante chamber some ten feet square. The ceiling was tented with the same patterned silk which covered the walls. Fully a third of the room was taken up with a large couch behind which was a mirror in an antique gilded frame. Carved cherubs, entwined in lascivious poses adorned each corner of the frame. I felt chilled the moment I entered, for there was no mistaking the air of decadence.

'His assignation room,' Ghia said. 'Take a closer look at the mirror.'

I stared at it.

'The cherub on the top right-hand corner. Look at the mouth. Do you see anything?'

'It's larger than the others?'

'There's a video camera behind it, with the lens concealed in the mouth. He filmed what went on in this room. I can show you a selection when we return to my office, if your stomach's strong enough. I'm talking about infants, some so young it's impossible to look at them without the heart breaking no matter what you've seen before. At the last count there were some four thousand known missing children in Italy. How many found their way here?'

We continued the tour of the house. Every room we were shown was lavishly furnished until we came to the old man's bedroom which, in startling contrast, was stark: stone walls painted white, a simple bed covered with a white counterpane, a small bedside table likewise draped in white cloth with a vellum-bound Bible on it. The only illumination would have come from two massive wrought-iron candle holders on either side of the bed. On the wall facing the bed Christ crucified hung from an enormous cross.

'A devout monster, as you can see,' Ghia said. 'Take a look in his wardrobe.'

He led me into an adjacent room, almost the same size as the bedroom, but fitted out like the closet of a Beverly Hills home. There were perhaps as many as twenty identical white suits hanging neatly on one side, and beneath them the same number of pairs of white shoes. Another section housed a collection of hats, others had socks, shirts and ties, all neatly arranged and I suddenly had a vivid recollection of the first time I had seen him. A sickly, pungent scent, like stale incense was all around us which made me want to gag.

'With all this to hand, why would he frequent brothels?'

'Who knows? Maybe he thought it safer to meet his dealer there.'

'Of course, you told me he died of a drug overdose.'

'The pity of it is we didn't get him alive. I would have enjoyed a session with him.'

'The boy taken out of the water, the one I saw at the airport, who was he?'

'Just another statistic. No papers, nothing to identify him by, just another death in Venice. Perhaps they killed him because they knew you'd spotted your friend. He was expendable.'

'But I took him for a girl. He was wearing unisex clothing and I would have sworn he was a girl.'

'So you said. Shall we go? A little of this place goes a long way, and I have something else to show you.'

He took me to police headquarters. There I was shown the computer room. Ghia rattled off some instructions in Italian and an operator keyed in at one of the machines.

'What am I going to see?'

'This is material we found in the old man's villa. He kept a record of all his activities, listing names, dates, the age of the children, fellow perverts – a methodical German, of course. But he used a code and at first it defeated us until one of my men identified it as written in a *Wehrmacht* code they used during the war. There might be references you recognise. I'll translate for you.'

He nodded for his operator to begin. The screen was split, one side showing the code, and the other the translation in Italian which Ghia interpreted. The operator cursored down a list of dates and names. Some of the names had asterisks against them. I stopped him.

'What do the asterisks signify?'

'That puzzled us too until we came up with one name that checked out with a dead child we fished out of the lagoon about two years ago.'

The list continued. None of the names meant anything to me until suddenly I spotted something.

'Can you ask him to stop it there? Tell him to cursor up two lines. That's it. Isn't that a reference to England?'

'Yes.'

'And what comes before it?'

' "See more of England." '

'Is that a literal translation?'

'It's how the code deciphered. Why?'

'Can I sit at the computer for a moment?' The operator relinquished his seat for me. 'Bear with me. If I change it slightly . . .' I backspaced to delete, then typed in *Seymour England*.

'What does that mean?' Ghia asked.

'Written that way it becomes an English surname. I know a

174

man called Seymour, I've met him, and he knew Henry.'

'You're sure of this?'

'Absolutely. And can I show you something else on another machine? I wouldn't want to mess around with this. Do you have one fitted with a modem?'

I was shown to an idle computer. 'If I get it right, this is something that came to light amongst Henry's papers. I'd no idea what it meant until I experimented. Ask your man to write these down as I put them in.'

I typed in the opening codes after the DOS prompt praying I remembered them in the correct order. It was a much faster machine than my own, a real numbers-cruncher, and seconds after I gave the last command the 'Lollipop' menu appeared. Ghia leaned over my shoulder to take a closer look.

'Have you seen one of these before?'

'No, but I know of them.'

'I never got any further than this,' I said. 'I'm not expert enough, but I'm sure somebody in your department can get beyond it.'

'Maybe not in my department, but somebody in Rome, certainly. How long since you discovered this?'

'Not long, a few days ago.'

'Did you show it to your friend at Scotland Yard?'

'No, I didn't.'

'Why not?'

'I was considering what best to do when I got your call to come here. It ties in, doesn't it – the old man, this Seymour, my so-called dead friend?'

Ghia stared at the screen without answering me at first. Then he said: 'There are times when I could wish these machines had never been invented. They've turned against us. We thought they'd solve everything for us and all they've done is bring a new dimension to crime. If billions of lire can change hands overnight at the touch of a button, why not apply the same technology to this? You can buy hair shampoo, CDs, any goddamn thing you choose sitting at home, why not bambino porn? What's the difference? It's just another commodity.' Blood flooded his neck and he swore fluently in his own language. 'I tell you something, anybody ever touched a child of mine, they wouldn't live. I'd find a way, even if it meant the end of everything else.'

He recovered his cool and instructed the operator to print out what I had fed into the machine.

'How long can you stay?'

'How long do you need me?'

'I'd like to have Rome cross-check this with their central records. They may come back with more questions which only you can answer.'

'Yes, OK, I'll stay.'

'I'll also get on to London and have this man Seymour checked out. For the moment you are safer here than anywhere. We've never had a single case of kidnapping.'

'You do have murders, though.'

'Well, if you feel uneasy, I'll detail one of my men to watch over you and arrange a hotel room, perhaps not what you're accustomed to, but somewhere comfortable and not conspicuous. Tonight you are my guest, you eat with my family, some good home cooking.'

'I'd like that,' I said.

'What you've shown us has been very useful.'

'Let's hope it stays that way.'

He arranged for one of his plainclothes officers, a saturnine-looking young man named Alessandro, to take me to the hotel and remain with me. Alessandro's English proved as sparse as my Italian, but we managed to establish a way of making each other understand the basics. I was installed in a small hotel with an unprepossessing façade, but my room was comfortable enough. After I had dumped my bag I wandered around shopgazing. Alessandro kept a discreet distance behind me.

Throughout that afternoon my thoughts never strayed far from the old dandy's villa and what I had seen there. I wished his life had never been revealed to me, that an impenetrable darkness could blot out the memory of those sybaritic rooms. At home, alerted by the Press and television I had been aware of the growing number of child abuse cases, for seldom a week went by without some new ghastliness being uncovered. Of all crimes these seemed the most despicable, the most inexplicable. Now the nightmare had crept in under my own door and I could never again shut it out. From the moment I had become convinced that Henry was not dead I had imagined that in all probability his fake disappearance had been dictated by some pending political scandal; it had crossed my mind that, because of the final Russian venue, he might have been involved in some covert intelligence mission which had gone hopelessly wrong and from which he could not be extricated without damage to others less expendable. Therefore he had been paid off and his demise stage-managed. I had no difficulty accepting that scenario; I owed the comfort of my existence to such plots for they were the stuff of fact as much as fiction. But now, confronted with the computer evidence and the positive connection between Henry and the old dandy I was forced to embrace the unthinkable.

I talked more about it after dinner that night in Ghia's home while his wife, also of ample proportions, was putting their two young daughters to bed.

'I know how hard it is to accept these things,' Ghia said. 'I had a friend once, a good friend, whom eventually I had to arrest. A model marriage, children, nice home, a responsible position, then one day he murdered his male lover. So, what do we know of anybody? Nothing. If my job has taught me nothing else, it's taught me that.'

That night, in the strange, cramped hotel room, I had the vortex nightmare, the one I am told most people have sooner or later, where we fall without end. Only waking saves us from an imagined annihilation. I fought to regain consciousness for every time I drifted back into sleep the dream resumed. When I finally forced myself awake my limbs were rigid. Cramp balled my calf muscles as I lifted my head from the skimpy pillow, the sure hallmark of cheap hotels. Damp with sweat, and for several moments totally disorientated, I massaged circulation back into my legs, then swung myself out of bed and went to the window. The cold air I gulped in helped steady my heartbeat and I stayed there, my head resting against the window frame, until the last fragments of the nightmare receded. Below me half a dozen cats skirted each other with the menacing precision of ballet dancers.

There is no worse time to take stock of one's life than in the middle of the night in an alien city but there was no escape, asleep or awake, from the starkness of my situation. I cursed my own folly, the fact that I had allowed myself to be ensnarled by an old passion: it had been the chance of winning back Sophie rather than any genuine grief for Henry that had led me to this point. I saw that now.

Ghia had no news for me the following morning so with Alessandro still tailing me, I spent my time revisiting some of my favourite churches lingering longest in the Basilica di Santi Giovanni e Paolo. Ghostly religious Muzak was playing to soothe the departed doges. Light filtered through the narrow, double-lancet windows, shafting across the nave and apse to fall on the monuments. I stood in front of the memorial to Marcantonio Bragadin, the martyred warrior who met such a hideous end from the Turks. I read the printed list of his sufferings: having had his ears and nose cut off, he was then incarcerated for three weeks before they finished him off in style, flaying him alive before they decapitated him. When I turned away from such fearful reminders of past cruelties, a woman rose from prayer in the Chapel of the Rosary. She was dressed in black, and as she turned I saw her full face. Despite the passage of time recognition flooded back: it was Eva, the ubiquitous Victor's twin. Doubtless she had had cosmetic surgery to preserve her looks, but the taut skin could not persuade me I was mistaken. Once again in Venice the past had caught up with me in a way that denied coincidence.

I followed her out of the church and kept her in sight as she crossed the Campo Dei Santi Giovanni, unnerved and undecided as to whether I should accost her. She made her way to a café. I took a table some distance away which gave me a discreet view of her. The faithful Alessandro went to the bar.

I became both the watcher and the watched as a jumble of memories made my heart race.

19

THE PAST

The last time I had seen Eva and Victor had been shortly after Henry's supposed death. I had been invited to a house party in Wiltshire, something I normally avoided, but I had declined my hostess's invitation twice in recent months and finally ran out of excuses. Kitty Marlowe was one of those women who had a face job done every three thousand miles and by now the skin was stretched so tight her scalp moved up and down like a venetian blind every time she spoke. Larry Marlowe, her husband, was considerably younger and it was an open secret that he preferred boys to girls, though possibly waking up every day to find Kitty on the next pillow had a lot to do with that. They had one daughter in her late teens but rumour had it that she was adopted; Kitty was said to have played out a phantom pregnancy, even to the extent of wearing successive layers of padding for nine months and checking into the London Clinic for the immaculate birth. That rather endeared her to me; I like people who go the limit. She had the money and Larry, like many gays, was an engaging companion who played the generous host to perfection. After a few of his own martinis the mask was apt to slip a little, the voice got higher and the bitchy comments nearer the knuckle. I guess the arrangement suited them both; despite everything they had been together for thirty years, Kitty's first husband being the source of her now considerable wealth, having dropped off the perch during a honeymoon cruise. They certainly knew how to entertain. Their weekend parties were lavish and always included some amusing people because they cast their social net wide. The beds were comfortable, the large, mostly Spanish staff well-trained and the food was rich, often too rich for my taste, since I have always had an aversion to crunching small birds, but on the credit side Larry liked to splash the contents of Kitty's wine cellar. Twice a year I made the effort and usually enjoyed myself once I was there, but for all their hospitality they were not the kind of people I could take in large doses, though I usually came away with some good copy.

This particular weekend they had eight of us in the main house and four more in the guest annexe. The house itself was Jacobean, but the interior had been degutted over the years and completely modernised, the décor tastefully exotic. Nothing ever seemed out of place and Kitty's collection of needlepoint cushions, antique quilts and rare china filled every corner. To be truly in with the Marlowes you had to have your photograph silver-framed on top of the Bechstein concert grand in the enormous living room. The ex-Shah of Persia, Kashoggi, Robert Maxwell, some tattered pretenders to lost European thrones stood cheek by jowl with a selection of yesterday's jet set. I had yet to make the Bechstein and was on probation in the library in a leather frame. I have to admit that copies of my novels were always in evidence, but I put this down to Kitty's stage management. Their coffee tables were piled high with those monster art books that nobody can lift and most people only buy when they are remaindered at half price.

I was one of the last to arrive that Friday afternoon. Being a hopeless navigator I had twice taken the wrong turning and in rural England that can be a nightmare. I sometimes have the feeling that we are still living back in 1940 when all the signposts were removed in preparation for the expected German invasion.

The usual collection of Turbo Bentleys and BMWs was parked on the immaculate crescent driveway and I squeezed my shabby Honda Accord in between them. Not for the first time I found myself making the association with Agatha Christie for at dusk the house had a slightly sinister air, accentuated by the creeper that covered most of the west façade. The Marlowes' butler who ran the show was waiting at the front door to greet me with a glass of champagne. Although welcome, this too struck me as slightly unreal like something you only see on television commercials.

The earlier arrivals were all gathered in the main living room – a couple of familiars, but the rest strangers to me and despite Kitty's careful introductions I immediately got confused with their names. The familiars were a couple I loathed: Brett Wakefield and his wife, The Honourable Susan, were a grotesque pair. He openly boasted that he had never done a day's work in his life and that evening put it to me more offensively: 'I never understand why anybody works, do you? Why bother, there are so many other interesting ways to spend one's life.' I resented the fact that he took it for granted that I would agree.

'Some of us have to,' I said.

'Yes, but I don't mean your sort of work, because I write a little myself. Never want it published, though.'

'Why not?' I said acidly.

'Well, I might get it done privately, just for friends. The thought of perfect strangers reading it would appal me.'

He was such a pretentious cunt. As well as sporting an obvious hairpiece he spoke in a bogus upper-class voice, rather like a bad actor auditioning for a role he was unsuited to play. I had no idea why they remained on Kitty's 'A' list, except that they were even richer than she was and a constant challenge for her to try and top. The Hon. Susan only showed signs of life when the conversation got around to jewellery. She always came overdressed and showing a lot of cleavage which, curiously, Brett liked to draw attention to. On more than one occasion I'd heard him say, 'I'm a tit man as you can tell from the wife.' The money came from cocoa, I believe, and he once confided that the rest of the family did not allow him to play any active part in the running of the company. 'They sort of pensioned me awff and gave me three a year to live on,' he said with glutinous pleasure.

I stupidly picked up the cue and asked, 'Three?'

'Three million.'

I was relieved, therefore, to spot Eric Walsham arrive. Eric was the genuine article, a gent as they used to say, who had written two highly readable and erudite accounts of the pre-Raphaelites, a period in English art that happened to fascinate me. A cultured, diffident man, he had no need to give himself airs. Whenever we met the conversation invariably turned to cricket. This usually ensured that we rehashed last season's games in minute detail, since he supported Yorkshire and I gave my total loyalty to Essex. That year's Test Matches had been a near whitewash for England against the West Indies, so there was plenty to discuss. We were reliving the final innings of the final Test ball by ball that evening when we were interrupted by the last guests arriving.

'Martin,' Kitty said, 'will you and Eric stop talking about that boring game and come and meet Victor and Eva. Poor darlings, they flew in from Monte and their private jet had to be diverted to Luton. Really they should move Heathrow, it's too tiresome for people to be constantly inconvenienced by fog.'

I suppose I should have recognised both of them, but it wasn't until Victor said, 'Martin and I know each other from way back, Kitty. How nice to see you again,' that the penny dropped. He had put on weight since the days when Henry was cultivating them. His sister, on the other hand, looked anorexic; when I kissed her, her heavily made-up cheek felt like parchment to my lips.

'How's the world been treating you?' I said.

'Badly last night,' he said.

'He lost a fortune at the tables,' Eva said. 'It served him right, I told him not to switch to roulette. Poor sweetheart.'

She reached for his hand, the action immediately reminding me that I had always thought their relationship was odd, even for twins. Now, as I studied Victor more closely, I noticed a pencil thin scar running down from his mouth to his chin. He seemed to sense me looking at it and as Kitty spirited him to the other end of the room it was his sister who supplied the explanation.

'He was badly hurt playing polo. He got kicked in the face, then the pony rolled on him. Of course he had the best possible treatment. Mother had him flown to the Mayo clinic within hours and they worked miracles. But he's still conscious of it,' she added as though reproving me for having forced her to mention it.

'A dangerous sport,' I said. 'It's getting more and more like cricket.' There was a pause and then I said, 'You heard about Henry, did you?'

I could have been mistaken but I could swear I saw something approaching fear in her heavily made-up eyes before she answered.

'Yes, I think a friend of Victor's wrote to him about it.'

'Had you kept in touch?'

Her reply seemed over-careful. 'Not for some time. We move around so much, it's difficult for us to keep track of everybody we know. We know so many people.'

'So you haven't seen Sophie, either?'

'Sophie?'

'Yes, his wife, the girl I was with the first time you and I met.'

'Oh, yes, her. No, we haven't.' The shutters came down and she reached into her handbag for a lipstick and applied it. I noticed how her Cartier wristwatch slid down on her painfully thin wrist. Later, at dinner, I sat across from her and several times tried to make conversation, but it was hard going. She ate nothing, merely pushing the food around on her plate.

Kitty, on the other hand, was in great form, monopolising her own end of the table for most of the meal with scabrous gossip; from where I sat it seemed that the weekend had been arranged for the sole purpose of exchanging malice about absent friends. I joined in the laughter out of politeness, but my thoughts were elsewhere.

The ladies retired while the cigars and port were passed round, but when we rejoined them Kitty immediately proposed we play one of her party games. This seems to be a characteristic of the British so-called upper class: it's either charades or, God forbid, that tiresome guessing quiz whereby one person goes out of the room and the others select an historical figure for the victim to identify in a set number of questions. I did my best to enter into the spirit of the thing, but my mind kept returning to Henry. Larry was in his element when his turn came and chose to be Madame du Barry, which was par for the course, I suppose. He was delighted when nobody guessed him. I elected to be Anthony Eden when it was my turn, a fairly bizarre choice but it was the first name that entered my head. Eric guessed it with no difficulty.

It wasn't until the following morning that Victor and I had any further conversation. We were both early risers and found ourselves alone in the breakfast room where an off-putting array of food had been prepared in heated silver salvers. Contemplating devilled kidneys, kedgeree, liver, bacon and eggs, I felt that I had drifted back to the Victorian age. I helped myself to coffee and a croissant, my normal fare. Victor, on the other hand, sampled everything going.

I am never at my best in the mornings and find chatty conversation irksome, so I was unprepared for his opening remark.

'It was a pity you had to worry Eva last night.'

There was something offensive about the way in which he addressed me and I answered stiffly. 'Did I worry her? I wasn't aware I had.'

'Talking of Henry.'

I put down my newspaper and stared at him, trying to remember what I had said to her.

'She didn't sleep all night because of it.'

'I'm sorry. I certainly didn't mean to upset her. It was just that it seemed natural to mention the death of a mutual friend. It was Henry, after all, who brought us together. But I'll apologise when she joins us.'

'She won't be having breakfast. She's gone to Mass.'

His whole attitude was so odd and perhaps because it was early in the day and I was feeling scratchy, I pursued the subject with him. 'Why would she get so upset?'

'Why? Isn't it obvious?'

'Well, no, frankly.'

'She and Henry were very close at one time.'

'Well, likewise. His death was a tremendous shock to me. He was my oldest friend.'

'It's still not quite the same,' he said, enigmatically.

What was it about him that induced an instant dislike? He was suave, with that self-assurance of somebody who had never had to ask the price of anything.

'Your sister gave me the impression that you'd both lost touch with him and Sophie.'

'Did she? Yes, well I suppose that's true in a way. People come and go in our lives.'

I helped myself to another cup of coffee, deliberately avoiding looking at him when I said, 'In that case I don't suppose you have any idea what sort of trouble drove him to do what he did?' before quickly turning around to catch his changed, anxious expression.

'Why do you say "trouble"?'

'For want of a better word. Presumably most people are troubled if they take their own lives.'

'Oh, I see what you mean. Yes.'

'It seemed to me so totally out of character for somebody like Henry to take that way out. He always had the ability to bounce back no matter what.'

'Perhaps Sophie drove him to it,' Victor said. I pretended surprise.

'Weren't they happy together? I always got the impression it was a successful marriage.'

'That's how little you know.' He replied a shade too quickly and I got the impression that he had revealed more than he had intended. Recovering, he added: 'Anyway, who really knows what goes on in any marriage? A lot of people don't mean to go through with a suicide. Often it's just a cry for help, they do it knowing they'll be found before it's too late.'

'Maybe, if they take pills,' I said, 'but hanging is more calculated, wouldn't you say? It carries a greater certainty of succeeding, especially if the place chosen is a hotel room in Moscow. That's a long way from the good Samaritan friends.'

The conversation seemed to have destroyed his appetite, and now he pushed his partially-eaten breakfast to one side.

'Well, speculation as to why won't bring him back to life.' He said this with deliberate emphasis and there we left the subject.

I did not see Eva until just before lunch when I wandered into the library and found her slumped in an armchair.

'I gather I owe you an apology,' I said, ignoring her brother's request to let the matter drop. 'I didn't intend to upset you by mentioning Henry.'

'What's Victor been telling you?' she said. 'Why doesn't he leave well alone? He's so bloody stupid sometimes.'

'How was Mass?' I asked, judging it best to change the subject.

'Mass? I haven't been to Mass in years. I went for a jog, that's all. One gets so fat in England, everybody eats so much. I've put on pounds since we got here.'

It was the typical answer of an anorexic. 'So how long are you staying in England this time?'

'Who knows?' Like her brother she was adept at cutting people down to size. When talking about each other they suggested a disgruntled marriage. They had all the material advantages, yet pouted their way through life, as though

187

everything not in their immediate circle gave cause for discontent. They intrigued the writer in me, for they were insulated against criticism and engendered an urge to pierce their armour of superiority, to shock and disconcert them. Not that I ever succeeded, for Victor and Eva had a total indifference to the effect they produced. In their own circle boredom and rudeness were social attributes to be assiduously cultivated.

Looking at Eva's drawn features, she reminded me of one of those elegant model figures that adorn the windows of expensive dress shops – they give the semblance of being human from a distance, but close to the illusion disappears.

I was about to put another question to her, this time concerning Sophie, when Victor came into the library.

'There you are, I've been looking everywhere for you,' he said. He shot a questioning look at her which I caught and which was obviously meant to be a warning. 'Kitty wants us to go riding with her.'

'Does she? Well, that's the last thing I want to do. I've just come from jogging and I want to take a bath.'

I couldn't resist saying, 'Eva decided to remain a sinner and skip Mass.'

Eva rounded on him. 'Yes, why on earth did you tell Martin I'd been to church? You piss me off sometimes, Victor, with your stupid lies.'

Her vehemence took him off guard and he seemed at a loss to know how to deal with it in my presence. 'I'll make your excuses to Kitty, then, if that's how you feel.'

'It's exactly how I feel. After my bath Martin and I are going to drive into the village. To buy all the tabloids. Kitty only ever has the boring heavies.'

'Well, good.' For a moment I thought Victor might burst into tears. 'Enjoy yourselves.' He turned and left the room.

'Did you see his face?' she said almost before the door had closed behind him. 'He was furious. He behaves like such a prick when he doesn't get his own way. I won't be taken for granted.'

'But you like taking other people for granted I notice. How d'you know I want to drive you into the village? I might have better ways of spending my morning, and I happen to like the boring heavies.'

'If I said "please"?'

'That would be a step in the right direction.'

'Please.'

'Oh, you can say it with more conviction than that, I'm sure.'

'*Please*, Martin, will you be sweet and drive me to the village?'

'That's better. All right, but don't take too long over your bath. I don't want to waste the whole morning.'

'I'm not taking a bath,' she said. 'That was just for him. Let's go now.'

We went outside to my Honda. Eva stared at it and remarked, 'These cheap little cars are such fun, aren't they?' She looked back at the house as I held the passenger door open for her. 'He's watching us, you know. He's up there somewhere, watching us. Desperate.'

'Why would he be that?'

'Can't you guess?'

'No, as you saw last night I'm not very good at guessing games.'

'He's jealous.'

'I don't think he has anything to be jealous about where I'm concerned,' I said as we drove off.

'Oh, you never know. Things change.'

I didn't answer that. When we got to the village shop I waited in the car while she bought all the gossip rags. She reappeared in the doorway and shouted, 'I've come out without any money.'

'How much d'you want?'

She thrust the bundle of newspapers at me. 'You add it up, I'm hopeless at arithmetic.' I gave her five pounds which she took without a thank you. The moment she got back into the car she scanned through the lot, throwing the streamer inserts advertising Victorian conservatories and package holidays on to the back seat while giving me a running commentary on the contents.

'They're pretty dull this week. Charles and Di are about to be reconciled again according to an unnamed close friend. How to revitalise your marriage with walnut oil. The secret life Madonna tries to hide from her fans. Not a patch on the ones you get in America. No holds barred and lots of lovely jollies, like Marilyn Monroe is alive and working as an au pair girl. I mean, that's what I call inspired. These British rags are just obsessed with tits. Look at this one.' She waved a page in front of me. 'Fifty-four inches and she's only seventeen. Gross. Does that sort of thing turn men on?'

'Some men, I guess.'

'Not you, though?'

'No, not me.'

'What's your type?'

'I don't know that I have one.'

'Didn't Sophie turn you on?'

'Once upon a time,' I said, staring straight ahead.

'She turned a lot of people on.'

'Yes, I'm sure she did. She was a very beautiful girl.'

'Was? Perhaps she still is.'

'Yes. I hope so. I haven't seen her in a long time.'

'So she was your type?'

'You could say that.'

'You're so uptight, aren't you?'

'No. I just find this an odd conversation.'

'Why? Because it's about sex? Don't you like talking about sex?'

'In the right company, at the right time.'

'So what's wrong with now? Would you like to fuck me, for instance? Or do you only get off like those characters you write about, with nice English girls who only do it in bed? See, I have read some of your stuff.'

I pulled the car on to the grass verge and killed the engine. Two can play at your game, I thought.

'And what's your scene, Eva? Is it the thrill of having it away in the back seat of a cheap little car? Or do you need your brother here?'

'My brother?'

'That's what I said.'

'What's he got to do with it?'

'I thought perhaps you'd tell me. You want to be careful, otherwise you'll end up in those tabloids you like so much. Now, I don't know what your game is, but I'm not a player.'

'Henry was,' she said.

'Well, good for Henry.' I tried to be flippant, but it was the first indication I had of what had gone on all that time ago, and I wanted to find out more.

'Henry wasn't your friend,' she said, 'he was ours. And your precious little Sophie didn't waste any time jumping into his bed,' she added spitefully.

'You're not telling me anything I didn't know already.'

'You don't know the half of it. Henry was my lover too. I was the one he really liked. I gave him what he wanted. He was bored with your Sophie. He only married her to get back at you.'

'Are these revelations meant to fascinate me? Because if so you're wasting your breath. And by the way I don't fuck anorexics. I like my women to have flesh on them.'

She slapped my face, but because we were sitting side by side the blow had little force in it. 'Don't you dare say that!'

I restarted the engine and put the car back on the road. We drove back to the house in silence. Neither she nor her brother spoke to me again for the remainder of the weekend.

20

THE PRESENT

Now as I observed her in the Venetian setting, fat pigeons, like old ghosts, fluttered around the tables. I watched her take out a mirror and lipstick to outline her mouth as though armouring herself for an encounter. Reflected light circled a portion of her face and our eyes met for the first time. I got up and walked to her table. Alessandro swivelled on his bar stool to keep me in his view.

'Hello, Eva.'

'Hello, Martin.'

I was strangely gratified that she remembered me.

'Can I join you?'

'If you want to.'

I sat down. At close range her face was skeletal, the skin stretched tight over her cheek-bones, as white as porcelain. Her nails were scarlet tipped, obscenely long.

'Are you both having a holiday here, like me?' I said by way of opening the conversation.

'Both?'

'Is Victor with you?'

She stared at me, then looked past me and I half expected Victor to appear. Finally she said: 'You wouldn't have heard, of course.'

'What should I have heard?'

Again the stare. 'Victor's dead.'

A child's balloon blew across our table at that moment,

brushing against her head and she jerked back in shock. I grabbed at it, but it was filled with helium and soared into the sky.

'I'm sorry,' I said. 'Truly sorry. How awful for you, you were so close.'

'Twins usually are.'

'He was very young to die, surely?'

'No,' she said, putting me in my place with her old hauteur. 'Lots of people die young these days. Happens all the time.'

I searched for the right words. 'It must have been very sad for your parents.'

'No,' she said again. 'If anything they were relieved. Anyway, I couldn't care less what they think.'

I glanced behind her to see Alessandro staring at me. He looked anxious.

'I saw you in the church,' I said, in an effort to explain.

'I wasn't praying for Victor, if that's what you were thinking. I was praying for myself. Will you order me another drink?'

'Of course. What would you like?'

'I don't care. Oh, grappa.'

I signalled a waiter. He took his time before coming to us. Venetian waiters do not waste charm on tourists. He cleared Eva's empty glass and made a perfunctory wipe across the table with his cloth. I ordered the grappa and a Scotch for myself.

'So what brings you to Venice?' I asked.

'We have a palazzo here.'

I nodded, thinking, of course you would have, I should have guessed. The very rich collect houses like others collect stamps.

When our drinks came I raised my glass. 'To lost friends,' I said.

'Who in particular?'

'Well, Victor, of course.'

'You think Victor was your friend? He thought you were boring.' She drank her grappa like a Russian toast.

'Well, we mustn't speak ill of the dead,' I said. By now her brusqueness was beginning to irritate me. 'I do have other friends.'

'Like darling Henry, is that who you're thinking of?'

'Look,' I said, 'it's obvious I'm not welcome and I'm sorry I inflicted myself on you.' I went to get up but she reached across the table and grabbed my arm.

'No, don't go,' she said. 'I didn't mean it. Stay with me. I need somebody to stay with me.'

Against my better judgement I sat down again.

'You mustn't take offence. I don't know what I'm saying most of the time.'

'I understand.'

'I'd like another drink,' she said.

I signalled for the waiter, but he refused to catch my eye for several trips. When the order finally arrived, her whole mood and voice suddenly changed. 'You are on holiday you said?'

'Yes,' I said. 'Just taking a few days off from work.'

'You're still writing?'

'Yes. Still at it.'

'I don't do anything,' she said. 'Nothing at all. Aren't I the lucky one?'

'Are you?'

'You think so?'

'I wouldn't know, never having been in that position.'

She stretched out a hand to touch mine. Another expensive wristwatch slithered down on her bony wrist.

'Are you with someone here?'

'No. On my own.'

'Let me show you our house. I'm sure you'd be fascinated to see how the filthy rich live – that's how you always thought of us, isn't it? You can use it in one of your books.'

I glanced towards Alessandro but he was turned away from me and talking to one of the waitresses.

'Would that interest you?'

'Yes,' I said, 'if you can spare the time. Let me go and pay the check.'

I went to the bar and stood beside Alessandro. Without looking at him I said, 'I've met somebody I knew in England. She's invited me to her house. Don't worry, I'll be back in my hotel by six.' I walked away before he could protest.

When I helped Eva into the waiting gondola I noticed how light and fragile she was. She said little during the journey but lay back in the faded plush seat as though exhausted. We travelled through the Dorsoduro quarter, where once the poor lived in wooden houses which had now been restored as weekend *pieds-à-terre* by the rich Milanese, until the gondola glided into a narrow canal, easing between two heavily decorated staging posts topped with gilded coronets. Glancing up at the Gothic façade I saw that, unlike its dilapidated neighbours, it had been lovingly renovated. The tracery of the balconies overlooking the canal shone white in the sunlight. As if they had anticipated their mistress's arrival with second sense two servants, dressed entirely in black, materialised from nowhere to assist us on to dry land. Eva ignored them; they were familiars who needed no acknowledgement. I noted that nobody paid the gondolier – presumably she owned that too.

Small windows shielded by ornate iron grilles flanked either side of the entrance and beneath them were stone paterae carved as votive plaques. I followed Eva into the dark interior as she led the way up a flight of stone stairs to the *mezzanino* where in bygone days the merchant would have had his offices. Now it was richly furnished in a strange mixture of styles, lots of uninviting Italian modern side by side with hung tapestries and, incongruously, a large telex machine.

We continued on to the *piano nobile* where the family wealth was abundantly in evidence. Six Murano chandeliers hung from the painted wooden ceiling. The furniture was baroque, the chairs covered in exquisite embroidery. There were numerous old masters on the walls including one magnificent Canaletto that dominated the far end of the room. I stood in front of it for a long time.

'You like that?' Eva said.

'Wonderful.'

'Everybody we know has a Canaletto, so of course my father had to keep up with the rest. It's all right, but why look at that when you have the real thing outside?'

I refused to be drawn by her snobbery. She left me studying the paintings while she poured herself a drink, then sprawled on one of a matching pair of sofas either side of the great fireplace, her skirt hitched up exposing her emaciated bare legs.

'You're impressed.'

'Shouldn't I be?'

'I don't see it any more. It's just another house.'

'Can I see the rest?'

'If you want.'

She finished her drink and got up unsteadily. 'I'll show you Victor's room. Would you like that?'

'I'm happy to see anything you want to show me.'

We went up to the next floor. A heavy aroma of incense penetrated my nostrils, my brain, as we reached the landing. In front of us was a carved wooden door with a wreath hanging on it. Eva stood aside to let me enter first. When my eyes became accustomed to the change of light I saw that the room was bare except for a covered trestle table surrounded by a dozen or more lighted altar candles. The table held a collection of ornate silver frames each with a photograph of Victor in it. Beyond the table, facing me on the far wall, was a large Warhol composite – a dozen or so multi-coloured images of Victor.

Eva said: 'This is my shrine to him. The candles are changed every day. You see how beautiful he was. He never lost his beauty, unlike some. God was good to him in that way.'

I went closer to the table. A single white rose, one petal of which had fallen, had been placed in the centre. As I studied the photographs I had to admit he had a kind of beauty, but mask-like with a hint of cruelty and there was nothing behind the eyes.

'Don't you want to ask me what he died of?'

I didn't speak, knowing the answer before she gave it.

'He died of the fashionable plague, the one that's going to decimate us all.'

She came and stood beside me and lifted the fallen rose petal with the tip of a scarlet nail.

'I hope he didn't suffer too much,' I said.

'What used to be known as the old men's friend ended it all. Pneumonia,' she added in case I did not make the connection. 'Yes, he suffered, but he was so brave, never complaining. I nursed him, I nursed him until it was over, we shared that just like we shared everything else.'

'I'm sure you did.'

She suddenly gripped my arm, turning me to face her.

'What do you know about it with your silly, safe little romances? You couldn't know about us, what we had, what we did. Henry was right about you. He said you couldn't understand anything outside your own boring little world. Everything pigeon-holed into neat little compartments that must never be disturbed. Aren't you glad you didn't sleep with me when I asked you to? I knew then, we both knew. That was the only reason I invited you to fuck me, it wasn't that you attracted me, I just wanted to share the good news.'

Her vehemence didn't shock me. The protective walls of privilege she had believed would protect them forever had collapsed. She carried more than the virus itself, she was infected with that hopelessness that comes from knowing there is no hope.

She raised her arms as if about to rake my face with her nails, but I caught and held them like twigs for there was no strength in her. The faint struggle caused the altar candles to flicker; soft ripples of light shimmered across Warhol's portraits so that, briefly, they ceased to be one-dimensional and had a semblance of life. A memory flashed into my mind – the time when Sophie and I had only been observers, when nothing had been corrupted.

I gently lowered her arms to her side and kept them there

until her body stopped shaking. Then I turned and left the room. As I closed the door behind me I saw her bend to kiss one of the photographs.

21

THE PRESENT

I woke up the next morning with the scent of that incense still with me. Even when I had showered and dressed it remained impregnated in my clothing. After breakfast I put in a call to Edna, my secretary, to see if there had been any urgent mail during my absence. When I was away she had the keys to my apartment and went in daily to check the fax and post. She was not usually hysterical, but the moment she picked up the phone and recognised my voice her normal composure vanished.

'Oh, Mr Weaver, I'm so glad you called. I've been so worried and I had no idea where to contact you. You didn't leave me a number, you see.'

'Why, what's happened?'

'Well, I went in yesterday morning, a little later than usual because my mother hasn't been well and I had to get her prescription, but I wasn't that late, and the moment I opened the door I knew something was wrong.'

A sense of foreboding entered me. 'Yes, just tell me slowly.'

'Everything was smashed, your computer, your tapes, the phone, fax machine. And your papers, all your research papers, they were torn up, and the post, even an Income Tax demand, thrown all over the place. It was awful. Nothing valuable seemed to be missing that I could see, it was just wanton damage.'

'Yes, well don't upset yourself, Edna.' I tried to keep my own voice calm. 'I'm just thankful you weren't there when they broke in. You informed the police, did you, and the insurance?'

'Oh, yes. The man next door let me use his phone.'

'Was there anything the police could do?'

'No, they just said that this sort of vandalism went on all the time. Motiveless destruction they called it and told me there's one every thirteen minutes in London, which just goes to show you the sort of world we're living in. That and the rapes and the bombs. Of course I gave them all the particulars they asked for, but they didn't seem hopeful about catching anybody for it. When they left I tidied up as best I could and I pieced together all the mail and Scotch-taped it.'

'Not the tax demand, I hope? I'm all for that being torn up,' I said in an attempt at humour I didn't really feel, but Edna was too wrought up to respond.

'Yes, I put that back together, I did everything I could find, and Mother helped, she was as upset as I was, I don't think I shall ever get over it.'

While she babbled on a familiar panic took hold of me. I was not so much concerned with the havoc done to my possessions – the computer was insured and I had a copy of work in progress on my laptop – but with the menace behind the act itself. It seemed the net was still being drawn closer.

'I've made a list of the letters. Would you like me to read it to you?'

'If they're important, but if not don't worry for the moment.'

'Well, there is a letter from your American editor which seems urgent.'

'What's that about?'

'You've been given an Edgar Award, whatever that is, and he's anxious for you to go to New York and receive it. He says it's the most prestigious prize and will help the sales of your next. Do you want me to reply for you?'

'No, I'll deal with it. Nothing else?'

'Nothing vital.'

'Well, now look, Edna, it's obviously been a horrible shock for you and I'm sorry you've been put through it. There's nothing more you can do, so stop worrying. Take a few days off and try and get over it. I'll be back soon and I'll cope with the insurance et cetera. OK?'

'I feel so responsible when you're away, and now this happens.'

'Yes, well lightning doesn't strike twice. You rest up. Give my regards to your mother.'

I might have pacified Edna, but my own fears remained. This latest incident alarmed me far more than the sad encounter with Eva. I could deal with deaths in Venice for the traveller knows that he will one day depart. But this was different. My own home had been entered and it was a matter of luck that I had not been there on the receiving end of the violence.

When Ghia called at the hotel later that morning I wasted no time in telling him what had happened.

'Who knew you were coming here?'

'Only my secretary.'

'And she's reliable?'

'To a fault.'

'It could just be an ugly coincidence.'

'Much though I'd like to think so, I doubt it. They took nothing, just trashed my computer and papers. That doesn't suggest an ordinary break-in.'

'No, I agree. You're back in the front line, it seems.'

'Have there been any developments at your end?'

'That's what I came to tell you. Like you, my news from London is not good. They followed up on this man Seymour, but . . . well, read it for yourself.'

He handed me a telex. It read: REFERENCE SEYMOUR NOTHING KNOWN STOP NOT AVAILABLE FOR INTERVIEW STOP ALL INDICATIONS ARE SUSPECT LEFT THE COUNTRY STOP ENQUIRIES CONTINUING END.

'You think that's just another ugly coincidence?'

Ghia shook his head. In my small hotel room he seemed larger than ever. 'In this case I think we can't rule out he was tipped off. It seems, my friend, that they follow all your moves and stay one step ahead.'

'You didn't get anything back about the network code?'

'Not so far, although it's been passed to them. Maybe the death of an old pervert in Venice isn't high on their list of priorities.'

'What about Rome?'

'Rome is something else.' He grinned. 'You have to understand they spend most of their time investigating politicians and keeping the traffic moving, the two most pressing situations. God forbid we get another *Duce*, but sometimes I wonder. Nothing works in Italy any more, so when a Venetian cop asks for help I don't expect them to jump. It will take time. But it's your situation that concerns me, especially in view of your latest news. That's not good.'

'What can I do? I tried to run from it once on good advice, but it didn't work.'

'Perhaps,' Ghia said, 'you didn't run far enough. As I see it, and I don't quite understand why, they are still playing with you. Others who get in their way they dispose of, but you – you they keep giving another chance. I ask myself why? Perhaps, my friend, you should now take those warnings to heart and retire from the scene. You're out of your depth. Leave it to people like me while you still have your health. Go somewhere a long way away, make them believe you've given up. That would be my advice.'

I thought long and hard after Ghia left me. If my every move was being monitored as now seemed obvious, his advice was sensible. I was scared and didn't relish returning to London. I now had a legitimate reason for going to New York, something easily checked by whoever was keeping tabs on me. I argued with myself that once I had received my award I could take off, hire a car and drive somewhere. Such trips had always paid off in the past: a foreign setting recharged my creative batteries and provided new plots.

Having convinced myself, I made the necessary arrangements, managing to get a seat on the evening flight to Paris. Somewhat self-consciously I bought a pair of spectacles and a hat as the simplest form of rough disguise.

The motor launch taking me to the airport was forced to throttle back to let a funeral boat pass. I knew that many years back the Austrian authorities had forbidden further burials in the city itself and had created the extraordinary Island of the Dead, San Michele, where the bodies of the poor are allowed to rest for a decade before their bones are exhumed to free the sites for others.

That day as I watched the funeral boat disappear into the haze it occurred to me how simple life would be if every ten years we could dispose of our mistakes and begin again.

22

THE PRESENT

New York seemed dirtier than ever, and the characters that swarmed around me the moment I arrived all had a manic, distracted look. My taxi ride into town from the airport was over roads designed for an army assault course, and the driver treated it as such, weaving in and out of the glutinous traffic with a skill that was as admirable as it was frightening. Detroit's orphans fought for position between the Mercs and BMWs – battered Chevvies with oversized tyres, their arses lifted high in the air like old whores, stripped-down Corvettes blotched with anti-rust paint jobs, the occasional shark-finned Cadillac that had somehow escaped being shipped to the Third World.

My driver, a Pole from his identity photo on the dash-board, was fortunately not a talker, he just swore constantly and leaned on his horn, sometimes pushing so close to the vehicle in front that death seemed imminent. State of the art graffiti blossomed, elaborate, multi-coloured, along the entire route; the trees on the debris-littered embankments, stunted things, their foliage withered and blackened by non-stop carbon monoxide fumes, looked ready to give up the struggle. After we had crossed the Tri-Boro bridge the Manhattan streets changed character again; now the pot holes were covered over with massive steel plates – hasty repairs done on the battlefield to terminal injuries. The entire population seemed on the move for my arrival had coincided with the lunch-hour. I spotted the normal quota of Big Apple familiars: the blind man selling pencils who had always been there, a black giant on roller-skates dressed as a Zulu, a priest on a Harley Davidson, several ignored junkies or drunks sleeping it off in the doorways of dead stores, a crazed bag lady wheeling a supermarket trolley laden with plastic flotsam and, best of all, somebody inside a chicken costume carrying a placard denouncing battery farming. The sight of this last demented soul caused my driver to hurl a fresh stream of abuse. For the first time during the journey he turned back to look at me through the protective iron cage that separated us. 'This fuckin' city,' he said, 'they should take out all those fat fucks. Gunge them off the streets with fifty-sixes. Who gives a shit about chickens?'

'Presumably, he does,' I answered. Jolted behind the wire cage I felt like a police dog.

'They gotta save my ass first before any fuckin' chickens.'

His pock-marked neck had turned an alarming shade of purple. It was time for conciliatory humour.

'You've got a point there, we all need saving. But you concentrate on what you're best at, you're a great driver.' The fake compliment was not well received and for the remainder of the journey he shot suspicious glances at me in his rear view mirror.

I booked into a middle-priced hotel on Sixth Avenue, taking a small suite in case I needed to give any interviews. A junkie attempted to panhandle me as I paid off the taxi and the rich scents of the city rose to meet me – a mixture of diesel fumes, burnt bagels and stale beer. Despite this and the hair-raising ride, I have to admit that I always get a kick of adrenalin whenever I set foot in New York. For all its extremes – squalor and magnificence in close proximity, flaunted wealth and abject poverty, greenery next to the fenced vacant lots, the abandoned old buildings within sight of the unreal glass towers, the daytime frenzy, the night-time uneasy calm – there is a powerhouse, anthill energy working all the time, a feeling of life in all its many guises.

My suite on the twenty-third floor (designated a smoking area) was pleasantly anonymous, though it had a slightly musty smell. I went to open a window but found it was sealed. I looked across the central well into an identical room where a man in shirt sleeves was talking on a cellular phone. I put the *Do Not Disturb* notice on the door handle and slid the security chain while I went to have a bath only to find it had a leaky faucet and the usual complimentary cockroach. The contents of hotel bathrooms always fascinate me. I have made a study of the free toiletries now universally provided. They often appear to have been exclusively designed for midgets. The free soap on this occasion was the size of a Communion wafer and when I tried to lather myself it shot out of my wet hand with the speed of an ice-hockey puck.

While soaking in the tub the idiocy of my situation suddenly came home. Splinters of doubt as to the wisdom of my trip pierced through my fatigue: had I fled all those miles only to keep an appointment in Samarra? In Venice, listening to Ghia's counsel, America had seemed a sensible choice. Now, as the wind funnelled up to whine through the air vent like a banshee, I was once again prey to self-doubt. They say it is a sign of incipient madness when you start talking to yourself and as I paced from bedroom to bathroom, muttering, I caught sight of my disturbed face in the mirror.

Having rung Bill, my editor, and arranged to meet in his favourite bar during the happy hour, I suddenly felt hungry because of the time difference and went in search of a meal in the nearest coffee shop. Afterwards I made a beeline for my favourite bookstore on Madison knowing that jet-lag would keep me awake and I'd need something to read. I bought the latest Updike and a couple of trashy paperbacks to give myself a selection.

Bill seemed edgy when we met. 'I'm wearing the patch,' he said in that holier-than-thou tone that recently dedicated smokers assume when the still-crippled light up in front of them. 'You really should try it.'

'Do they work?'

'Well, the clinical studies say you've got a better shot than going cold turkey.'

'Well, good for you. I'm impressed. How long have you been wearing them?'

'Two days.'

'That long. You've got it licked then.'

He downed his martini and ordered another.

'How's the new novel? Got anything to show me?'

I stalled. 'Not really. I'm kicking around a few ideas.'

'Did you ever make use of our Venice trip?'

Even as he said it in that crowded bar I felt panic return.

'No,' I said, avoiding looking at him. 'It didn't gel somehow. Maybe one day.'

'I still think about that murder. When I show people those shots I took they just can't believe I was there when it happened. Jesus! Such a pretty girl.'

'Yes,' I said. 'Yes, she was.'

'Did they ever get anybody for it?'

'Not that I know of.'

'You were so on the ball, I was impressed.' He finally changed the subject. 'So are Marie and I gonna see something of you while you're here? How long are you staying?'

'I'm open-ended.'

'That's good. How about dinner tomorrow?'

'Sounds fine.'

'The presentation is next Tuesday.' He was eyeing my cigarette. 'They're really delighted you made the trip over. I've told our publicity department to make sure they set up some interviews. Boy! It ain't easy to sell books these days. Been a dull season so far. The bestseller list is nothing but junk, we're all waiting for the big one. And of course there's been another shake-up at the office. The predators are stalking the canyons. Everybody thought Murdoch was going to bid, but he backed off at the last moment. Charlie

Goodwin went to Viking – remember Charlie? – and Gloria who ran our cookery division, she got cancer, died in three weeks. Left two kids, it was a trauma for us all, believe me. I tell you, the place is not the same.'

All the time he was talking I was trying to make up my mind whether I should reveal the true reason I was in town.

'But you're still there?'

'Hanging in. Call me in the morning, huh? What d'you like to eat? Fancy some pasta or what? No, maybe that would remind us both too much of Venice. I can still taste that food. There's a new Thai place on Third everybody says is sensational. Maybe we'll give that a try. I'll make the reservations. Tomorrow you should come to the office and talk to some of the guys. Never hurts to show you're still alive. Sorry, I can't take you out tonight, but the in-laws flew in from Cleveland. They'll probably mean I'll start smoking again. Hey, tell you what. We've been invited to Vince and Eleanor O'Hara's this weekend. You met them once with me. They've got a gorgeous place up in Roxbury and they'd love to see you. Lots of writer chums live around there, Bill Styron and Terry Southern. No problem getting you an invite and we can drive up together.'

'Great.'

'I know they'd love to have you. They're your sort of people.'

I wondered what sort of people enjoyed the idea of a total stranger dropping in unexpectedly for the weekend.

We parted company on the pavement. I took myself to Third Avenue and bought a cinema ticket for the latest French import. There was comfort in the darkness and the film took my mind off my problems for a couple of hours. Back in my hotel room I checked to see if anything had been disturbed, but apart from the bed being turned down and a fresh Communion wafer of soap in the bathroom, all seemed as I had left it. I switched on the television but between black and white films from the dark ages, every other commercial was aimed at either curing the female masses of vaginal infections and the men of something disturbingly called Jock Itch, or everybody else of volcanic headaches; an alien arriving from space would have been persuaded that the majority of Americans needed immediate emergency treatment. I suffered all this for a short time, then turned to the sanity of John Updike before finally falling asleep.

The following day I paid a visit to Bill's lair. Whereas my first publisher had always received me in his dingy little office crammed with dog-eared manuscripts, Bill had a partitioned space in an open-plan labyrinth. The windows extended down to the floor giving me immediate vertigo. I was introduced to Sales, Marketing and Publicity in quick succession all of whom exuded that special New York brand of confidence which, in large doses, I find exhausting. I drank too much at the lunch they hosted and by the end of the meal had begun to believe in the hype they gave me, always dangerous for an author. True to his word, Bill had fixed the weekend – Vince and Eleanor were 'thrilled' I was to join them.

The ride to Roxbury was a pleasure once we had shaken off the Friday evening traffic. Bill was too fond of his Jaguar to take chances and we purred gently up the scenic Merritt Parkway as far as Westport, before taking the secondary roads, the countryside growing ever more lush and my previous unease diminished with each passing mile. I liked Marie, Bill's wife, she was smart and attractive with none of that brittle snappiness which characterises some American women. For much of the journey we chatted aimlessly about the state of Broadway theatre and whatever happened to Edward Albee and who was he afraid of?

On arrival Vince and Eleanor's house proved to be a pristine white Colonial set in about ten acres complete with pool and a clay tennis court. Vince was some hot-shot C.E.O of a leading line of cosmetics and the connection was he and

Bill had been at Princeton together. He and his wife greeted us dressed as Ralph Lauren clones and indeed the entire house seemed to have been done over in Mr Lauren's style, no expense spared. I was shown to a bedroom at the top of the house that had dormer windows overlooking the pool and tennis court that was immediately welcoming. My spirits brightened for they had gone to immense pains to make me feel at home, even to the extent of providing recent English newspapers and a bottle of twelve-year-old malt.

That first evening it was warm enough to have a barbecue and the meal was served without any of the pretentious trimmings some people give to alfresco meals – just superb rib-eye steaks, baked potatoes, a well-mixed salad and a good domestic wine. I could start to believe that my recent nightmare experiences were a figment of my imagination.

'Now there's an idea for a book,' Bill said, as Vince recounted a few of the hazards associated with his line of business. 'Pick Vince's brains over the weekend and then do an exposé novel. Reveal how women are duped into thinking they can stay young forever by ruthless types like our host.'

'Thanks a lot,' Vince said.

'Yes, Bill,' Marie said, 'thanks a lot, Mr Tact.'

'Just kidding.'

'Actual fact our products do have an anti-aging effect, you cynical bastard. Come to think of it, you could use a little of our newest moisturiser which is packed with liposomes.'

'What the hell are they?'

'Quite frankly, I don't know, but our R and D people swear they work miracles on skin like yours. I'll give him a free sample, Marie.'

'As long as he doesn't turn into Dorian Gray. I don't want to end up with a toy boy.'

'Listen, Martin, in all seriousness,' Vince said, 'I'd be happy to show you around our factory if it would interest you.' Later that first evening he gave me a glossy magazine containing a feature about a new beauty centre his company had just opened in Arizona.

It was all good humoured, for they were relaxed with each other and I envied them their friendship and casualness. As the weekend progressed I detected a touch of Gatsby about Vince O'Hara and I could well believe that there was a more ruthless side he employed in his pursuit of the American dream. Certainly he played a killer game of tennis with no allowances made towards his guests.

I took the magazine up to my room to read in bed. The majority of the articles extolled the quality of life to be found in the unique communities of the high desert. The feature Vince wanted me to read had a large colour photograph showing various local socialites standing in front of a modern building with a caption proclaiming, *Gala Opening of the new Carefree Institute of Cosmetic Therapy*. I skimmed through it more out of politeness than anything else and was about to put it to one side when a woman in the group photograph caught my eye. She had short, dark hair fashionably styled and was wearing expensive designer clothes, but something about her was familiar. I took the magazine to the bedside lamp for a closer examination. The more I studied the photograph the more I became convinced I had found Sophie at last. The years had taken their toll of her hour-glass figure and her features had coarsened, but it was her, of that I was convinced. I went to the captions on the opposite page and, yes, she was listed as Sophie Gregory, which I dimly remembered had been her mother's maiden name. The shock was such that my whole body began to shake and I sat on the edge of the bed forced to take slow, deep breaths until the spasms eased. I tore out the page, folded it and put it in my wallet, and during the rest of that disturbed night I started to work out a plan.

By the time we drove back to New York on the Sunday evening I knew what I had to do as soon as the Edgar awards were over. The next morning it was as though all the symptoms of a long illness had been lifted from me. I went to my bank and drew out a large amount of cash, then purchased a road atlas and pinpointed the location of Carefree. It appeared to be some twenty miles to the north-east of Phoenix at the foot of the mountain region.

I remained in this mood of optimism throughout the Edgar ceremony. The awards are given by the Mystery Writers of America, and I guess those who spend their lives devising plots for thrillers are a fairly odd group who speak to each other in a language foreign to most. The craft of writing anything is difficult to explain to others for with the dis-appearance of the literary salon we are not given to much in-breeding and tend to remain isolated within our shells unless brought together for such a gathering. Bill and his colleagues had taken a table and were obviously delighted I was to be the winner of one of the trophies – a ceramic bust of dear old Edgar Allen Poe himself which still stands on my desk as a constant reminder of both folly and achievement. It was the first award I had ever won and I confess that I enjoyed the experience and the company of my peers.

Several press interviews had been arranged for the follow-ing day at staggered intervals and by the time I had got through the first I had already run out of things to say about myself. The second appointment proved to be with a formidable lady who pitched into me with a metallic mid-Western accent that twanged around my hotel suite like a zimbalin.

She opened with, 'Have you read Elaine Showalter's *Sexual Anarchy*?'

'No, that hasn't come my way.'

'Read it, it has a lot to say to you, and about you.'

'Really? In what way?'

'She hits it right on the nail. Her chapter on Stevenson. Could have been written about you. Has it ever occurred to you that your protagonists are all middle-aged bachelors who have no relationship with women except as chattels?'

'Well, I try to be accurate and the majority of spies tend to be loners. It goes with the job. But I'll certainly look for the book you mention. Always willing to learn.'

There was no stopping her. She talked a lot about 'sexual ghettos' where most male writers placed their female characters. 'Hemingway began it and the novel has never recovered from it.'

'Really? It's an interesting theory.'

'Read your own books again.'

'Curiously, when I finish a book I seldom look at it again.'

'You should.'

In an attempt to divert her in mid-flow I asked if she'd like some tea.

'Now that's an example, if you'll pardon me saying so. Subconsciously you think of women in the kitchen. The association with food, domestic chores.'

'I was going to send for room service,' I said with a smile, piling on the charm. 'I didn't intend you to make it. Not even subconsciously.' The joke went nowhere.

'In my class we term it "kitchen-sink pornography".'

I had lost the thread by now. 'What class is that?'

'I teach the anti-feminist structure of the modern novel over in Queens. Are you going to be here long? Come and take in a session.'

'I'd love to, but unfortunately I leave tomorrow.'

'Too bad. Well, I've certainly enjoyed talking to you. You've told me a lot about yourself,' she added ominously as she gathered up a woollen portmanteau and stuffed her unused tape-recorder inside. I had no great hopes for what she would write about me.

My last interviewer was a smooth young man who arrived unannounced.

'Sorry to do this to you at the end of the day, but my editor suddenly sprung it on me.'

'That's OK. Who are you from?'

'We're a new literary magazine called *In Focus*. Haven't been going long, but we're building, and we like to meet visiting celebrities.'

He sat himself in one of the armchairs and I couldn't help noticing that he was surprisingly well-dressed for somebody working on an obscure magazine.

'I was just about to have a drink. Would you care to join me?'

'Yeah, good thought.'

'Courtesy of my publisher, I might add.'

He examined my Edgar while I fixed his glass.

'Any prize money go with this thing?'

'No, just the honour. Cheers.'

'Cheers.'

'I needed this.'

'I bet. What we like to zero in on is not so much the books because we're snobby enough to assume that our readers are familiar with those . . . and in any case don't you hate those crappy pieces that look for hidden meanings behind Daniele Steel's latest? . . . We go more for how you separate your public and private lives. By the way, I don't take notes, I find people talk more freely without somebody scribbling all the time. But I have a good memory.'

For the first ten minutes or so until he had finished his drink he questioned me amiably and seemed to have no particular axe to grind unlike my previous interrogator. Then, abruptly, as he put his empty glass down, the line of questioning changed.

'You're unusual in that you travel a lot,' he said.

'Do I?'

'You seem to. Most modern American writers put their roots down someplace and stay there, excluding the immediate post-war collection, the ones that stayed on in Europe under the GI Bill.'

'Yes, now you mention it, you're probably right. No harm in that, though. Tolstoy never wandered far, but that didn't cramp his talents. The reason I travel is the sort of books I write depend on exotic locations.'

'Like Moscow, for instance?' He slid the question in under my guard.

'I wouldn't call Moscow exactly exotic.'

'Maybe that was a bad example. How about Venice?' he said and for the first time his smile seemed frozen. 'I've never been there myself, but people tell me it's none too healthy.'

'It depends when you go,' I said.

'Or when you leave.' He looked me straight in the eye and the smile was no longer in place. 'But I'm sure you're very sensible about taking care of yourself, a seasoned traveller like you. It's important to stay healthy.' He shot back his cuffs and consulted a gold wrist watch. 'I bet you've had enough for one day, so why don't I get out of your hair? Been good talking to you.'

'Likewise.'

'Where're you off to next?'

'Home,' I said.

'Yeah, there's no place like it. That way you stay out of trouble.'

I showed him to the door and the moment he'd gone I rang Bill. He wasn't in his office so I had my call transferred to Publicity.

'What d'you know about a magazine called *In Focus*?'

'In what?'

'Focus.'

'Never heard of it.'

'I've just been interviewed by them,' I said.

'What a nerve! They weren't on my schedule. Let me check it out.'

'No, don't bother, it's not that important.'

'How did the rest go?'

'OK. Will you do me a favour? I tried ringing Bill, but he's not there at the moment. Tell him something came up and I have to leave tonight.'

'Gee, that's too bad. Sure, I'll pass it along. You going back to London?'

'Yes, back to earn my living.'

'Well, have a safe trip. It was great meeting you.'

I hung up and started packing. Rather than risk booking a

flight from the hotel I took my chances of getting a seat at Kennedy. I was in time to catch a red-eye Delta flight to Phoenix with a stopover in Dallas. The first leg of the flight was turbulent, which I find more alarming at night and I was relieved when we put down at Fort Worth. Airports in the middle of the night always resemble waiting rooms in hospitals: a lot of weary people sagged into hard seats, their fates in somebody else's hands and nothing they can do about it. In addition it seems all the clocks go into slow motion. My plane developed a technical fault which took a couple of hours to fix. I went to the rest room and shaved to kill some time until our flight took off again. Several of my fellow passengers had the same idea.

The temperature was in the high eighties when we landed in Phoenix and once outside the air-conditioned terminal the dry heat enveloped me like a blanket. Like most airports, Sky Harbor was being enlarged, rebuilt, updated, you name it, but Phoenix was squeaky clean compared to New York and the smog-free, cloudless blue sky a welcome change from LA. I went to the Hertz desk to hire a car. The girl behind the counter put on a smile even at that hour and offered a brand new Thunderbird which she said only had ninety on the clock. I reached for my credit cards, but the jacket pocket where I kept them was empty. I searched all the other pockets, then checked my money wallet. Nothing. I looked in my overnight case on the chance that I had put them away there and forgotten. Again nothing and by now I was panicked because I kept my driving licence with them as well.

'I'm sorry,' I said to the girl. 'I seem to have lost my credit cards. I have money, of course.'

'We don't take cash, sir.'

'Not even if I paid over the odds?'

'No, sir.'

I should have known. Cash is less and less welcome in America; if you don't have plastic you're suspect.

'Can you remember when you last used them?' the girl

said, still pleasant, but already bored and looking to the next in line.

'New York,' I said, 'but I'm fairly certain they were in my pocket when I caught the plane.'

'Well, I hope you find them. Excuse me, sir.' She moved to the next customer. I carried out another search to no avail. And then I remembered using the rest room at Dallas and hanging my jacket on a hook while I shaved. I could only think that somebody had lifted them while I wasn't looking. I walked away from the desk; the others in line stared at me and I could feel they regarded me as a credit leper.

I queued outside for a taxi angered by my own stupidity. As luck would have it I chanced upon a taxi-driver who immediately latched on to my British accent. He proudly revealed he had served in the US Navy and had been stationed at Holy Loch in Scotland for a period. I listened politely while he gave his enthusiastic verdict on the local girls and a less favourable opinion of our beers. 'They ain't ever heard of ice up there. That stuff, you could shave in it on a cold morning.'

The reference to shaving /reopened the self-inflicted wound.

'Where are you from?' I asked, waiting for the right moment to pick his brains for my own needs.

'Can't you guess? I'm from the Bronx. Got meself in a spot of trouble when I came out of the Navy, needed to put some miles between me and the Big Apple. That place is too heavy. Got divorced, came out here, been here ever since. How long you gonna be here?'

'I haven't made any fixed plans. This is my first trip. Just want to see the country.'

He took a business card out of his shirt pocket and handed it to me. It read: *Eddie Kuhl – Airport Limousine 24 hour Service, Pool and Garden Maintenance, Plumbing.*

'Fast Eddie,' he said with a grin. 'See what I mean? You want somebody to show you around?'

'What I actually need, Eddie, is a car,' I said. 'See I got

ripped off. Somebody stole my wallet with all my credit cards in it. Don't worry I've got cash to pay you.'

'No shit! Well, don't surprise me. Every place you go nowadays you run into slime bags. You say you're looking for a car?'

'Yes, but I can't rent anything without a card. So I'm looking to buy one for cash.'

I could almost feel his brain working. I was sure I had picked the right man.

'What're you looking for?' he said with a new note in his voice.

'Just something reliable on four wheels for a couple of weeks.'

'Well, I've got a spare '87 Olds. Yours if ya wan' it. Nothing special, but it runs OK.'

'Really? Would you let me have that?'

'Sure. Wan' to see it? I live over in Mesa. Want for me to stop the clock and run you there?'

'I should also tell you I don't have a licence either. Does that bother you?'

'Don't mean shit to me. Tell ya what though, they're hot on speeding around here. Even got remote cameras – ya get a photograph in the post with the hundred-dollar ticket so take it easy. Go over ninety and they hang ya.'

He lived in a trailer home that reminded me of our post-war pre-fabs. I examined the car he was offering. It had four reasonable tyres and apart from the odd dent seemed roadworthy and admirably suited to my needs. I wasn't looking for anything flash. After we had settled on the deal and I had paid him cash in advance, he invited me in for a drink. By now we were on first-name terms. The interior of the trailer held few surprises. Most of the furniture was built-in, the upholstery scuffed and torn. There was a cage with a torpid gerbil in it on a shelf alongside a model of a nuclear sub, and when he fetched two cans of cold beer from the ice-box, he fed the gerbil some scraps from a saucepan in the dirty sink. I noticed several gun magazines and a couple of Micky Spillane paperbacks lying around and there was a Penthouse calendar pinned to one wall.

'Here's to Scotland,' he said, as he broke the seal on his can.

At that moment a very well-built girl appeared in the doorway carrying a bag of groceries. She was wearing a brightly-patterned smock dress that barely reached her crotch and her legs were long, bare and tanned. Her hair was the thin, blonde, unwashed variety. She paused in the doorway and stared at me.

'Honey, this is Martin, Martin, meet Sally.'

'Hello. Pleased to meet you,' I said.

'Hi,' she responded without overmuch enthusiasm and as she came inside and dumped the bag on the table, her bra-less breasts almost fell out of her dress.

'Martin's from England. Bet you could tell from the way he speaks. Wanna beer, honey?'

'No, gimme a Coke.'

Eddie went to the ice-box. 'Martin here's gonna have the Olds.'

'What for?' she said.

'What for? To drive, what else?' He gave me a wink.

Her face was expressionless and her eyes stopped taking me in. She kicked off her sneakers and curled up on the one armchair, affording me an interesting view of her endless legs.

'One of these days I'm gonna get me a bigger place.'

'Which day?' Sally said. The opened can of Coke sprayed over her neck and dripped into her cleavage, but she appeared not to notice. 'Like tomorrow?'

'Maybe, who knows, hon? Things could change around here real fast. Think positive. Martin, you wanna stay for a bite to eat? What'd you buy, hon?'

'Not enough for three.'

I jumped in quickly. 'Don't worry about me. I should be getting on my way.'

'Where you thinking of goin'? Why don't you head on up to Sedona, that's real pretty up there.'

'Sedona sucks,' Sally said. 'Mexico, that's where the action is.'

'Whadda'you know? Just stay out of it, hon.'

It seemed a good moment to leave. I said goodbye to Sally which she acknowledged by waving the can of Coke in my direction. Outside Eddie was apologetic. 'She's a good kid, don't think I'm pussy-whipped. Only thing is she's lookin' to see a wedding ring and I'm not about to take that walk down the aisle again.'

He put my case in the trunk and tossed the keys to me. 'Probably needs some gas, so check it before you go any distance. The desert ain't the place to run dry.'

'Thanks, I'll do that.'

'If you wanna go to Sedona, your best bet is to take 17 North. Don't be listening to her, it's real artistic up there.'

'Yes, I've heard good things about it.' Caution once again dictated all my moves. I wasn't anxious for anybody to know my itinerary. 'Thanks again for all your help.'

'My pleasure. Have fun. When you head on back here maybe we can have us an evening together. Sally's got a friend, we could make it a foursome, get us some real Western food.'

'That sounds good.' I found myself aping his accent.

I didn't take Interstate 17 to Sedona. Instead after filling the tank with gas and buying a map, I picked the most direct route to Carefree, heading across town until Camelback intersected with the Scottsdale Road. The landmark Camelback mountain, incongruous behind the huge shopping centre, dominated the urban landscape. I passed joggers sweating their weary path towards the American dream of eternal youth. The developments bordering the main road were shielded by giant oleander hedges; orange and grapefruit trees, their trunks painted white, decorated the sidewalks on either side and there wasn't a billboard to be seen. Once I had crossed a road named Thunderbird, the houses thinned out. Small private planes, their wings trembling in the hot air like unsteady gnats, drifted soundlessly across the sky ahead of me on their descent to Scottsdale airport. The air-conditioning fan in the Olds clattered its metal blades against something, and I switched on the radio to drown it out. The DJ's soothing, well-oiled voice told me I was listening to K-Light, the station that promised to get me home safely with light rock. The road seemed endless, running in a straight line as far as the distant mountain range. By now there was scrub desert on either side, the terrain dotted with giant Saguaros pointing up into the azure sky. For some reason they called to mind the gesture you get when you cut up Italian motorists. Frequent signs warned against shooting or driving off the road. I passed a couple of roadside stalls selling bleached steer skulls, tin cut-out coyotes and Indian jewellery which was probably made by a lost tribe of Taiwan Navahos. After a fake cowboy town the road narrowed to two lanes, switchbacking dramatically for eight miles or so. Apart from a few adobe houses the countryside was deserted. The street signs echoed what a rube like me imagined the old West to have been: Lone Mountain, Never Mind Trail, Sleepy Hollow, Long Rifle. As I approached the Carefree city limit the road dipped again and ahead was an awesome pile of boulders, precariously balanced. A tall Cross rose from the base of the rocks and as I drew closer I saw the futuristic church it belonged to was integrated, chameleon-like, into the background. Carefree turned out to have no beginning or end. I imagined that on their premium lots, secure in their million dollar, custom built, showcase homes the well-heeled inhabitants were counting their golf balls, for there was nobody to be seen anywhere.

Slowing down to obey the new speed limit I suddenly realised that the impulse that had brought me here had been misguided; I had no idea how to set about finding Sophie, or what I would do if indeed I succeeded in locating her. The alien landscape, the stillness everywhere and absence of any human life around me all added to my feeling of unease. I had arrived with no thought out plan, which was rash to say the least remembering all that had led up to this moment. I had brought myself to uncharted country for what? Some foolish Quixotic quest to recapture a lost love? Did I really imagine that, single-handed, I could alter anything? I pulled over on to the sandy soft shoulder to try and get my thoughts in order. The harsh light gave the enormous boulders a new and sinister appearance; in my present mood I could readily imagine them slipping from their precarious balance to roll down and crush me as surely as the stupidity of my situation.

After smoking two cigarettes I decided that my first priority was to get a bed for the night, working on the theory that nothing ever looked so black after you'd slept on it. At first sight Cave Creek suggested a manufactured ghost town, for in contrast to the barren terrain I had just passed through, Main Street was a scattered collection of squat wooden buildings with an air of *fin de siècle* Western style about them. The first store I came upon was appropriately called The Town Dump, and there were a number of eating houses with exotic names like The Horny Toad, The Buffalo Chip Saloon and El Encanto. I drove to the end, then did a U-turn and drove back again having spotted the only hotel. This was The Tumbleweed Hotel and its large sign said it offered phones, cable TV and casitas, whatever they were. There was a modest entrance, just a door in the wall, but the proprietor greeted me warmly and the room I was shown to was clean and cheerful. I took a shower, felt much better, then decided to sample some of the local atmosphere. By now it was dusk and lights dotted the slopes of Black Mountain. The Horny Toad's parking lot had twenty or thirty cars in it, which I took to be a good sign. Always eat where the natives eat.

It was dim, noisy and crowded inside, the walls hung with cowboy memorabilia. The scrubbed wooden tables betokened nothing fancy, and the simple menu was chalked up on a blackboard. I ordered the house speciality, chicken, little suspecting that I would be faced with a whole bird and a mountain of home fries – there was nothing skimpy about the

Horny Toad portions. When I finally had to admit defeat my elderly waitress scolded me.

'Why you ain't ate nothin'. You want a doggy bag for that?'

'I don't have a dog,' I said.

Back in my room, too bloated for sleep, I flicked through the TV channels until I hit the late-night religious marathons. One preacher asked his flock, 'What does Jesus have to say about styrofoam?' which must have sent scholars scuttling back to the Gospels. The camera kept cutting to a crazed old biddy done up in a Civil War ballgown sitting on a sofa in a mock Louis Quinze studio set. From the way she kept squeaking 'Hallelujah' in a little girl voice you could tell Jesus had really got to her. Apart from salvation the Lord had also provided her with about four inches of Max Factor and a Marie Antoinette hairpiece which looked as though it might have been made of styrofoam and hence the reference. I also had to admire the preacher's sales pitch. Slotted into his repeated plea for sinners to surrender their will to the spirit of God Almighty, he also asked them to surrender their hard-earned bucks to keep the mission afloat. 'Send me a prayer and tuck a big note inside. Amen.' Then he gave us a rendering of that rousing old football song, *Jesus kick me gently through the goalposts of life*. The studio audience was visibly affected. It was vaguely comforting to know I was in Indian territory and the good old white medicine men were still at work conning the natives.

23

THE PAST

I woke up in the middle of the night to find my room suffused with an unearthly light. Tottering to the window I discovered the source. The clear, pure black, desert sky reminded me of the Elton John song, and as the lyric has it, I was amazed by that big fat yellow moon. It brought back the time in France, when once before brightness fell from the air and Sophie and I ended our affair.

We were in Aquitaine, staying in the Château de Rolland, a small, private hotel on the outskirts of Barsac which sits in the centre of the Sauternes country. Sophie was there for the ride, but I was working, researching the history of one of the local vineyards which had recently been purchased by a consortium of London businessmen with money to burn who wanted to boast of their acquisition. They had commissioned me to write one of those non-books which are never career-enhancers, but which pay better than reviewing and don't make enemies. They had given me two thousand up front plus generous expenses which enabled me to take Sophie along. I can't pretend that she was ever crazy about making the trip. She didn't share my love of the grape, in those days her taste buds only sparked when Coke hit them, so the thrill of sampling some fine vintages for free was lost on her. The mystique surrounding the great châteaux really fascinates me, so the book was not the chore it might well have been. I spent most mornings finding out why certain years produced the great wines while others proved a comparative dud. A certain amount of bullshit surrounds anything to do with wine, but the local growers I interviewed willingly allowed me to explore the various techniques and took a delight in my interest.

This meant that Sophie was left to her own devices for the best part of the day and the attractions of Barsac soon palled for her. I tried to make allowances, and made time to show her some of the châteaux in the surrounding countryside. One in particular, the Château de Roqutaillade held a particular fascination for me; it had been curiously decorated in the style of Camelot by Violette le Duc and to my eyes was steeped in romanticism, but sightseeing bored her. Maybe our affair had run its course in any event. Maybe too much passion at the start of an affair has to burn itself out and without marriage and children to cement the relationship, chinks open up which we can never plug.

The end came, as they say, with a whimper rather than a bang. No fireworks, no punishing slugging match à la Edward Albee, just the worst kind of slow death. I returned to our room before lunch one day to find her packing. She was tired of being left on her own with nothing to occupy her, so she was going back to London.

Initially I could not bring myself to take her seriously.

'But this job's not forever, I shall have finished in another week, but it is a job I have to do. I've had the money, that's what paid for this holiday.'

'How can you call it a holiday? You have fun on a holiday.'

I could not swallow the enormous improbability of it all ending there in that hot, circular room. But she had made her decision and nothing I said, no promises I made, could deflect her. Her calmness was a weapon she had never used before. I could have overcome anger, I could have mastered tears, but it was impossible to counter her icy resolve.

'Is it just this place, or something else, something I've said or done? What? Tell me. Stop packing that case for a moment and look at me.'

She did so, reluctantly. 'You care more for your work than you do for me.'

'That's a stupid thing to say. And untrue. Nobody's ever made me happier than you. I know I'm withdrawn sometimes, maybe too often, but that's the nature of the beast, the blank sheet of paper I face every day. But that never bothered you before. I thought this would be a treat for you – a different country, some great food, new places to visit.'

'It's all so old,' she said.

'What is?'

'Just everything. This place is dead.'

'So that's it, is it? Just this place?' I reached for any strand of hope.

'No.'

'What then? Something must have happened to make you act like this. What's changed? I haven't changed.'

When I found that I could not move her I squandered what remained of caution. 'If you can't be bothered to stick it out for another few days, then you're right, you'd better go,' I said, not meaning it, still hoping for a last minute reprieve. 'I'm the last person to want to make you unhappy. But if you go, where does that leave us?'

'How d'you mean?'

'Well, it's obvious, isn't it? People don't just up and go without good reason, not if they feel anything for each other. The reasons you've given don't make any sense. Will you be there when I get back?'

'Yes.'

'Then why put us through this, darling?'

'I don't know,' she said, and cried, and it was then that I first saw love's ending.

We ate a last tortured lunch together, then I drove her to Bordeaux airport.

'I'll wait until your flight's called,' I said.

'No, don't do that. I hate long goodbyes.'

We kissed at the barrier and I tried to convince myself that

226

the moment she arrived home she would ring to say that she missed me and all would be the same as before.

But she didn't ring. Instead she wrote, a few lines in her immature, sloping handwriting on pink notepaper decorated with teddy bears such as schoolgirls use. All it said was, *Dearest Martin, just to say I arrived safely. I'm sorry about it all. You deserve better than me. I hate myself sometimes and wish I was different. I shall always love you. Nothing was your fault, it was all me and I never wanted to hurt you. Take care of yourself and enjoy what you're doing. Sophie.* Something after that had been heavily crossed out. I held the letter against a strong light, but I could not decipher what had been deleted.

I rang the apartment, but there was no answer, only my own voice on the answering machine, mocking me. In the following days I must have rung twenty times with the same result. Even then I could not bring myself to believe that it was the end of the affair. When I returned to London there was no sign of her. I went straight to our bedroom closet, but nothing of hers remained. It was like going home to a house where somebody had died; their presence can be felt everywhere, but there is something lifeless about every inanimate object they ever touched. The only traces of her were in the bathroom – spilled face powder on the wash-basin, a twisted tube of her toothpaste, an empty packet of the Pill. This, more than anything else, induced a different ache. Perhaps the remembrance of lust, rather than love, is more wounding when the object of our desires has vanished.

I called some of her friends at the ballet school knowing that amongst them there would be somebody only too anxious to tell me any bad news – isn't that what friends are for? – but she had not been back to class and they could tell me nothing. It was one of those illusionist acts you see on television when they make impossible objects disappear: now she was there always by my side, now she was no longer on the same planet. I paid visits to all our old haunts, but that proved too painful and in any case I had to explain her absence with a casualness I did not feel. I even rang Henry, the final humiliation, knowing it would give him the satisfaction of having the last word about Sophie's true character, but he surprised me.

'Oh, that's terrible. You must be feeling awful,' he said.

'Yes, I am.'

'I'm so sorry, chum. I always thought you two were a permanent fixture. You seemed Darby and Joan material.'

'I'm just so worried about her. You can't think of anybody who might know where she is, can you?'

'Not offhand. I'll ask around. I still bump into her old girlfriend occasionally – what was her name, Melissa?'

'Melanie.'

'That's right, Melanie. I'll call her, I think I have her number in the office.'

'Would you? And tell her to ring me.'

'Of course. You sound really rough. D'you want to have lunch? I can't manage tomorrow, but how about Thursday?'

We did meet and Henry did his best to cheer me up, even to the extent of suggesting he provide a couple of companions for a night on the town. But my hurt was too recent for a blind date. Later he was as good as his word and got Melanie to phone me. My hopes there were short-lived; now married with two small children Melanie could give no comforting news – she and Sophie had drifted apart and she had no idea of her whereabouts.

They say a writer can capitalise on anything, but it isn't always true. Sometimes we are too close to the realities that strike us down and if we attempt to purge them on the page they destroy us twice over. I did attempt a short story using elements of our parting in Barsac, but it died on me. I suppose I went on searching for another month or so, but gradually I stopped sifting through a ragbag of memories to find the one incident that would explain everything and began to pick up the threads of a new life. I dated other girls, but living with Sophie had ruined me for casual one-night stands. I did take up with one girl, a researcher I met at the London Library. She rekindled something for a time but then took a job in

Brussels and the effort of keeping the affair alive at long distance proved too much for both of us. It was a curious, aimless period in my life, not far removed from those empty years of adolescence when everything is anticipation and nothing is realised.

I rattled around in my apartment increasingly dissatisfied with my lot, although ironically my writing went well. The next novel I wrote was the Book of the Month alternative choice and for a few weeks figured in the bestseller list. As a result I allowed myself to be talked into one of those publicity tours of the main cities, and was invited to speak at half a dozen literary luncheons. I gradually worked some jokes into my set speech, and duly signed copies to gushing matrons, but the novelty of daily journeys on British Rail soon wore thin. It was a long time since I had visited the provinces and I often felt I was passing through an England I had never known.

I was accompanied by an earnest young publicity girl who found it all thrilling and by the time we got to Aberdeen, fatigue and disillusion had brought me to the low watermark of the entire tour. I drank too much the night we arrived and made a half-hearted pass at her which sensibly she laughed off. It was there that I chanced upon a copy of *Country Life*, a fine magazine which although primarily concerned with real estate and the arts, somewhat incongruously always features a full page photograph of a bride-to-be at the start of the text section. That was how I learned what had happened to Sophie and the extent of Henry's duplicity.

The caption under the photograph read: *The marriage has been announced between Miss Sophia Herbert, only daughter of the late Mr and Mrs Stephen Herbert of Northampton and Mr Henry Blagden, the popular young Member of Parliament. The couple will honeymoon in Barbados.*

I had little doubt that Henry had instigated the change to 'Sophia' from the more mundane 'Sophie'.

At the time the hurt and the hatred were evenly divided,

but gradually hatred for them both took over, though I confess that the night I discovered the magazine I wept in my hotel room. Somebody, I think it was Mauriac, wrote: *Such are the inexplicable workings of our hearts that it is with horrible anguish we leave those by whose side we have lived without pleasure*, and in my initial anguish I convinced myself that this was true. Only much later was I able to acknowledge that Sophie had entered my life at that moment, which comes but once, when we are perfectly equipped for love.

24

THE PRESENT

Standing by the window of the Tumbleweed Hotel, I relived some of the agony of that time, aware that I was once more close to her, that somewhere out there in the desert landscape she slept in somebody else's bed. I knew how she slept, curled inwards against her partner, one hand flung upwards as though to ward off a blow from the creatures of the night. I remembered, too, the patterns of her lovemaking, sometimes demanding, at other times demure with a show of false reluctance, or else daring all, her lips wanton, wandering, giving way at last to the wrenching cry she always made when she could no longer stay the ultimate pleasurable pain of coming. There was always violence in her final spasms, the need, it seemed, to mark me with her talons, just as animals stake out their territory against intruders. And in the aftermath, if I displayed my scars, she would deny all knowledge. 'That couldn't have been me,' she would say, 'you must have done that to yourself without knowing,' regarding me, it seemed, as a stranger without connection to her recent surrender. Sometimes she would force me to withdraw at the last moment and come on her breasts as if only then could she be sure that my pleasures equalled her own.

It was a long road to have travelled from innocence to uncertainty, a journey that, until now, had been without maps. I thought back to the deaths along the way, beginning with Henry's sham suicide that had launched the whole sorry business. I knew I was still in the territory of the unknown but I was driven by something stronger than fear: that strongest and most powerful of motives, sexual love, which devises daily the most entangled and worst actions, manages to pervert all reason and sooner or later makes idiots of us all. The plan I had devised in New York after the discovery of Sophie's whereabouts had wilted, for part of me realised that I was committed to a fool's errand. But having come that far I was compelled to go on regardless of the risk. If I had ever stopped to consider my real motives, I doubt I could have explained them, I was consumed with that kind of desperation that must drive some to murder. I had to put an end to loving one way or another, write *finis* to those lost chapters in my life which had begun with a chance meeting on an English road many summers ago.

After breakfast I again went through my clothing and belongings searching for my lost credit cards on the off chance that I had overlooked something, but again drew a blank. Then, before taking to the road, I put the Olds through a car wash, topped up the oil and gas and bought a more detailed local map. I convinced myself I was in no immediate danger provided I took reasonable precautions, since nobody connected with Seymour or Henry had any inkling that I was in the area. I had been tracked to New York, that I knew, but the flights to Dallas and Phoenix had been without incident.

I don't suppose I had driven more than two miles when the heavens fell in. There were frequent signs warning of flash floods, and they weren't kidding. Monsoon rain obliterated the landscape in a matter of minutes and because the ground was rock hard none of the water penetrated, it just lay there four or five inches deep in great muddy swirls as the dips filled. A few minutes later, with sheet rain continuing to fall, the level was halfway up to my fenders. The windshield wipers on the Olds gave up and I did the sensible thing and eased blindly off the road and parked. Bits of debris started to drift past me. It was frightening while it lasted, as though a dam had burst. Water started to leak inside the car since most of the rubber seals had perished. My breath had fogged the windows making it difficult for me to see much. I could only sit and listen to the rain beating on the roof like percussion from a ghetto-blaster.

It was some fifteen minutes before the downpour eased off, though streaked lightning persisted in the distance. When I judged it safe I started the engine and after a few anxious moments the back wheels stopped spinning in the mud and found traction again. Using the low gear I eased the car back on to the road taking it slowly through the pools and trusting to luck that I didn't suddenly disappear into a hidden dip. For the next half hour I drove aimlessly, for I had no idea where Seymour's house might be. Some of the roads led nowhere and twice I had to reverse out with my wheels spinning in the red mud. I passed a couple of sodden joggers, but few other signs of life. It was an area where most of the houses were built on large plots, many of them cantilevered into the hillsides – to my eye perilously, for above them massive rocks seemingly bunched together at random were silhouetted against the looming sky. I could not help wondering how the early settlers had navigated such inhospitable terrain in their covered wagons.

I was about to abandon the search when the rains began again with a vengeance, as though a powerful faucet had been turned on. This time I immediately pulled off the road into a gully. Steam rose from the ground, swirling around the giant phallic cacti with their plumed hats, transforming them into the illusion of solitary figures standing sentinel. This time the cloudburst was short-lived and when my windshield cleared I made out a horse and rider sheltering under a large eucalyptus at the end of the gully. I wound down my window for greater visibility as the rider moved from cover and came towards me. It was then, as the last spatterings of rain drummed against the car, that the past finally caught up with me: as the horse drew alongside I looked up into Sophie's amazed face.

233

I can't remember which of us spoke first. Dressed in cowboy jeans that, rendered sodden by the rain, clung to her figure, she stared down at me, momentarily nearly dismounted as the horse slithered on the wet rocks. She jerked on the reins, recovering her balance, then pulled the beast around and for a moment I thought she was going to ride off without a word.

'Martin?' she said, just as I spoke her name at the same time, the difference being there was no query in my voice. Then, 'How could you be here?' as she brushed strands of dank hair out of her eyes.

When I found a normal voice, I said, 'I suppose if I told you I came here looking for you it would sound too far-fetched, wouldn't it? But that's the truth, God help us.'

'Why?'

'Why did I come? That's complicated. Come and sit in the car, we can't talk like this.'

She hesitated, looking around, then dismounted and tied the reins to the tree. I opened the passenger door for her and she slid on to the sagging bench seat. Close to she gave off a scent of horse and a heady perfume with a lily of the valley base.

Nothing was said for a few moments. I didn't touch her; we sat apart and just looked at each other. The rain began again, this time a softer rain, shrouding the surrounding countryside like a fine mosquito net. The scene reminded me of a French film: the enigmatic Gabin whose thin lips never seemed to move when he spoke, and Simone Simon, I think, portraying two doomed lovers in one of those wonderful post-war black and white classics. They always had unhappy endings, yet for some reason the trite words of love, despair and anguish they exchanged in the inevitable farewell scene, those words we all use when searching for ways to explain human failings, sounded so much better in French. Now, I wanted that same sad intimacy, framed gently like the rain, that would not alarm Sophie, but the words did not come. I was afraid to say too little, afraid to say too much too soon. It seemed that everything in my life had been a preparation for this moment and I was not equal to it.

Sophie was the one who finally broke the silence.

'I shouldn't be here. It's too much of a risk.'

'For me or for you?'

'For both of us.' She made a move to open the car door and I put an arm across to restrain her. 'I know Henry isn't dead,' I said. My arm remained across her and I could feel her heart beating. 'Where is Henry now? Is he here with you?'

She did not answer.

'Is he here?' I repeated.

'They're all here, that's why it's so dangerous.'

'Who's "they"?'

'Seymour and the others. You should never have tried to find me again.'

'But I did, so it's too late for that.'

'There's nothing you can do. Nothing. Nobody can help. It's gone too far.'

'What has?'

'Everything.'

'People have died along the way since I first spotted Henry in Venice. Did you know that?'

'Don't tell me,' she said, but I was relentless, torn between an old longing for her and the need to find out as much as possible. 'And do you know why?'

'All I know is that if they found out I'd seen you they'd probably kill us both.'

'But do you know why?' I insisted. 'Do you know what you're mixed up in?'

'Some of it,' she said. 'Enough.'

Again she tried to get out of the car, but I restrained her.

'Don't,' she said. 'For all I know they're watching us now I mustn't stay here any longer, they'll come looking for me.'

'Have you never tried to get away?'

'Where would I go?'

'I'd find somewhere safe for you.'

'No, it's too late for that. Too late for both of us now. Don't

235

you see, we can't go back. I'm sorry for what I did to you.'

The panic in her face was real enough.

'Fuck that,' I said, 'I can forget the past if you can. If you let me, I'll find a way to get you out of this.'

She shook her head over and over again.

'Well, then promise me one thing. Let me see you again.'

'How can I? Anyway, what's the use?'

'There must be times when they leave you on your own, aren't there?'

'Not here they don't. I sneaked out today because that house, those people, drive me mad.'

'Are they always around?'

'They're supposed to be going to Chicago next week. At least, that's what I overheard.'

'So?'

'But it couldn't be here. They have watchers.'

'You say, I'll go anywhere, meet you anywhere.'

She thought for a moment. 'Seymour has a chalet in Flagstaff, which he uses when he goes skiing. I might ask if I could go there while they're away.'

'Good. Then I'll go to Flagstaff and wait. Tell me a place, a restaurant or something, where we could meet.'

'Supposing I can't make it?'

'Then I'll think of something else. And by next week I'll have got help.'

'What d'you mean?'

'Never you mind. Tell me a place. Is there a Macdonald's up there? We need somewhere ordinary.'

'There's a Howard Johnson's just off the freeway.'

'I'll find it. I'll go there for breakfast every day and wait. Next week, you say. What day are they leaving?'

'They said Tuesday.'

'Fine. I'll be there from Tuesday. You go now.'

She got out of the car and I watched her mount the horse and ride away, watched her disappear through the fine rain, wondering yet again why it was, despite her contagious fear, I still felt the same about her.

25

THE PRESENT

I suppose I had only gone ten or so miles on the road to Flagstaff when I spotted a police car in my rear-view mirror. It came up behind me with its lights flashing and I wasted no time in pulling over and stopping.

The patrol car drew in a short distance behind me. As far as I could see in my mirror there was only one man in it. He used his bullhorn to direct me.

'Would you step out of your car, please.'

Politeness, I thought, as I complied, politeness at all costs, play it very British. I watched as he got out and walked slowly towards me. He was a big, handsome fellow in his twenties, wearing the smart uniform of the Highway Patrol, his gun arm swinging loosely. He paused at the rear of my Olds and studied the licence plate before coming to me.

'This your vehicle, sir?' he said with no particular menace.

'No. I rented it from a friend. I'm just here for a few weeks on holiday doing some sightseeing. Was I speeding, I didn't think I was?'

He ignored this. 'Can I see your licence?'

He had quickly dropped the 'sir' I noticed.

'Well, that's a problem. I don't have one. I'm from England.'

'Show me your British licence then.'

'I don't have it.'

He stared at me.

'Somewhere on the way here I had my pocket picked. I lost my licence and all my credit cards.'

'So what identification do you have?'

'My passport.'

'Show me that.'

I handed it to him. He studied it without any appreciable change of expression.

'Says here you're an author.'

'Yes.'

'What d'you write?'

'Novels mostly.'

He nodded. I got the feeling he was not overly impressed. 'You say you rented this vehicle from a friend, Mr Weaver?'

'Yes.'

'Where was that?'

'In Mesa. Is that how it's pronounced?'

Again no response. Don't press so hard, I thought.

'Did you get any papers with the car?'

'Papers?'

'A title document.'

'No, he didn't give me anything like that.'

'Well, he gave you something, Mr Weaver. He gave you a stolen car.'

'Stolen?'

'Stolen in Tulsa 'bout four weeks back. This friend of yours, you known him long?'

'No. Perhaps I shouldn't have called him a friend. Just friendly. He was the taxi-driver who drove me from the airport when I arrived in Phoenix. He volunteered to let me have his spare car.'

'Do you have his name?'

'Yes. He gave me his card.' I produced it for him.

'I'll keep this if you don't mind. Now I don't disbelieve you, Mr Weaver, but it looks like your holiday is gonna be interrupted until this thing is sorted out. Gonna have to ask you to accompany me back to the station and answer some more questions. You have the right to remain silent of course, but anything you do say can be used against you. Do you understand that?'

I nodded. I was in shock by now.

'If you'd like to take your personal belongings and hand me the keys.'

I did as he instructed and he locked my car.

'Now I'm gonna have to search you.'

'Fine,' I said. 'Go ahead.' I raised my arms. By now everything had taken on an air of unreality. I couldn't believe it was happening to me.

He frisked me. Then he told me to get into the back seat of the police car. The round decal on the side panel stated it belonged to the Sheriff's Office, Maricopa County. Shortly after we set out he radioed a message, giving Fast Eddie's details and asked for a computer check. I sat quietly, doing my best to appear at ease. Although I made a couple of attempts to voice my opinion of Fast Eddie, he didn't seem inclined to engage in any social conversation. I stared at the sweat ring in the centre of his immaculate shirt. I could feel my own sweat running down my arms.

When we arrived at the police station I was searched again and made to empty my pockets. My suitcase was also taken away and I was then put into a room and told to wait. It was nearly an hour before anybody came near me. Then a plainclothes detective came in, a squat individual with a jowly face that betokened few comforts. He introduced himself as Sergeant Wexler as he sat opposite me.

'Can we run over this again, Mr Weaver? You're British, right?'

'Yes.'

'On holiday?'

'Yes.'

'When did you arrive in Phoenix?'

'Yesterday morning.'

'From where?'

'New York, via Dallas. Which is where I think I lost all my papers and credit cards.'

'But not your cash?'

'No, I had that in another pocket.'

'Why so much cash? You had over five thousand dollars.'

'Is that wrong?'

'Let's just say it's unusual. Most people use plastic.'

'Well, in my case, it was just as well then.'

'You could say that. So when you arrived in Phoenix, you hired a car from this guy?'

'Yes.'

'Prior to arriving at Phoenix airport you'd never seen him before?'

'No, I've never been in Phoenix before.'

'Why didn't you go for an ordinary rental car?'

'I did. But they don't take cash.'

'But the guy did, huh?'

'Oh, yes.'

'How much did he charge you?'

'Four hundred dollars a week for two weeks.'

'Hell, you could have bought the heap for that. I thought you British were smart.'

'Not this one, apparently,' I said with an attempt at lightness.

'You sure this is your first trip?'

'To Arizona, yes. I've been in the States before.'

'Then you should know our laws. I guess in this case they ain't too different from your own. Imagine driving a stolen car is a serious offence over there. Am I right?'

'Of course.'

'Makes you an accessory. Plus you can't produce a licence, or an insurance certificate.'

I remained silent.

'Did you know this guy Kuhl has a record? He served two terms for armed robbery, one for assault, and he's currently out on parole.'

'No. How could I possibly know that?'

'Well you know now. You're sure you've never seen him before?'

'No. Never. He was a total stranger to me. It was stupid of me to trust him.'

'Yeah,' Wexler said laconically. 'You said it. Nothing else you want to tell me?'

I hesitated a fraction too long, my mind racing to try and decide whether I should reveal the true story. In fiction and in the movies it has always irritated me when innocent victims don't use the first opportunity to clear themselves. It was a question of saying things in the right order.

'I realise I've put myself in an awkward situation, but I do have somebody in London who'll vouch for me, a fellow cop, on Scotland Yard's Anti-Terrorist Squad, Superintendent Clempson. You could ring him.'

Wexler stared at me. 'Why would I want to do that?'

'I think he could explain some things.'

'What needs to be explained?'

I was getting near the precipice. Wexler knew it too, he was no fool.

'Well, my story as to how I came to be driving the car is absolutely true,' I said slowly, 'and I know nothing about this man Kuhl except what you've just told me. But there are other aspects.'

He seized on the word. 'Aspects?'

'Yes.'

'What's that mean?'

'Well, I think Clempson could explain them better than me.'

'How's that?'

I was floundering now, getting more and more out of my depth. 'Because he carries a lot of weight.'

'Over there, maybe. Here, he doesn't mean shit. I get the feeling you're holding out on me. I wouldn't want you to fuck with me, Weaver.'

'I wouldn't dream of it,' I said at my most British. 'But if you'll take the trouble to ring Clempson I'm sure he can convince you on certain matters that don't tie up at the moment.'

'Certain matters. Aspects. What the hell do they mean? You tell me first, then maybe I'll ring this guy.'

'All I'm trying to say is, I don't have a lawyer or any friends here and he's my only hope of convincing you that I'm not involved in any other way. You have to take the word of a top-ranking British policeman, surely?'

He regarded me in silence for several moments and I met his look. 'This better not be a gag,' he said, then he got up and left the room. I sweated it out for another half an hour before he returned. There was nothing in his expression that gave comfort.

'Did you get him?'

'No, I didn't as a matter of fact.'

'Wasn't he there?'

'No. You gave me the name of a dead man, Mr Weaver.'

'Dead?' I said.

'Your friend, if he was your friend, was killed by an IRA bomb two weeks ago. Nobody else there knows anything about you.'

The shocking news took some moments to register.

'You got any other bright ideas, Mr Weaver? Don't fuck with me, I'd hate to think you were some bullshit artist. Now I suggest you think it over, think it over real good and come up with some better answers. I'll be back.'

This time he was gone nearly an hour. When he returned he was accompanied by a man I had never seen before who didn't introduce himself, but steamed right in aggressively. From his general manner I took him to be Wexler's superior.

'I hear you're trying to be too smart, Mr Weaver, giving us the runaround.'

'No.'

'You think we've got nothing better to do than make long-distance calls? That we're some chickenshit outfit you can fuck with?'

'No, sir.'

'Know what I think? I think you're a phoney, that nothing about you adds up. And we're getting a little pissed off. Let's start over, shall we? I want some straight answers to straight questions. See, what I'm looking at so far ain't too healthy for you. For all I know, your British passport could be a fake. What we've got is a guy driving a stolen car he says he bought from a con. A guy with a lot of cash, but no credit. Now, I'd say that puts you in a whole heap of trouble.'

During this I was desperately searching for some plausible way out, but everything I thought of seemed likely to plunge me deeper into the pit. I still hadn't recovered from the news of poor Clempson's death.

'I've told you the truth,' I said.

'Like hell you have.' He turned to Wexler. 'Book the fucker, give him a night to think things over, I've got better things to do.'

He left the room.

'Big mistake,' Wexler said. 'Captain Travis don't like being riled and you riled him.'

After being charged I was put in a cell. I sat on the stiff mattress and cursed myself for being so trusting where Fast Eddie was concerned. Ordinary common sense should have told me that nobody in their right mind lets a total stranger drive away a car with no guarantee they'll ever see it again, but at the time the thought that I was being suckered hadn't occurred to me. Now I was paying for my gullibility. It came home to me that I had never known real fear before but now it seemed with me for life.

Suddenly the cell door was opened and another man was pitched inside, a very big man who at first glance appeared to have been in a road accident. His plaid shirt was ripped in several places and his jeans were covered in mud. He had an ugly cut over one eye and there was another rivulet of blood running down from his scalp that was almost the same colour as his short red hair. He fell to his knees, burped, then opened his flies and proceeded to relieve himself. After that it was some time before he focused on me.

'Got my ass stomped,' he said. 'I'm drunk as dawg shit. You ever been drunk as dawg shit and had your ass stomped by a woman?'

I decided not to answer and swung my legs up on to the bed as the pool of urine snaked towards me. I could see it was going to be a long night.

'Them women, they're all bitches, whaddya say? I say they fuck you up, stomp on yer every which time, ain't that a fact? Ain't I right? Tell me I'm right.'

Whether my lack of interest in his problem annoyed him, or perhaps because he was so loaded, his mood and expression changed abruptly.

'Who you lookin' at, mister? I've seen you before, you're a friend of hers. If you're a friend of that little cunt I'm gonna bury you.'

He made an effort to get to his feet, but they had removed the belt from his gaping jeans and he tripped and fell sideways in slow motion. He lay there muttering, then threw up. I got off the bed and skirted round him and the mess on the concrete floor to hammer on the door. After making a hell of a din it was opened by an elderly policeman. He took one look inside and cursed.

'That lousy scumbag, he does that every time.'

He slammed the door closed. The drunk was still lying where he fell, but I had a nasty feeling that when he came to I'd be in for a repeat performance. I never took my eyes off him while I gathered up my things, but it was another fifteen minutes before the old officer returned. This time he carried a bucket of water and doused the drunk with it, though it produced no immediate effect. 'Let him lie in his own shit,' the officer said. 'He can clean it up himself in the mornin'.'

The cell remained fetid all night, but happily my drunken companion slept it off and did not bother me again. In the morning, nursing a monumental hangover, his personality had changed; now he was a contrite, shambling wreck forced to clean up his mess before he was taken away. I had spent most of the night thinking things through, trying to decide on the most sensible course of action. If I was ever to extricate myself from my present situation, I had to somehow convince Travis of the true facts. I certainly did not fancy a stretch in an American jail and that now seemed a very real possibility.

After being given breakfast I was allowed to use the washroom to shave and began to feel vaguely human again. My mind made up, I requested another meeting with Travis, stating that I was now prepared to make a statement and around mid-morning Wexler came for me and took me to Travis's office.

I began my rehearsed dialogue by saying that I had been shaken by the news of Clempson's death. 'That threw me for a loop,' I said, 'and accounts for my behaviour yesterday.'

Travis brushed this aside. 'Yeah, OK, Just get to the bottom line.'

'My name is Martin Weaver. I *am* an author, and you can check on that. Your local bookshop will almost certainly have a copy of my latest paperback. There's a photo of me on the back of the jacket which will confirm who I am.'

He studied me. 'Give me a title.'

'The Sixth Column.'

After a slight pause Travis said, 'Waste our time again and I'll get really mean.' He turned to Wexler. 'Go see if you can find it.'

After Wexler left the room, I said, 'I am prepared to make a full statement.'

'Don't do me any favours, will ya? I don't wanna sit here and listen to another slew of bullshit.'

During the night I had decided that the only person likely to extricate me was Ghia and I wished I'd had the sense to think of him before. More than poor Clempson, he knew the genesis of the whole sorry mess. Even so I knew it would still take a lot to convince Travis, given my current situation. I had made so many mistakes already and this would be my last chance.

'Can we tape it?' I said. 'I'd like it to be on the record.'

'Yeah, so would I.'

He activated his tape machine, going through the normal procedures by prefacing it with the time and date.

'Go ahead, give your name, then start.'

I began slowly, sketching in my past relationship with Henry and Sophie without sparing myself, then coming to Henry's supposed suicide and my subsequent sighting of him in Venice. This revelation finally gained Travis's full attention.

'Hold it there,' he said. 'If you were so certain about seeing him, why didn't you go to the police right away? You say he was a member of your parliament, so he was an important guy, right?'

'Well, he had a certain public standing.'

'Are your politicians as crooked as ours?'

'I wouldn't know.'

'I wouldn't piss on ours if they were on fire.'

'The fact is, I wasn't a hundred per cent certain, it was only subsequently, after the first murder, that I was sure I was right.'

'You're talking about the murder of the boy in Venice, right?'

'Yes.'

'You said "first" murder. There were others?'

'Yes.' I took him through my trip to Moscow and the episode with the Golitsins leading to my being warned off and virtually escorted on to the plane at Moscow airport.

'Even after that you still didn't go to the police?'

'Yes, I did, well not officially, but the next best thing. I contacted my friend Clempson, the one you say is tragically now dead, and told him what I've just told you.'

'If he was the top-ranking cop you say he was, why didn't he take action?'

'Well, I don't know how your force works, but it was outside his brief. He was Anti-Terrorist and this would have been something for the criminal division. I'm sure he did follow it up, he was a man of his word.'

'So how come nothing happened?'

'I don't have the answer for that and now he's dead we'll never know.'

'That's kinda convenient for you. You've got to do better than that, Mr Weaver,' he said, stopping me again. 'See you strike me as an intelligent guy, and what you've said so far don't make a lot of sense. If I'd been in your situation, I'd have made damn sure I got to the right people. Why didn't you?'

'I did try, but as I've told you the so-called "right people" weren't prepared to help – everywhere I went I got stone-walled – and in the beginning all I was trying to do seemed innocent enough to me. If one of your best friends committed suicide I'm sure you'd be the same. I couldn't understand why everybody closed ranks – at that time I genuinely thought he was dead. It was only subsequent events in Venice and Moscow that convinced me otherwise.'

Travis shrugged. 'OK, I'll give you the benefit of the doubt on that one. So what happened next?'

I described how I had traced Seymour, and my eventual chance discovery of the computer code amongst Henry's papers. 'I'm just a three-finger man, not an expert, I use my computer purely as a word processor to write my novels on. But I called in a man who gets me out of trouble when the bloody thing goes haywire and he showed me what the code meant. At that time we both imagined it was just a way of getting some of the Continental porno magazines and videos that are banned in England. Sleazy, a skeleton in my friend Henry's closet, but nothing more than that. It wasn't until later that the realisation I was looking at a paedophile network came home to me.'

Travis was sitting up and taking notice now. I judged it my turn to ask him a question. 'Do you know of the existence of such networks in your own country?'

'I've never come across the computer bit, no, but paedo-phile rings, sure. Those sick bastards are everywhere. We have our share, believe me. OK, go on.'

I explained that immediately after that piece of the puzzle had been revealed I had been called back to Venice to identify the old dandy, describing my experiences there in detail and explaining how Ghia's computer operator led us further into the maze.

Travis interrupted me there. 'Why didn't you give me his name instead of your Scotland Yard buddy? You could have saved yourself a lot of hassle.'

'Yes, I realise that now, but can I finish? Now there was a chain linking them all. Henry, the old guy and the boy in Venice, Seymour, the computer code, a hideous connection was emerging.'

'So why come here? Why not stay there and see it through?'

'I had a legitimate reason for coming to the States, to New York. I'd won an award, an Edgar, from the Mystery Writers of America. Have you heard of those?'

'No, but I'll take your word for it. Even so, why Phoenix?'

'In one sense I was running scared . . . I believe I was followed to New York . . . and at the same time . . . well, you've been through my wallet. You must have seen a cutting from a magazine I happened to find while I was on the East coast. It's a picture of my ex-girlfriend, Sophie, and it was taken in Carefree. I came here to find her. She's now living with this character Seymour. Just by chance I came across her while she was out riding during that freak rainstorm you had. We had a brief reunion but there wasn't time to find out much and in any case she seemed too frightened to talk. We arranged I'd meet her again next week in Flagstaff. She told me Seymour, and maybe Henry too for all I know, is going to Chicago on Tuesday. I was on my way to Flagstaff when your highway patrolman brought me in. The plan was for me to have breakfast at Howard Johnson's every morning and wait until she showed – *if* she showed.'

'What made you think you could trust her?' Travis said. 'Seems she two-timed you once, why not again?'

'I don't know that I did trust her, but I was prepared to chance it.'

'You were going to show up regardless?'

'Yes.'

'On your own?'

'Yes.'

'Despite all that's happened?'

'Yes. Another of my foolish moves.'

'Foolish is the word.' Travis stared through me, then turned off the machine and reached for a pen. 'Tell you what I'm gonna do. Give me the name of this Italian cop. If he checks out and gives you a clean bill of health, I'll buy the rest. But if he turns out to be another stiff, watch your ass.'

There was a notice board behind Travis's desk and pinned to it were three sheets of small photographs, all three headed *MISSING*. They were photographs of young children of both sexes, crudely reproduced by a copier machine – sad, haunted little faces such as might have been taken in one of those do-it-yourself booths you find at airports. I pointed to it. 'That's part of the same, isn't it?'

Travis got up and poured us both a mug of coffee from his machine. 'These hit my desk from all over the States as regular as junk mail. You any idea how many kids go missing in any one year? Would you believe thousands? I've had three reported in the Phoenix area in the past week. And usually the ones we find are dead. There was a time when one missing child made the world headlines, but today it isn't Lindburgh's baby that presses the conscience button. Nobody presses the button. Out there they're more interested in whether some member of your Royal Family gets a divorce, or one of our yo-yo presidential candidates humped his secretary ten years ago.' He paused, studying one particular photograph. 'Four years old. Four years old,' he repeated, 'and the sick fuck who took her will get some fancy lawyer to plead an unhappy childhood if we ever catch him.' All this was said without histrionics, though his face had become mottled and emotion had gravelled his voice.

Catching my eye I think he suddenly became conscious that he had revealed too much of himself. 'This country is full of shitheads and freaks. The other week in Phoenix they had a guy who wrapped himself in tinfoil and painted air force signs on his house to scare off aliens. When they finally nabbed him they found he'd blown his mother and father away with a Magnum. How does that grab you?'

Wexler returned at that moment and much to my relief had one of my American paperbacks. Travis examined it closely and compared me to the jacket photo.

'Taken a couple of years ago,' I said as I waited for his verdict.

'OK, so you are who you say you are, that's a beginning. If the rest checks out we could be in for some excitement round here.'

He turned to Wexler. 'How was he charged last night, Al?'

'Accessory to a theft.'

'Well write it up that the charge was subsequently dropped for lack of evidence. If there's any comeback I'll deal with it.'

'Thank you,' I said.

'Don't thank me, I ain't let you off the hook yet. I can always write up another charge sheet, paper's cheap. You've just seen the good side of me, but I can turn real mean if anybody takes me for a ride.' He examined my paperback again, studying the blurb.

'Could be, of course, you've just got a fancy imagination. This worth reading?'

'I think so.'

'Autograph it for me. No, better still, autograph it to my wife. Her name's Audrey.'

I borrowed his pen and signed the book.

'Gonna be worth something one day? Hey, hey!' It was a curiously mirthless laugh. 'If everything you've told me is on the level, we're gonna have to involve the Feds.'

'The Feds?' Wexler questioned.

'Yeah, I'll explain. First off I want you to trace a guy named

251

Seymour who lives local. He's almost certainly not listed. Don't move on him, just find him.'

'Seymour?'

'Spell it for him,' I was told. I wrote it down.

As Wexler started to go Travis stopped him. 'Oh, and another thing, give Mr Weaver a bed at your place. He sure as hell don't want another night here and I want to keep him safe.'

Wexler didn't embrace this suggestion with any enthusiasm. 'Have to clear it with my bride.'

'That gonna be a problem?'

'No.'

'So don't make a Dreyfus case of it. Just tell her.'

When we were alone again Travis said: 'Seems to me you backed losers with your friends.'

'It began because I saw a man I thought was dead. Wouldn't that have sucked you in?'

'Maybe. But from where I'm standing seems to me that what sucked you in is not that, but this broad you were once involved with. Chasing pussy has buried a lot of guys. Nearly buried me twice. I'm on my third wife and the future ain't too rosy neither. Let's hope your book sweetens her up.'

By now I was totally confused. At one moment he seemed well disposed towards me, the next moment he turned off the charm. He was a man on a short fuse, pleased with himself and anxious to come out on top. I was left to my own devices in another office until Wexler returned and drove me to his house.

'Can't say you're a welcome guest,' he said. 'Don't know why the fuck Travis couldn't have had you in his place if he's so concerned for your comfort. And you'd better be on the level, mister. Any trouble and I'm gonna cuff you.'

His house proved to be a small adobe set in about half an acre of land that was mostly sandy desert spotted with cacti. There was a basketball net fastened to the side of the garage.

'Do you play?' I asked, making conversation.

'My kid does. He's in his college team.'

252

I was introduced to his wife, a pert little blonde wearing a halter top and faded jeans. She said nothing to me when I introduced myself and thanked her, merely tightening her thin lips as she looked me over. Like her husband, it was clear she didn't think much of Travis's idea. I was shown to their son's room at the rear of the house. It was festooned with baseball pennants and posters of Madonna and Cher and smelt vaguely of stale sweat.

'This ain't likely to remind you of home,' Wexler said with what, for him, was a glimmer of humour. 'Kids have their own tastes these days. You like Madonna?'

'I can get to like her,' I said. 'She's better company than the drunk I shared with last night.'

Wexler checked the small adjoining bathroom. 'I'll bring you fresh towels. You got everything else you need?'

'Yes.'

He hesitated in the doorway. 'You married?'

'No, I'm not.'

'Well, don't take this the wrong way, but my bride don't want you to eat with us, so I'll bring your food in here. Nothing personal, you understan'?'

'Sure.'

'Strangers bother her.'

'Yes, you don't have to explain.'

He appeared about to say something else, then thought better of it and left me to my own devices. I took stock of my new surroundings. The single bed seemed comfortable and as with most American houses there was ample closet space. Half a dozen pairs of ragged sneakers were lined up under a bookcase which contained mostly paperback copies of the collected works of Stephen King. A ghetto-blaster stood on the window-sill alongside a stack of cassettes.

When Wexler returned with the towels I took a welcome shower, then lay on top of the bed and thought about the way Clempson's luck had run out. My own luck was holding – just – but I still felt like somebody caught in a Kafkaesque nightmare who had crossed a frontier too far.

26

THE PRESENT

I was under 'house arrest' for the next two days without any inkling of what was happening in the outside world, then on the morning of the third day I was taken back to Travis. Wexler drove me to the station with his siren screaming, an experience I confess I enjoyed.

'You allowed to use that any time you like?'

'Why not? Scares the shit out of all these little old ladies driving their dead husbands' Caddies,' he said, blasting through a red light. He seemed in a good mood for once.

When we arrived Travis introduced me to a new man. 'This is Special Agent Robb Kemelman from the Bureau's Sex Crime Unit.'

Kemelman didn't look the role, rather he suggested an academic who had somehow wandered from his natural habitat. He wore the sort of clothes that would have passed muster on the campus: creased linen jacket, a button-down shirt, conservative tie, grey flannels and scuffed brogues. The contrast between him and Travis was marked. I placed him in his early forties, though in truth he looked older, he looked in fact as though he had a bad liver, for there were dark circles under his eyes. Perhaps he was a heavy drinker, perhaps given the job he did every day hitting the juice was the only respite. When he spoke he framed every word carefully. I also suspected that he dyed his hair, for it was an unnaturally intense black. I had seen an ad on the local television station which demonstrated a new product that sprayed fake hair on to bald patches. Maybe he used that.

'Let me bring you up to date, Mr Weaver,' Kemelman began. 'Travis here has located this guy Seymour's house and his men have managed to get inside the grounds.'

Travis interrupted to explain that most of the casual labour in Arizona – gardeners, pool men, cleaners – was ethnic. 'I guess we white Americans have lost the urge to perform menial tasks.' (This said with the ghost of a smile, as though even inverted racialism demanded an apology.) 'Mostly Mexican or Japanese. They can lay waste to a garden if you don't watch 'em. Green fingers they ain't.' Again, like Wexler, he seemed very chipper.

'So,' Kemelman resumed with a trace of irritation in his voice, 'if I can continue, two ethnic officers have been brought from the Tulsa force and infiltrated as an undercover "gardening" team. They've scouted the grounds and established how many people are in the house. They've also pinpointed the security arrangements and installed listening devices, plus they've managed to photograph some of the residents. So I'd like you to take a look at what they got, see if you can identify anybody.'

He slid some prints across Travis's desk to me.

'That's Seymour,' I said, 'and that's the girl, Sophie, with him.'

'How about this guy?' Kemelman indicated a man wearing dark glasses who stood on the patio of the house some distance from Seymour and Sophie. I peered at it. Travis handed me a magnifying glass.

'Use this.'

I studied the photograph again. 'No idea,' I said. 'Never seen him before.'

'Didn't really expect you to. He's a known hood out of Chicago. Look at the others, maybe your bogus dead friend is amongst them.'

There was a closer shot of Sophie and further shots of Seymour talking to three other men, but no Henry. Looking at Sophie and Seymour again in such alien surroundings pushed a sliver of ice into my mind.

'I can't see Henry in any of these,' I said.

'Pity, that would have been a real break,' Kemelman said. 'Never mind, we're making some progress. We now know what Seymour looks like.' He ringed Seymour with a marker pen. 'Let's make enlargements of him and the girl and get them circulated.'

'Have you heard anything back from the Venice police?'

'Yes,' Travis said. 'You'll be happy to know that your story checked out. Better late than never.'

'That's a relief,' I said.

'Your guy there seems on the ball. From what he gave us, Immigration were able to trace that the old guy you described, the one who OD'd on drugs, made two trips over here last year. He was logged as entering the country in Chicago, which again ties in with what Kemelman will tell you. Go ahead, Robb.'

I sensed that Travis was keen to let me know that Federal agents or no he was still making his contribution.

'The Chicago trip your ex-girlfriend mentioned could be connected with an outfit based there we've been watching for some time. It calls itself *The Looking Glass Club* and publishes a magazine just this side of pornography – suggestive nudist material which comes within what we call the "constitutionally protected" area. Its real function, we know, is to provide a flea market for the buying and selling of photos of young children. What we have done is to answer some of the advertisments in the classified section to try and smoke out the hard-core paedophiles. We have to tread carefully since the Supreme Court overturned a conviction we'd worked on for two years on the basis we obtained the evidence by entrapment. They're so bloody concerned to protect the guilty they've forgotten the victims. We're fighting with one hand tied behind our backs.'

Again Travis interrupted him. 'Yeah, only last week the LA force set up a tri-state bust on a guy. Hit him with a SWAT team and netted a truck load of child porn hidden in a crawl space under the house. Turns out he was on a local school Board of Governors. He'd photographed himself with some of the little kids. For some sick reason the majority of the hard cases do that. I guess it feeds their fantasies, gives them a permanent record of the children they've had sex with, so that they can relive the moment. And what happened? He's out on bail. Here. Read this.' He pushed a copy of *USA Today* towards me.

The item he pointed to stated that there had been a hundred-and-thirty-one thousand cases of child abuse reported in New York State during 1991.

'Gives you some idea what's happening out there. Hell, that's more than the population of Scottsdale.'

Badly concealing a burp, Kemelman reached into his pocket to palm and swallow a couple of pills. 'The need we have,' he said, 'is to tie all the ends together, make the connection between what's happening here and elsewhere, that's why your involvement is so valuable. You could be a key witness if we make the bust. I say "if" because nothing's cut and dried any more. We're dealing with guys who know their way around the law and have the money to square things. Our justice system is screwed up, has been for years. When Hoover could have done something about organised crime, he backed off and the battle was lost. This country is ready to go up in smoke.'

'Backed off?' Travis said. 'The fucking old hypocrite was gay. I've just been reading a new book that blows him wide open.'

'Well, be that as it may,' Kemelman said through another burp, 'we have to play the cards we've been dealt. And move quickly because these birds could fly the coop any day. Now we've set something up for you to take a look at, Mr Weaver. It means a trip to Phoenix.'

When we left the station Kemelman drove me in an unmarked car to a small airfield dotted with those tiny craft that always remind me of the rubber-band, balsa-wood models of my childhood. Standing waiting for us was a police helicopter. I'm a touch leery about flying at the best of times; I am incapable, for instance, of comprehending how a 747 ever gets off the ground let alone stays in the air, and the aeronautics of helicopters are beyond me, except they inspire total fear. However, there wasn't any choice so I followed Kemelman meekly and took my seat behind the pilot. We rose, dipped nose forward at a sickening angle, then skimmed over the terrain at an alarming speed.

On arrival at Phoenix my legs were still trembling from the chopper ride. At police headquarters we were shown into a room in the basement where a sixteen-millimetre movie projector was set up. Kemelman introduced me to two other agents from the Bureau, much younger men than him – snappily-dressed, neat suits, collars and ties – the late J. Edgar would have approved. I was given but immediately forgot their names. As soon as we were seated one of the young agents doused the lights and started the projector.

Even before the images started to flicker on the portable screen I felt uneasy; it was like sitting down to face a meal you knew would be repellent. The focus was out in the early sequence and whoever had been operating the camera had a shaky hand when using the zoom lens. We were inside a room but since the only light source was a single lamp, it was difficult to make out details. Later the camera appeared to have been placed on a tripod and the general quality improved. Music was playing, a theme that reminded me of Villa Lobos, and repeated with chilling insistence. There was a sudden close-up of a face hidden by a mask, a white pierrot's mask with black diamond-shaped slashes dissecting the eyes vertically. The gash mouth was outlined in black and sloped upwards at both corners, giving it a leer. The camera zoomed out revealing more of the room, going with the figure wearing the mask, now shown as a naked male. Glimpses of a pouched stomach and spindly legs denoted an elderly man and as he turned his back to camera this was confirmed by a head of sparse white hair.

'Stop it at any point if you think you recognise anybody,' Kemelman said. 'We can go back if you need a second look.'

As he spoke the film broke and the agent switched off the current abruptly. 'I can fix it, I've got a splicer,' he said.

While we waited I asked Kemelman the origin of the film.

'It was part of the haul found in a deconsecrated church, overlooked at first because it had been hidden in a pair of Wellington boots. According to the code numbers on the edge of the film – Agfa negative stock by the way – it was part of a batch sold in Milan. Have you recognised anybody so far?'

'Not really. It's possible the nude figure could be the old man I first saw in Venice. The mask certainly reminds me of Venice, though that in itself doesn't mean much. I daresay you can buy them in a lot of places.'

The room lights were extinguished again and the projector restarted. 'We've lost about seven frames,' the agent said. 'The film's very brittle, so it might break again.'

'Will it hold up if you run at slow motion?'

'We can chance it.'

'Do that.'

The agent adjusted the speed and when the action resumed the nude pierrot minced his way past a mirror to a couch. There was a very young boy lying on the couch, also naked, his puny little body garlanded with vine leaves like a sad Bacchus. The child was then shown in a closer angle. His eyes were dilated as he stared vacantly into camera and it seemed obvious he had been drugged. The pierrot figure bent over the child, firstly fondling the torso, then moving his hands down to caress the immature genitals. Then there were black frames and when the film resumed the elderly pierrot was seated on the couch with the child kneeling between his thin legs fellating him. A sense of revulsion swept over me and I had an overwhelming urge to close my eyes. Even though none of us were there as voyeurs I felt we had no business extending the horror. Forcing myself to watch this scene to its conclusion, I was suddenly riveted by a

259

cut-away to a third figure, another man, again nude, seated on what, in theatrical terms, is called a Hamlet chair. This onlooker was wearing an elaborate butterfly mask.

'Stop it there,' I said.

'We can't hold one frame for very long,' the agent working the projector said. 'The heat of the lamp will burn it out. What we can always do is have our lab blow up a frame, and print it. Then it can be computer enhanced.'

'Risk it,' Kemelman snapped. He turned on me. 'What made you want to stop?'

'The mask, the butterfly mask.'

'What about it?'

'I think I mentioned that when I visited Seymour that one time I found out he was an avid butterfly collector. That could be a clue, but again it could just be a coincidence.'

'You think it's Seymour behind the mask?'

'No. Seymour's not the same build. This is a much heavier man.'

'Who then?'

Something so monstrous was beginning to form in my mind that I found myself unable to articulate clearly.

'Can I see it again, please?'

'Rewind it and run it again,' Kemelman instructed.

The film resumed. There was more disgusting footage of the child being abused and violated, but it wasn't until near the end that the man in the butterfly mask came back into the picture. He was shown urinating on the child who remained limp and passive throughout like some discarded rag-doll. I prayed that he had been drugged.

When the lights came on Kemelman sat hunched forward, covering his mouth with both hands, looking at me expectantly.

'Do you want to see it through again?'

'No.'

'Well, any conclusions?'

I thought carefully before answering. 'It certainly reminded me of that house I was taken to in Venice. The covering on the couch, for instance, struck me as similar to some of the furnishings. I think, but obviously I'm not sure, that the first man could be the one found dead in the brothel.'

'And the second man?'

My mouth was dry as though I had bitten on cotton wool, and I found that I was crying, though whether from compassion for the small child or the realisation that nothing in my life would ever be the same again, was impossible to say. 'If I was under oath,' I began haltingly, 'I couldn't swear to it, but I believe . . . I think the second man . . . could be my friend, Henry.'

Kemelman betrayed no elation. It wasn't a time for elation. He just stared at me for a long time, then nodded and thanked me. 'If you're right, then the sighting of him at Venice airport would make sense. The old man in the white suit, the villa with his hidden rooms . . . all circumstantial at the moment, I grant you, but more than we had before.'

He turned back to the two agents. 'I want as many good frames as you can isolate blown up and then computer enhanced. Concentrate on the two men, rear views, side face, anything you think might provide us with clues. Also close-ups of the child. We'll send them to Venice and see if they match with a missing kid.' Then to me: 'He was an MP, you said?'

'Yes.'

'Then it shouldn't be too difficult for London to provide us with photographs?'

'No, I'm sure.'

He snapped another instruction to the agents. 'Get on to that as well. Do it through our London embassy, I don't want any leaks.' For the first time there was a trace of emotion in his voice. He poured himself a glass of water and took another of his pills. 'There's one other thing I want to try on you while you're here. As you know we've got a phone tap on the house, but they're smart bastards. They don't use the phone much, we believe they use mostly computer talk, and we haven't hacked into that yet. However, they did get one incoming call. Play him the tape.'

Like most phone taps, it was recorded at slow speed to improve the quality. It then needed to be run at the correct speed. The first part contained little of interest – a woman's voice which I took to be Sophie's, ringing the local cleaners to enquire about a missing skirt, then a man placing an order with a liquor store – and it wasn't until there was a ringing tone denoting an incoming call that Kemelman nudged me.

'This one,' he said and handed me some headphones. I listened carefully. The phone was picked up by a man with an accent I couldn't place. The caller then said, 'Give me Seymour' in a voice that was unmistakably British. There was a pause and then Seymour came on the line. The conversation went as follows:

'Anything new?'

'No, it's all quiet. How about you?'

'That new client is prepared to buy the whole Chicago stock.'

'So is the trip still on?'

'Unless he gets cold feet at the last moment.'

'Is his money good? It's got to be cash, remember.'

'Sure, he knows that.'

'How's Sophie?'

'Don't worry about her.'

'I do worry, and so should you. What else, any more feedback from London?'

'No, they've lost the trace at the moment. Pity that wasn't taken care of in New York.'

'We'll get to it. Have you changed the codes?'

'What d'you take me for? We did that immediately.'

'Just checking. So unless you hear from me, I'll meet you at the funeral parlour as arranged, but don't call me.'

The line went dead. I removed my headphones.

'What did you get?' Kemelman asked.

'It's a British voice for certain, even though there's a trace of an American accent, but people often assume that if they stay in a country for any length of time.'

'Your friend Henry?'

I took my time before answering. 'It could well be.'

'Can't you do better than that?'

'Difficult. Can I hear it again?'

I listened once more, hunched close to the speaker. 'Yes,' I said, when the tape finished. 'I'm fairly certain that could be Henry.'

I felt my heart begin to race. 'And the dialogue ties in with what Sophie told me about them going to Chicago. He seemed anxious about her, do you think they've got wind of anything?'

'Your guess.' He paced the room while questioning me. 'Funeral parlour,' he said. 'Why funeral parlour?' Then he left the room abruptly. I hesitated, wondering if I was supposed to follow him. I exchanged a look with the two agents. One of them said: 'These cases always freak him. Guess it has a lot to do with his daughter.'

Before I had time to ask more, Kemelman returned.

'Let's go,' he said.

I followed him out to the helicopter pad. This time he talked all the way. 'We've got a team installed in a partially built house half a mile from Seymour's place conducting round the clock surveillance. We're lucky it's a cul-de-sac and there's only one road up to it. I know that shook you in there, but let me tell you about the sort of thing we're up against. I had a fax in from Florida this morning. A lad went missing in a theme park there. When that happens a full security alert goes into operation. They seal all exits, nobody allowed in, nobody allowed out. Luckily, this time they found the kid – little boy aged seven – after about twenty minutes, but even in that short time the kidnappers had managed to cut his hair, dye it another colour and give him contact lenses. They were just about to change him into girls' clothes when they cornered them.'

'Jesus!'

'Man and his wife, looked as homespun as a Norman Rockwell cover. Turned out they were wanted in three States on related charges. Filth like that aren't entitled to any mercy. I'd be happy to pull the switch and fry them in the chair.'

I had plenty to take my mind off the trauma of the return chopper flight. The film had revealed a world of perversion I had never before allowed myself to admit existed. I suspect Kemelman was quite a dab hand at reading people's thoughts, because on the car journey back to my motel he jolted me by suddenly saying: 'You don't want to go through with this, do you?'

'Why d'you say that?'

'I understand you were once involved with the girl, so I know what's going through your mind. You don't want to be the one who turns her in, do you?'

'No, it's not that.'

He gave me a look.

'Believe me, it's not that,' I qualified. 'I know they have to be stopped. I've seen enough, learned enough in the past few weeks to know that I have to play my part. What worries me is I might blow it when it comes to the crunch.'

'Just think of the kid in the film, and all the others like him.'

We pulled into the forecourt of the motel and Kemelman killed the engine. The academic mask suddenly dropped and I was looking at a different man, a man possessed. 'Let me tell you something,' he said. 'I'll use anybody, anything, risk playing every dirty trick in the book if need be, to save any kid from going through what we just saw.'

His vehemence startled me. Just why he felt the need to reveal his hidden anger wasn't clear at the time, it was only later that I began to understand. By then, of course, it was all too late.

27

THE PRESENT

The break came when the Bureau's hacker finally broke into their computer system. He came up with a list of names and addresses, some of which were duplicated on the one Venice supplied. The hundred or so names proved a catholic cross-section of prominent American citizens: a judge in Oklahoma, the headmaster of a school in Maine, the vice-president of a Savings and Loan bank in West Covina, California, a stockbroker in New York, a well-known sports commentator on network television, an evangelist operating out of Texas and, believe it or not, a fashionable paediatrician in Memphis, together with correspondents in Panama, Columbia, Mexico, even Alaska.

I don't know if I was the only one to notice the dramatic changes in Kemelman, but his behaviour became more erratic, some of which could be put down to the hours he was working but left me with the feeling that he was disquietingly hyper. Increasingly he distanced himself from the local police, challenging everything Travis suggested. The print-out of the computer list was a case in point. The moment he saw it he wanted to move in and make wholesale arrests. When such action was blocked by his superiors he took it out on everybody around him.

To an outsider the American judicial system, rather more than God, moves in mysterious ways, often complicated by conflicting Federal and State legislation, rivalries between the various law enforcement agencies and always subject to the demands of the political scene. Because this case not only involved the Bureau and the Arizona officers, but also Interpol, there was a reluctance from all concerned to act unilaterally. The recent Supreme Court ruling on entrapment had had a demoralising effect. Kemelman was the only one prepared to chance his arm and the fact that he was constrained on all sides fuelled his frustration.

The surveillance on Seymour's house produced no sightings of Henry, nor did the phone tap record another call from him. Travis instigated a search of all hotel registers in the greater Phoenix area and credit card companies were under instructions to report all transactions in the name of Blagden, a pointless exercise in my opinion since Henry would hardly be so stupid as to use his given name. It was a further example of everybody going round in circles grabbing at straws. I suppose Travis was trying to show initiative faced with outsiders on his territory calling most of the shots. As a result of the chance coincidence of one of his officers flagging me down on the highway he had suddenly been catapulted into the limelight and I think it had gone to his head.

On the Saturday morning of the weekend I was scheduled to travel to Flagstaff the surveillance team reported that Seymour and two other men not yet identified had left the house. Sophie was not with them. They were discreetly tailed to Scottsdale airport where they boarded a private Lear jet operated by a legitimate firm, properly registered and with a clean record. The Control tower reported that the flight plan they had lodged routed them direct to Chicago. The police there were alerted to take over surveillance at O'Hare and follow the trio's every move. Kemelman and his team took off an hour later to be in on the kill. Before leaving he reluctantly agreed to a plan Travis put forward for my trip to meet Sophie in Flagstaff.

Sunday evening, Henrick, one of Travis's men drove me to Flagstaff. He used an unmarked police car with a hotted-up engine and wore civilian clothes. There was a concealed radio fitted in the car and a lethal-looking pump-action rifle fixed beneath the dashboard. Heavily built, Henrick proved a taciturn character who had the radio on for most of the trip, listening to a baseball game, the intricacies of which he tried to explain to me, in what might just as well have been a foreign language – describing cricket to the ignorant provokes like incomprehension of course. I daresay I was still regarded as a passing curiosity from England who would never be on their wavelength and would soon disappear from their orbit.

Originally a lumber town, Flagstaff lies some hundred and fifty miles to the north of Phoenix on the Coconino plateau. Beyond are the Grand Canyon and the Painted Desert. Being seven thousand feet above sea level, in winter it is a popular ski resort; during July and August when the temperatures in Paradise Valley daily soar over the 100 mark and the old joke about frying eggs on the sidewalk comes true it provides a cooler watering hole for the parched inhabitants of Phoenix and Scottsdale. The countryside around is a mixture of green forests and high desert plateaus and the city sits at the base of Humphrey's Peak, the State's highest mountain. The only piece of local folklore I gleaned from my driver as we reached the outskirts was that Flagstaff was sometimes known as The City of Seven Wonders.

'Why is that? What are the seven?'

'Well,' he drawled, 'it sits in the middle of seven national parks. Y'ever bin to the Grand Canyon?'

'No. I've flown over it on the way into LA.'

'Have to see it at sunrise. Get up real early and stand on the rim. Makes yer balls go cold looking down. Course, y'can take a 'copter flight or a mule ride to the bottom if that's y'fancy. Most folks do that.'

He took me past the Howard Johnson's on the way to my own hotel so that I could get my bearings. I was deposited at a small one-storey motel.

'Is this it?'

'This is it.'

'Is it even open?' A mangy dog lay on the entrance porch and even as I surveyed the shabby exterior a ground floor window was opened and somebody threw out an empty beer can. Somewhere a radio blared Carly Simon singing 'Nobody Does it Better'.

'Yeah, it's open.'

'What do I do now?' I asked.

'Understan' the boys up here'll be in touch.'

'You're not staying?'

'No, this ain't my patch. You take care now,' was his not too encouraging parting shot.

I stepped over the dog and went inside. When I had checked in I enquired whether anybody had left a message. No, there was nothing. I also discovered that there was no restaurant or bar on the premises, it was just a staging post for travellers who wanted a bed for the night. Rather than sit in the unprepossessing room by myself I went back to the reception desk and asked the middle-aged clerk to recommend someplace where I could get a meal and a drink. He directed me to a Mexican restaurant about half a mile away. Having no transport, I walked. So far nothing about my welcome to Flagstaff inspired confidence.

Many of my women friends have confessed that they would rather starve than eat alone in a restaurant and that night I began to appreciate what previously I had always thought was a female affectation. Stuck in my corner, I was an island surrounded by chattering groups of tourists. They produced in me the strongest impression of life changing, of the mortal yesterday that had been lost to me: isolated, I felt like somebody with a contagious disease and I stared at the laughing faces with uncharitable envy. The waitress who served me was a pleasant enough girl, darkly attractive with beads of perspiration above her upper lip. As she walked away to place my order I saw that her shoes were shabby, the backs of her ankles reddened, which somehow made her desirable in my eyes. I was desperate enough for company to have considered asking her to join me for a drink after she finished work. I didn't, of course.

During my solitary meal I tried to anticipate whether I was going to save Sophie, or return her betrayal. Part of me dreaded the meeting: I wanted an end to uncertainty but not at any price.

When I got back to the motel, there was a message that a man named Hochstein had rung three times, asking for me. The desk clerk gave me the number he had left and I went to my room to place the call. The phone at the other end was picked up immediately.

'Hochstein,' a terse, nasal voice said.

'Martin Weaver, Mr Hochstein.'

'Where the hell have you been?'

'I went out for a meal.'

'You fucking idiot, you were under orders not to leave the hotel.'

'Was I also supposed to starve?' I said, immediately annoyed by his aggressive tone.

'I've been detailed to keep tabs on you. I came round twice.'

'Well, if somebody had told me. Nobody told me anything.'

He didn't answer at once. I heard him sneeze several times.

'Fucking hay fever,' he said. 'The pollen count is out of sight. In future, don't make a move without checking with me.'

'Fine,' I said. 'Now I know. I'll do that.'

'What time did you arrange to meet this broad?'

'I didn't. It was a very loose arrangement. I said I would be at Howard Johnson's every morning for breakfast and wait for her to show.'

'Better make it early. People get up early around here.'

'What d'you call early?'

'Seven.'

'OK, I'll put in a call. That is if they give wake-up calls in this place, they don't give anything else. How will I recognise you?'

'You won't. But I'll be around.' He sneezed again.

'How will I get there?'

'I left a car for you in the lot. Red Chrysler Le Baron convertible. The keys are under the seat, together with a gun.'

'A gun? I don't want a gun.'

'You may need one. It's a small automatic and fires ten rounds. Carry it at all times. Go outside and collect it now. I'll be around tomorrow morning for your meeting, in the meantime keep a low profile.'

He barely managed to finish the sentence before he had another sneezing fit.

'You should take something for that,' I said, but he rang off abruptly.

I went outside to the parking-lot and sure enough there was the red convertible. I sat inside it and made sure nobody was watching me, then felt down under the driving seat. I found the keys and then my hand closed over a small package which I lifted out gingerly and put in a pocket. It wasn't until I was safely back in my room that I opened the package. The only time in my life I had ever handled a weapon was as a teenager when I owned an air pistol, a much heavier specimen than the one I now held. This, the real thing, seemed too small to be capable of killing anybody. Making sure that the safety catch was on I released the magazine and examined the bullets. I found my hand was shaking.

As it happened I didn't need a wake-up call the following morning – some reflex triggered me awake from a dream in which I was aiming the gun at somebody I could not identify. For several moments I had no idea where I was, the window was shuttered and the room was fetid. Stiff in every joint, I felt as though I had slept on the floorboards and when I rubbed a hand over my stubbled cheeks I found several raised weals from mosquito bites. Stumbling to the shower I stayed under it until my muscles relaxed.

After dressing I examined the gun again, and removed the magazine before putting this in one side pocket and the gun in the other, conscious of the extra weight.

Outside the sun was already up, hot on my shoulders. The same old mangy dog was limping along the path to the parking lot, holding one back leg off the ground. I spoke to it and it paused, slowly turning its head in the direction of my voice; for the first time I saw its eyes; they were two milky dots and I realised it was blind. It suffered me to stroke its wiry head for a few moments, then collapsed in the shade of a tree.

The only new vehicle in the lot was one of those enormous Winnebagos that people tour America in. I couldn't imagine why anybody owning one would sleep in a motel, since I knew they were luxuriously appointed with all mod cons. I made my way past it to the red convertible, which I now checked had a full tank of gas and only two or three hundred miles on the clock. It took me a good fifteen minutes to find my way to the Howard Johnson's and I memorised the route for subsequent journeys.

The coffee shop was already half full and I had no sooner taken a seat when a teenage waitress with flawless brown legs rising out of clean white tennis shoes immediately came to my table and poured a cup of piping hot coffee, told me her name was Sharon and said she would be straight back to take my order. I looked around and could see no sign of Hochstein, then I heard a sneeze. He was seated on a stool at the counter in a position which gave him a clear view of the entrance.

When my young waitress returned her charm was such that she persuaded me to take the special breakfast – a mistake as it happened because I found myself confronted with a monstrous pile of waffles saturated in maple syrup, together with an omelette large enough to push my cholesterol level past the terminal mark. 'Enjoy,' Sharon said. As she walked away I stared at her perfect legs like a condemned man.

One hour later Sharon was topping up my fourth refill of coffee but Sophie had still not put in an appearance. Several times I looked across to Hochstein hoping he might give me a signal, but when he caught my eye he stared back without any change of expression. At half past eight I decided to make a move, paid the bill and sauntered out. I lingered in the lobby studying some tourist brochures until I saw Hochstein leave. He walked straight past me without a word. When I returned to the motel parking-lot I found he was already there, the hood of his car open while he made a show of checking the oil level. I was suddenly struck by a sense of the ridiculous: none of it seemed real any more – my being in a place called Flagstaff, staying in that utility motel, paired off with a minder while waiting for a reunion with a girl who had left my life years ago. I had never felt more isolated.

'We go through the same routine tomorrow, I guess,' he said, his head still inside the open hood. Even the subterfuge of pretending to tinker with his engine had an air of unreality. It was obvious that he did not intend to stay around all day, though this was not what Travis had promised.

He closed the hood and drove away. The prospect of spending the rest of the day cooped up in my motel room was infinitely depressing. More than anything else I wanted to return to the calm of a writer's routine where the agonies of love and hatred could all be plotted and solved on the word processor screen.

It was in that frame of mind, ignoring Hochstein's warning, my heart thumping from a surfeit of coffee, I convinced myself there was no immediate danger if I took a sightseeing trip around the town. I parked my convertible just off the main street and went in search of a bookshop, pausing to browse in the boutiques selling Indian artifacts, many of them tourist-orientated kitsch of dubious origin, but here and there something of genuine originality.

Then, crossing over to the shaded side of the street I suddenly became conscious that a black Ford Bronco with darkened windows was keeping pace. I paused to look into a shop window and the reflection showed that the same car had stopped a few paces ahead. There was nothing particularly sinister about it; the majority of vehicles had darkened windows to help keep out the blistering heat. When I resumed my walk and drew level with it, the driver opened the passenger door. A voice called my name.

I stopped and peered inside and there, unbelievably, was Pearson, the man Roger had introduced me to.

'How the hell. . . ?' I started to say but Pearson made a cautionary gesture. 'Don't say anything. Get in quickly.'

Without stopping to think I did as I was told. The interior was ice-cold from the efficient air-conditioning yet the shock of our reunion immediately made me break into a sweat.

'Put your belt on.'

While I fumbled with the seat-belt strap he put the car into drive and accelerated away, jerking me against the headrest.

'I can't believe you turning up like this,' I said.

'Oh, I expect there's a lot more you won't believe. This isn't your last surprise. We've got plenty more in store, not all of them too pleasant. I'm sorry to say.'

It was only then that I became conscious there was another man in the rear seat. I turned around to find a gun pointed at me.

'Just sit back,' Pearson said, 'and don't do anything stupid. You're not at home now. These boys don't play around, that piece in his hand will blow a hole in you the size of a dinner plate.'

I found no voice to answer him with. We drove for about half an hour until Pearson turned off into a dry riverbed well hidden from the road and brought the Bronco to a halt. The first thing I saw when I got out, parked a short distance away behind a clump of stunted trees, was the same Winnebago I had noticed at the motel earlier that morning. The man with the gun got out first and stood waiting.

273

'Take it slowly,' Pearson instructed, 'don't make any fuss, it's not worth it.'

I was motioned towards the Winnebago, Pearson going ahead of me and the other man following. Pearson opened the aluminium door and stood aside to let me enter first. The interior was divided into sections – a dining area, a fully-equipped kitchen, a shower and a sleeping area. Pearson followed me and closed the door behind him. I saw he now had the gun.

'Sit there.'

He indicated one of two swivel armchairs, then took the other himself and swung it round so that we were facing each other.

'Want a drink?'

I shook my head. His gun was no longer pointing directly at me, but he held it in his lap.

'Take a drink, you'll feel better. The bottle's beside you. And pour me one too, I guess we both need one.'

I slopped some of the whisky as I poured. Pearson reached out and took his glass with his left hand. I heard the sound of the Bronco driving away.

Pearson said: 'I don't suppose you ever expected to see me here. You really haven't been too smart, you know. Despite the warnings they gave you, you still kept pressing your luck. I think this time your luck's run out.'

I stared at him, trying to collect my wits. The only thought in my head was that at least they hadn't searched me. I kept my hands well away from my pockets and made no attempt to touch my drink, although Pearson downed his.

'Guess old Roger didn't do you a good turn, did he, introducing you to me? Silly old queen. Brilliant scholar I'm told, but not too bright when it comes to picking people. Still, mustn't blame him, poor soul. He thought he was doing you a favour. I think he has a soft spot for you, you must have been his type when you were younger.'

I let him talk.

'Just in case you get the wrong idea, I'm not tarred with the same brush. Never fancied the chocolate punching, know what I mean? Just as well seeing as how things have turned out. I gave it all a miss years ago, not worth the candle, I'd rather read a good book. Funny that God started off making the whole business so pleasurable and then decided to move the goal posts. Vindictive of Him.'

'I didn't know you were a philosopher,' I said.

'Oh, I'm a lot of things. As you've now found out.'

A sudden shaft of sunlight hit his face and I noticed that one of his eyes was watering. Watching me, he got up and adjusted the venetian blinds.

'Want to know my philosophy? I'm in it for the money. It's all economics, isn't it? You make yours writing books, I take it where I find it. You don't imagine I walked out of the Met with a fat pension, do you? I got sod all, but when this is over, I'll have more than enough to last me out. I'll probably piss off to somewhere a bloody sight warmer than jolly old England. I hear good things about the Cayman Islands, they have a nice relaxed attitude towards tax.'

I let him finish, then I said: 'So what happens now?'

'Don't ask me. My job was to pick you up and bring you here. Unlike you I don't ask too many questions.'

I can't remember how long we sat there with nothing further to say to each other. It was like being in a hospital waiting for the surgeon to return with the results of a test for cancer.

Then I heard a car draw up outside. Pearson's face tightened. He stood up, keeping his gun pointed at me. A car door slammed, then another, after which there was a pause, then footsteps coming closer. The door of the Winnebago opened and I found myself staring at Sophie in the doorway. As she stepped inside she revealed Henry behind her. His appearance had undergone subtle changes since the last time we had seen each other. His hair had been dyed much lighter and although the interior of the Winnebago was too dark for

275

me to be certain, I had the feeling he was wearing coloured contact lenses: they gave him a slightly maniacal look. He had always had clear skin with scarcely any beard line, but now the cheek-bones were mottled by a network of small veins – the sort of complexion which suggests a fondness for drink. His jowls were pudgy and he had put on a lot of extra weight, for the smart city suit, so incongruous in Arizona's heat, was tight across his middle.

Coming inside, he grinned at me before taking the seat Pearson had vacated. 'Well, old chum, who would have thought it – you and me catching up with each other in a place like this? You haven't said hello to my widow,' he added with gallows humour. 'As you know, she didn't act as is customary for a widow. No sackcloth and ashes or to a nunnery gone for our Sophie. No, you moved in with the celebrated butterfly collector, didn't you, sweetheart? Though we couldn't really blame her in the circs, it's difficult to go on loving a corpse, isn't it? Look at me when I'm talking to you.'

Sophie raised her head and looked at him with dead eyes.

'That's better.' He turned back to me. 'No, she forgot me with unseemly haste, and I can't say all is forgiven. However, that apart, here we three are again.' He spoke in that slightly plummy voice many politicians affect.

I looked at Sophie. She was twisting a ring on the little finger of her left hand.

'You've caused me no end of trouble, you know, chum. No end of trouble. Why couldn't you keep your nose out of my business? What good has it done either of us? All it's done is bring us to this pretty pass.'

'Is that what you call it – business?'

'Everything's business, just a way of making a crust. Isn't that what makes the world go round?'

'I should tell you the police are on to you.'

He grinned at me. 'Do you mean that pathetic joker with hay fever? Really, Martin, you mustn't think this is an episode from one of your books. I grant you they're very

276

readable, but hardly true to life. Your trouble is you still believe the good shall inherit the earth.' He shook his head. 'Wrong. The world is a cesspit. The trick is never to tread in it, always tread round it. My shoes are clean, I'm not personally involved, I'm just the merchandiser, the satisfier of needs. And you'd be surprised who are out there buying the goods. All out of the top drawer, Martin, with the money to pay for it. Clients with a lot to lose if anything should go wrong. I'm talking people with clout who can't afford anything to go wrong.'

He helped himself to a whisky. 'A touch more for you? No? Oh, Martin, Martin, I'm really not enjoying this, we go back too far, you and me, but you surely didn't think I would go to such extreme lengths to remove myself from circulation just to have you spoil it all? Surely not? You must know me better than that?'

'I've never known you,' I said.

'Don't blame me for that. We had something going once and I remembered that – you can't say I didn't give you more than one chance to pull back, beginning with that business in Venice. People got hurt there because of you, Martin, you and your fucking keen eyesight. The moment we spotted each other it was really the end, but I still held off any final solution where you were concerned, despite my associates urging me differently. The problem was even after Moscow you didn't take the hint, did you? I never wanted it to come to this. We shared some good times together, and believe it or not I'm a sentimentalist at heart. That's why when Pearson's name came out of the hat – a coincidence by the way, your gay Cornish friend isn't on our mailing list – I told him to try and head you off, play it down, convince you there was nothing more to find out. I hoped the message would get through, but it didn't, you always were a persistent sod, always inclined to question everything.'

'Well, you were right, weren't you?' I said.

'Yes, I was. Unfortunately for you. The pure in heart don't inherit the earth, Martin. You should know that by now.'

'I thought purity was your thing, not mine. Going all the way back to when we first met Sophie.'

'Well, we change, don't we? Sometimes for better, sometimes for worse. Take Sophie. She's changed too. I saw her for what she was, unlike you. Look at her. When she's had her goodies she turns into a real little performer in front of the cameras. Her tapes are one of our bestsellers. You should have forgotten her, chum, she forgot you long ago.'

'You did a good job on her,' I said. 'You and the butterfly collector between you.'

'Ah, yes, dear Seymour, an odd bedfellow but he payrolls my operation, so I mustn't criticise his secondary hobby.'

He paused and studied me for several seconds.

'A shame you're such a moral person. Does anybody turn a hair when all those Stock Exchange shits deal in wheat futures while two-thirds of the world are starving for a loaf of bread? Course they don't. Well, I deal in sex futures – the one commodity that never goes out of fashion, there's always a demand. All I do is satisfy that demand. It's like running a lending library: when one of my clients finishes with a book, they exchange it for another. So, sometimes the pages get torn, sometimes it gets damaged beyond repair.'

'Even you can't say it, can you?'

'Say what?'

'You can't say you're peddling children, that your distinguished clientele with their clout are just the worst kind of filth.'

'Whatever way the world spins somebody gets fucked. I learned that in the best school of all – the Palace of Westminster. I didn't invent the game, chum, I'm just a player who refined the technology. Some people get rich supplying Cruise missiles or plutonium. Did you really think that by nailing me you could change anything? While we're having this little heart to heart a few thousand more children have died in Ethiopia, Calcutta, Somalia, Mozambique, you name it, and I'm sure your heart bleeds for them every time you tuck into your *foie gras* at the Gavroche or whichever watering-hole you frequent these days.'

He had worked himself up by now, his voice getting louder as though sheer volume would somehow bolster his case. Then we both became aware that Sophie was crying. Henry rounded on her. 'Don't start that!'

She smothered her sobs immediately as though programmed.

His manner changed again, abruptly. He rounded on Pearson. 'Right, let's get it over.'

He left the Winnebago locking the door after him. I heard the tow-bar being fixed to the Winnebago and shortly afterwards we bumped back on to the road. From the late sunlight coming through the blinds I calculated we were heading north. Pearson sat watching us, the gun still handy in his lap.

I looked at Sophie and said her name. Her head came up slowly. I wanted to feel sorry for her but somehow nothing from our past seemed to work any more.

'I waited for you at breakfast,' I said. 'It was a good breakfast, sorry you missed it.'

Her expression did not change.

'I suppose it's too late to suggest a deal?' I said to Pearson.

'A good deal for you would be a bad one for me.'

'Just thought it was worth asking.'

'Can I give you a top up now?'

'Yes, I probably need one.'

I held out my glass. As he got up and went for the whisky bottle I took the opportunity to slip the magazine into the same pocket as my gun. I had no idea whether, if the chance came, I would find the nerve to use it, but the touch of metal gave me some comfort. I swallowed my whisky quickly, but my body burned the alcohol immediately and I remained clear-headed. We must have driven for two hours at least and perhaps I dozed off for a while, coming to again to find Sophie staring at me. Her eyes seemed to flicker in and out of focus

'I'm sorry,' she said. 'I got you into this.'

'No.'

'Yes, if it wasn't for me you'd never have come this far.'

'Well, if it's anybody's fault, it's my own.'

She shivered. 'I'm cold,' she said.

Pearson got up and adjusted the air-conditioning. This time I managed to slip the magazine into the gun and pushed it home while his back was turned.

'That better?' he said. 'Use a blanket from one of the beds.'

She got up unsteadily, clinging to the fitments as she made her way to one of the bunks. There she huddled in the fetal position.

'It takes them like that,' Pearson said softly. 'I've seen them go cold turkey. Rather her than me.'

Watching her curled on the bunk the years retreated for in sleep she appeared to me no older than when we had first shared a flat, but the innocence she had once possessed was no longer there. All I saw was but the shadow of a girl I had loved. Staring at her, remembering so much that had gone before, I wondered what the end would be. It took a conscious effort for me to keep my hand away from the gun as I considered, then rejected, desperate measures to free us both.

It was dark when the Winnebago finally bumped to a stop, and a few moments later Henry unlocked the door and came inside. He went straight to the freezer and took out a cold beer which he drank from the can, American style.

'Ever been to the Grand Canyon?'

I met his bright look.

'No.'

'It's a tourist must,' he said, then turned away from me and went to Sophie.

'Wake up!'

'Please,' she said.

'Please what?'

'Help me.'

'Course I'm going to help you. That's what I'm here for.'

He went to the freezer again and this time took out a hypodermic. 'Take your clothes off,' he commanded.

She still hadn't focused on him, but he waved the hypodermic in front of her. 'Come on, do as I say, then you'll get your goodies.'

She sat up on the bunk and robot-like began to disrobe, never once looking at any of us. It was like watching a hired act at a stag party. When she was completely nude I could see the tell-tale marks of previous injections on her thighs, arms and legs. I guessed it was heroin he gave her, or maybe some new cocktail – an extension of hell is always made available to those in need. She gave a small cry as the contents of the syringe went into the vein, though whether it was from relief or pain I couldn't tell.

Henry deposited the spent hypodermic into a trash can beneath the sink. Sophie's whole body shuddered several times as though possessed by an alien force, then she lay back on the bunk, supine and seemingly content. Shamefully, I found her nakedness disturbingly erotic and felt sickened not only for her but by myself.

'Now we have to take care of you, don't we?' Henry said to me. 'You're not the only person who can devise a plot, and I've come up with a real good one. There's a slight snag: it doesn't have a happy ending though, just a kind of poetic beauty which should appeal to your sense of the dramatic.'

Going to the freezer again he took out a second hypodermic. 'The great thing about this stuff, especially to somebody like yourself who hasn't tried it before . . . You haven't, have you? No, of course you haven't, a solid citizen like you . . . The great thing is the first taste is the best. You might say it's the only time it *is* the best, and you're not about to become an addict.'

He tested the syringe, squirting a little of the liquid it contained.

'Sorry you won't see the Canyon in all its glory, because everything you've ever heard about it is true. Quite awesome, especially if you witness it at sunrise, which sadly isn't on the agenda, old sport.'

His use of the word 'sport' framed us both in a time-warp of absurdity. I had a feeling of deadly emptiness, made all the more chilling by the fact that Sophie was now a contented witness. My hand was beside the gun pocket as he moved a step closer.

'This place is rather like Beachy Head, a place lovers frequently use for their final solution. Did you know that?'

I shook my head, my eyes never leaving the syringe in his hand.

'Well, this is how my story goes. You brought her here for one last lovers' tryst, to try and rekindle an old passion. Not too far-fetched, after all she was your first love. Unfortunately, because of what will ultimately be found in both of your bloodstreams, you weren't quite in control when you parked this thing. It was dark and you put it much too close to the edge – the sort of mistake anybody who shoots up a few cc's of this stuff might make – and it toppled over.' He waved the hypodermic in front of me. 'Not as subtle as your own efforts, but then I'm a beginner. So, to make it look authentic, we have to get you in the mood. Take your clothes off and lie beside her.'

I did nothing.

'Come on, it's not a bad ending. And painless.'

I walked past him and sat on the edge of Sophie's bunk. Slowly I started to remove my shoes, knowing that it was now or never. Henry was in front of me, partially blocking Pearson's view. I pushed my shoes to one side and stood up as though about to loosen my belt and drop my trousers. Using my left hand to free the buckle, I pushed my right hand into the pocket and without removing the gun fired two shots straight at Henry. The force of the bullets staggered him backwards into Pearson. Despite this Pearson managed to let off one round but it went wild, slamming into the air-conditioning unit. By then I had my gun out and was screaming for him to drop his. I shall never know whether he would have obeyed me because, in the panic and the fine trigger pressure on the automatic, I loosed off another two rounds. The first caught Pearson in the shoulder, spinning him around, and the second hit him in the neck close to the jaw-bone, the spent bullet cases zinging against the metal walls. Blood sprayed in a wide arc across the windshield as Pearson collapsed against one of the swivel armchairs and pitched towards the dashboard, hitting the steering wheel and setting off the horn. He made a bubbling noise for a few minutes then went silent. I found myself retching and sank to my knees close to where Henry lay twitching, my lungs filled with the acrid smoke of the explosions mingled with the smell of burnt cloth in that confined space. It seemed an age before I had the strength to pull myself upright. There was no sound from Pearson and I was too far gone in shock to examine him. I stepped over Henry and opened the door, taking in great gulps of air until the pounding of my heart lessened. It was only then that I thought of Sophie.

I forced myself to go back inside. Sophie had pulled herself into the corner of the bunk, knees drawn up to her breasts, staring straight ahead with dilated eyes. I reached for the blanket to cover her, only to find it saturated with blood. Going to the second bedroom, I splashed my face with water and, as I raised my head, the mirror over the basin showed a madman. I took a fresh blanket and wrapped it around Sophie. 'Come on,' I said. 'Come with me.'

She began to laugh, just as she had during that drug-soaked episode on the twins' yacht years before. I slapped her two or three times until the hysteria subsided, then lifted her in my arms and carried her outside, putting her into the passenger seat of the Bronco and securing her with the seatbelt. I suddenly became aware that I was barefooted. It took an effort to go back inside. Henry and Pearson were exactly as I had left them. As I momentarily turned my back on the two bodies and bent to ease on my shoes I felt a sudden stab of pain and spun round to find the hypodermic sticking in my right calf. Against all reason Henry was still alive. I chopped down on his arm holding the hypodermic but he had demonic strength. Even when I struck his Adam's apple several times with inexpert karate blows, he still didn't relinquish it, but made desperate efforts to press the plunger home. The macabre struggle continued until, with one hand pressed into his face, I finally knocked the syringe from his grasp and sent it flying. He rocked backwards and forwards like some clockwork toy running down, then blood gushed from his mouth. His eyes opened wide and he seemed about to say something. But before he could frame the words he toppled sideways and was still.

It took me a time before I could breathe normally again. I collapsed on to the edge of the bunk and watched him until convinced that he was finally dead. Only then did I make any move, backing all the way to the door. Once outside, I locked the door then sat on the metal steps until my heartbeats slowed. Later I found the strength to un-couple the tow-bar. This accomplished, I reversed the Bronco with infinite care for the headlights picked out the rim of the Canyon only twenty feet or so away. Henry had carefully positioned the Winnebago rear-end towards the drop; a nudge from the Bronco would have sent it into oblivion.

I drove from the scene searching for a road, any road, then when I found one, headed for a distant glow in the desert sky that promised human habitation. It proved to be a small supermarket and gas station. Sophie was comatose, so I parked and locked the car and used the public phone booth, making a 911 call and asking the operator to get me the Carefree police.

For the first time during the whole nightmare my luck was in and I got straight through to Travis. I found I couldn't stop myself crying as I told him the story.

'Stay where you are,' he said, as though there was any-where else to go. 'We're on our way.'

I went into the supermarket and bought a fifth of Scotch. Then I went back to the Bronco and got under the blanket with Sophie.

'It's over,' I said. 'You're safe now,' telling her the last lie. I put my arms round her but her naked body was cold to the touch and it was like embracing a statue.

POSTSCRIPT

For a long time after the events of that night I felt like an amputee: the stricken limb was no longer there, but the sensations kept returning to remind me of the loss.

No charges were brought against me for the killing of Henry and Pearson; Travis saw to that. At the inquest the verdict recorded was that I had acted in self-defence – the fact that Pearson's revolver had been fired told in my favour – and once Henry's full story had been revealed, the jury's opinion was that I had done society a good turn. I don't know about that, a death is a death however you justify it.

I suppose the saddest twist to come out of it all concerned Kemelman. He proved to be the last victim, but not before he had extracted his own form of justice. It was Travis who told me exactly how it all happened, beginning with the episode in Chicago, the rendezvous that Henry never kept.

Before Kemelman arrived, the Chicago police had done the groundwork. Seymour and his two sidekicks were still inside the airport having been tracked to a bar in the International Arrivals area. Seymour apparently stayed put but every so often one of the other two went to the Information desk. A Bureau agent discovered they were enquiring about the delayed arrival of a scheduled flight from Hong Kong. The passenger indent was produced, but nobody on the flight checked out with any of the names on the computer list, the only thing that suggested a tie-in with Henry's telephone call was that the plane was carrying a coffin. They established that the dead man was a Pole named Peter Rojak, forty-two years old, a sales rep for a shirt firm who got most of their products out of Taiwan and Hong Kong. The death certificate stated the cause of death was a brain haemorrhage and that a post-mortem had been conducted. All apparently legit, signed and witnessed by the authorities in Hong Kong. Once they had the name the Chicago boys moved fast, contacted the shirt company who confirmed, yes, they had employed a Peter Rojak as their Far East salesman, and that they had paid for his body to be flown home. The cops traced where he lived, turned out he was a married man with three kids, no criminal record.

According to Travis, Kemelman wanted to move in there and then, but the Chicago Police Commissioner wasn't having it. The Polish vote carries a lot of muscle in the windy city and with a local election in the offing the Commissioner wasn't prepared to mess with a legitimate corpse.

When the Hong Kong flight was on final approach Seymour and the other two left the bar and went up on to the observation terrace. While they were there a police photographer got shots of all three. One of the sidekicks turned out to have form, a small-time hood who worked for one of the Mob families. The trio waited until the coffin was off-loaded, then left the airport and checked into a suite at the Ritz Carlton. An undercover team was fed into the adjoining suite using sophisticated bugging devices.

After the coffin had been cleared through Customs, it was taken to a funeral parlour, followed all the way, just in case they pulled a switch. The dead man's family was waiting to receive the body, together with a priest. It all looked on the level at that point, Travis said. After another face-off with the Commissioner Kemelman decided to go his own way and run a strictly Bureau operation that night with the Chicago police kept in ignorance. He assembled a team of a dozen agents including a pathologist with X-ray equipment the only concession he made was not to disturb the body unless something showed up on X-ray.

Breaking in that night was no problem and they immediately X-rayed the corpse using the latest fast plates which were developed outside in an unmarked van.

'There was something inside him,' Travis said. 'Well, to be accurate when they first took a look at the plates they didn't know what it was, just a square object, but it sure as hell wasn't part of his guts. And it was at that point they got word that Seymour's two hoods had left the hotel. Seymour stayed where he was, too smart to get involved in any of the dirty stuff. The Bureau team had radio contact all along the route and knew exactly when to expect them. Everybody outside the funeral parlour was under orders to leave them well alone. Kemelman wanted them taken inside with the goods.'

As Travis came to the climax I remember he got up from his chair and started to act it out.

'Let me give you the picture. Kemelman and two of his team took up position behind the small altar in the Chapel of Rest, the backup were hidden in the adjoining waiting room. Say I'm Kemelman, the trestle with the coffin on it was roughly where you are. The two hoods came in from over there. They knew exactly what they had come for and they worked fast, prised open the coffin, tipped the corpse out and slit him open. The moment they had what they came for, Kemelman gave the signal and took them red-handed.'

'And *was* it a can of film?'

'Tape. A tape cassette, the miniature long-running type. We ran it later. The worst – Chinese kids as young as maybe three or four, both sexes,' he said in a changed voice, not looking at me. 'The poor little sods were being fucked and tortured every which way. They say life is cheap out there and, Jesus, their little lives were cheap enough.'

I listened appalled, for just when I had thought the horror had ended in Arizona, it was back with me.

'What about Seymour?'

'Oh, they picked him off easily enough. He's out on bail fighting a deportation order. The one I felt most sorry for was poor Kemelman. They busted him that night.'

'Busted him?' I said.

'On the spot. He took the rap for acting without authority on somebody else's pad. Like I said, the Polish vote counts in Chicago and the stiff had been sliced open. They had to appease the family, the Commissioner, the Bishop, you name it.'

Travis told me that after his dismissal Kemelman tried to get a licence as a private investigator, but that was blocked and he eventually ended up as a security guard for a quarry firm – a deliberate move as later events proved.

Some six months later when I was back in England Travis sent me a newspaper cutting. It was a report of a murder trial and Kemelman was the accused. Apparently there had been a series of seemingly unrelated deaths of prominent citizens in various parts of the country. In each case the victim had received a letter bomb, and six men died before anybody made the connection. Then it was spotted that the names checked out with the computer list of paedophiles Travis had once shown me, and that was traced back to Kemelman. After he had been busted from the Bureau he must have decided to take the law into his own hands. At the trial it was revealed that his daughter had been raped and murdered ten years previously and this was entered as a plea in mitigation by his attorney, but it failed to impress and he was given life. I've often thought of the irony of that, for it is such a contradiction in terms.

Following receipt of the cutting I made it my business to find out which jail he was in and wrote to him. He never replied.

As for Sophie, I paid for her to have treatment in one of those places where they dry out alcoholics and drug addicts. I believe it worked in her case and that subsequently she married her counsellor and now lives quietly in a suburb of San Francisco.

I read the other day that it is possible to create diamonds from peanut butter. You take any carbon source, add hydrogen gas and heat to 2000 F. The heat and hydrogen disengage the carbon atoms from the peanut butter and they reassemble as diamonds. I have never understood the mysteries of physics, to me it is all inexplicable, but for some reason this item took me back to Henry. I can no more comprehend how he did what he did than I can the home-made polyhedron – it is a black hole that allows of no understanding. What terrible fires transformed the friend I once thought I understood into the man I needed to kill? I wish to God I knew. But I have no answers except the certainty that we all die unknown.

Henry was right about one thing. Somewhere out there there are always going to be willing sellers and willing buyers, not those who stalk the school playgrounds and shopping malls – the shabby mackintosh brigade of popular imagination with their sad, twisted urges – but those who prey with more cunning and clout, as he put it. The hidden ones who will always find ways to satisfy their perversion until our society chokes on its sexual materialism. Somebody, another Henry, will always be around to supply the product. That, God help us, is presumably how they must justify their acts, thinking of their tender victims, not as children, but just a product, as disposable as the plastic food that nourishes everything but our souls.

I have a new life now. No cities, no word-processor or fax machine, no inclination ever to write another thriller. I bought Roger's coastguard's cottage when he died. For the last two years I have occupied myself writing a commissioned biography of Turgenev, a subject as far removed from my previous work as I could think of. I have a placid, but not unpleasant existence and seldom travel. Nowhere is safe these days.

A DIVIDED LIFE

It would be a mistake to describe this mordant, though often wildly funny, odyssey as just another show business autobiography, for, as might be expected, Bryan Forbes tells his story with the directness and honesty that have characterised his 'divided life' as an actor, author and film maker of distinction.

Marshalling his recollections with humour and compassion, he writes incisively of his enduring friendships with Dame Edith Evans, Graham Greene, Peter Sellers, Katharine Hepburn, Elton John, Bette Davis, Terence Rattigan and Enid Bagnold, to name but a few of the famous who punctuate his personal narrative. He also does not spare himself in the telling of the turbulent years when he was head of production for EMI at Elstree studios, and is equally frank in giving his version of the now infamous production of *Macbeth* with Peter O'Toole at the Old Vic.

Whether he is writing with affectionate warmth of his wife and family or describing the many hilarious exploits that have bestrewn his long career, the author employs an unerring photographic eye for intimate detail.

FAMILIAR STRANGERS

'Written across the photograph were the words *To Theo with too much love*. One corner was torn, obliterating most of the signature, but I had no difficulty identifying the face. It was a photograph of Guy Burgess.'

Foreshadowing the exposure of Anthony Blunt, *Familiar Strangers* is the provocative, highly acclaimed novel of betrayal, deceit and divided loyalties in the world of British espionage, in which Bryan Forbes so uncannily anticipated the scandal of 'the Fourth Man'.

'Mr Forbes has cleverly combined actual events as background to the fiction, and aptly shows how a man can die slowly from "the incurable drug of deceit itself"'

Daily Telegraph

'Brutally frank and compulsively readable . . . a major novel not to be missed'

Bookseller

'One of the best books I have read this year'

Oxford Mail

THE REWRITE MAN

'She wore a loose-fitting shirt of patterned silk which outlined her young breasts as she walked. She walked with that easy grace of those who are accustomed to admiration. Her face was haloed by dense, black hair – a gentle mouth, slightly crooked when she smiled. But even now I can't be certain that I am describing her with any accuracy. All I know is that I was stunned by her beauty'

Down on his luck and licking his wounds, Hollywood scriptwriter Harvey Burgess thinks he has landed a windfall when he is summoned to the South of France to rewrite a stalled film about the French Revolution. What he finds is a tawdry script, a fractious film crew – and Laura . . .

'Marvellously readable, funny and poignant . . . Bryan Forbes has created some splendidly living characters, sparkling dialogue and a truly touching novel of obsession and jealousy'

Sunday Express

'Bryan Forbes has written a very good book indeed, based on all his experience in the film business . . . it's a long time since I felt such enthusiasm about my bedtime reading'

Mail on Sunday

'Forbes's dialogue is magnificent – there is no other word for it. It's clever, fast-moving and totally absorbing'

Pittsburgh Press

NED'S GIRL

Edith Evans resisted all requests to write an autobiography and had previously refused to grant permission for an authorised biography before making Bryan Forbes her literary executor. Together, they worked on *Ned's Girl*, the title that she herself chose for the first full-length account of a life, a love story, and an unequalled career on the stage.

Bryan Forbes is the first person to have unrestricted access to papers and unpublished correspondence from Bernard Shaw, George Moore, St John Ervine, Sybil Thorndike, Enid Bagnold and many other famous contemporaries. *Ned's Girl* is a warm and entertaining portrait of the greatest English actress of this century, and is all the more important for faithfully adhering to Edith Evans's one all-consuming passion – the truth.

Books by Bryan Forbes available from Mandarin

While every effort is made to keep prices low, it is sometimes necessary to increase prices at short notice. Mandarin Paperbacks reserves the right to show new retail prices on covers which may differ from those previously advertised in the text or elsewhere.

The prices shown below were correct at the time of going to press.

☐	0 7493 1452 4	**The Distant Laughter**	£4.99
☐	0 7493 1386 2	**Familiar Strangers**	£4.99
☐	0 7493 1387 0	**The Rewrite Man**	£4.99
☐	0 7493 1845 7	**The Endless Game**	£4.99
☐	0 7493 1850 3	**A Song At Twilight**	£4.99
☐	0 7493 0835 4	**Ned's Girl: The Life of Dame Edith Evans**	£6.99
☐	0 7493 0884 2	**A Divided Life (autobiography)**	£5.99

All these books are available at your bookshop or newsagent, or can be ordered direct from the address below. Just tick the titles you want and fill in the form below.

Cash Sales Department. PO Box 5, Rushden, Northants NN10 6YX.
Fax: 0933 410321 : Phone 0933 410511.

Please send cheque, payable to 'Reed Book Services Ltd.', or postal order for purchase price quoted and allow the following for postage and packing:

£1.00 for the first book. 50p for the second: **FREE POSTAGE AND PACKING FOR THREE BOOKS OR MORE PER ORDER.**

NAME (Block letters) ....

ADDRESS ....

....

☐ I enclose my remittance for ....

☐ I wish to pay by Access/Visa Card Number

Expiry Date

Signature ....

Please quote our reference: MAND